MW01107366

MURDER BY PROXY

A NOVEL

MURDER BY PROXY

A NOVEL

ROBERT PAUL SZEKELY

Rutledge Books, Inc.

Danbury, CT

Copyright© 2000 by Robert Paul Szekely

ALL RIGHTS RESERVED
Rutledge Books, Inc.
107 Mill Plain Road, Danbury, CT 06811
1-800-278-8533
www.rutledgebooks.com

Manufactured in the United States of America

Library of Congress Cataloging in Publication Data
Szekely, Robert Paul
    Murder by Proxy

    ISBN: 1-58244-092-1

    1. Fiction.

Library of Congress Card Number: 00-103216

MURDER BY PROXY

A NOVEL BY ROBERT PAUL SZEKELY

A novel with a twist,
in more ways than one.

INTOXICATING PRINCIPAL
CHARACTERS

THE LAW FIRM OF DANIELS AND RUMM

JACQ DANIELS, owner
JACKIE DANIELS, JR., owner's son

"A" LAWYERS:
> JARVIS RUMM, co-owner
> AMY AMONTILLADO
> RICHARD PORT
> MARCUS LAMBRUSCO
> SHERRY WEINSTEIN
> GINA COLLINS

"B" LAWYERS:
> CHARLES COGNAC
> MAI TAI

LEGAL ASSISTANTS:
> TONY MARTINI
> BRANDY JONES

SECRETARIES:
> KRISTIE CLARET
> IRIS WHISKEY

INTOXICATING PRINCIPAL
CHARACTERS

THE LAW FIRM OF DANIELS AND RUMM

LAW LIBRARY PERSON:
MARGARITA LOPEZ

RECEPTIONIST:
ROSIE ROSÉ

PRINT SHOP/MAIL PERSON:
HARRY HEINEKEN

SECONDARY CHARACTERS

DeDe Daniels	Paul Stout
Lt. Miller	Dr. Amaretto
Donny Dos Equis	Mrs. Sarah La Grande
Guinness	Mr. Royal
Dan Dewars	Schlitz
Labatt	Sheriff Jim Malt
Tony Tequilla	Bobby Bombay-D.J.
John Vodka	Sadie Smirnoff
Julie Champagne	Perrier Funeral Home
Miss Bordeaux	Brenda Ballentine
John Coors	Nathan Colby
Ricky Molson	Judge Forest Glen
Tom Beers	D.A. Taittinger
Bud Porter	Jenny O'Doul
Johnny Walker	Jean Hennessy
Colada Jones	Mindy Michelob

CONTENTS

CONTENTS

CONTENTS

CHAPTERS

ACKNOWLEDGEMENTS

I want to thank my circle of family and friends for their wonderful support and encouragement during the writing of this book.

A special thank you to Stephenie Steele, Director of the Writer's Digest School, for her kind words and sound advice. She was always there to answer my questions with a phone call or timely letter.

Thanks to George Edward Stanley, my writing instructor, for his help in character development and dialogue. He emphasized the importance of concise chapters for today's reader resulting in a page turner.

A heart-felt thank you to Lauren and Ryan, two of my five grandchildren, for reading parts of the book and helping to convince me that you don't need offensive language to have a good story.

To my son Mark, a heap of thanks for the lunches that helped put the writing and publishing of this book in the proper perspective.

Finally, I want to acknowledge my Uncle Paul Mandy, a veteran of WWII, to whom I sent short stories during his tour of duty. He was an avid reader, poet and writer who peaked my interest in storytelling.

DEDICATION

I would like to dedicate this novel to the thousands of writers who have written a book of their own, believing as I did that once it was finished, the struggling had come to an end. Little did I realize that the real work was yet to begin.

I want to encourage every writer who believes in his or her work to continue writing and never give up. Do not ever get discouraged, There is a way to become a published author, thanks to people like Rutledge Books, Inc.

I also want to dedicate this book to my daughter, Lisa, who is by far a more talented writer than I, but her priorities lie with her husband and three young sons at this time in her life.

Lastly, I dedicate this book to my wife, Iris, who helped develop the story and refine the characters. She did much of the editing and proof-reading and supported me every step of the way with her tact-ful critiques. There would be no book without her.

SUNDAY, OCTOBER 18, 1998-11:45 P.M.

The curved blade of the knife flashed forward and deep. Repeatedly, as the rage increased, the thrusts grew in intensity, gouging into the smoothness. Crazed criss-cross slashes.

How does it feel, huh? Feel good? Well, too bad! This one is for **YOU KNOW WHO!**

The whispering stopped. Then silence, except for the shallow breathing. A hand-held flashlight cast an eerie shadow on the paneled wall. The knife remained imbedded, its handle carefully wiped clean with a fine-stitched linen handkerchief. Just another Sunday in Chicago.

Not a bad night's work!

X

A 1999 BMW careened around the corner and came to an abrupt stop on Clark Street behind the National Bank Building. Jacq Daniels, chief executive officer and a managing partner in the law firm of Daniels and Rumm, flicked off the latest stock report on the monitor. He kicked the door open on the stretch limousine before the chauffeur could get around to the curb.

Jacq brushed off the croissant crumbs from his lapels, tightened the belt on his cashmere coat and swung his athletic body out of the limo. He was impeccably dressed and deeply tanned from his latest trip to Zaire. His rugged features and full silver-gray hair made him appear far younger than his early sixties.

Tall blue steel, glass, and marble penetrated the rare blue October sky in mid-town Chicago. The early morning rays cast jagged shapes on the east side of Clark Street. Jacq shook off the last of the crumbs.

"You're getting old, Guinness," said Daniels. "Thirty two minutes today. Not good!" He fiddled with the collar of his handmade English shirt. "I got a gut feeling it's going to be a lousy Monday, thanks to you!"

"Ah, but you are the 'top brass,' shall we say, sir." Guinness forced a smile and fluttered his eyes. "YOU can never be considered late." Guinness was holding the door open, dressed in the standard black attire, complete with boots and a snappy hat. He was slight of build, with a grayish pencil-thin mustache.

"Yeah, yeah—tell me about it. Listen—don't forget to..."

"Yes, SIR—pick up your Brioni suit. I have the address."

"If you don't, I'll have to answer to DeDe. And you'll answer to me!" Daniels approached a steel door at the back of the building. Next to the door was a small computerized unit fastened to the marble wall. Jacq quickly accessed the lid of the box with a code and punched in his four-digit number. The door buzzed, he pulled it open and turned to his driver. "We don't need her whining, do we?"

"No, sir," said Guinness. "Madam WOULD be rather upset."

"Get lost," countered Daniels. "I'll call you when I need you."

"Yes, SIR."

Poor schmuck, thought Guinness. *I'm probably the only friend he has in Chicago.*

Tommy Guinness had the rest of the morning to run his errand.

At noon he was scheduled to pick up Jackie Jr. at the O'Hare Airport. Jackie had gone to Columbus, Ohio, where he had hoped to find additional information pertaining to the Colby case. Guinness walked to the rear of the limo to shut the door. He leaned into the back seat.

Damn! he thought. *It's going to take me an hour to clean up from last night!*

X

The law firm of Daniels and Rumm occupied the top three floors of the National Bank Building. Entering the high-rise from the rear, Jacq took one of several freight elevators to the twenty-first floor. In this way, he was able to circumvent all the TV reporters in the parking garage. The Colby fiasco was a hot issue with the press and he wasn't in a friendly frame of mind, knowing the media was waiting for him at the front doors, too, along with more camera crews.

Jacq exited the elevator, walking quickly down a short hallway and through the back stairwell door. To his left, near the main marbled hall, he approached Iris Whiskey's cubicle. The high-resolution video cameras, one panning each corridor, taped Jacq as he marched toward his secretary. His image was being observed at that very moment on the main-floor monitor by a security guard, in between bites of her hidden glazed donut.

"Morning, Iris. What's going on?"

"Good morning, Jacq," said the administrative secretary. Iris shared her duties between Jacq and his son Jackie. She was busy sorting the morning's mail. "Mr. Lambrusco wants to talk to you about a possible motion to dismiss in the Colby case."

"Yeah, okay. Get me some coffee! Anything else?" Jacq loosened his silk designer tie.

"Yes. Sherry called at eight-thirty and said she has car trouble. She won't make the ten o'clock meeting. She didn't elaborate."

"Hell! We've got to finish the pre-trial documents for Gina's case." Jacq stormed into his office. "Now she'll have to do it herself!" He threw his cashmere coat on the leather loveseat. His scarf and suede sherling gloves flew across the room against the sterling coffee urn. "Call Gina. Let her know what's happening. I want that paperwork finished by four!"

"Yes, right away." She picked up the small stack of Jackie's mail and pushed Gina Collins' extension. Iris wore a dark Armani suit, open at the neck. A thin gold necklace with a flower pendant completed her tailored look. She was a young-looking fifty-eight.

Jacq Daniels' office was finished with matched panels of Honduras mahogany, polished to a high luster. The desk in his office, also mahogany, was an antique that had belonged to his father from the 1930s. A pearwood cabinet, stained in light and dark brown with black accents that DeDe had purchased at the Dorotheum Auction House in Vienna, was the other highlight of his office. J.D. always spoke affectionately about his favorite piece—his desk.

Looking out of the mahogany-trimmed picture windows, to the right of the Art Institute overlooking the Chicago Harbor, Jacq's clients could spend quiet moments alone, between meetings with lawyers and plaintiffs, comtemplating their fate. The harbor looked remarkably clear today.

Jacq, with his partner, Jarvis Rumm, were the principal stockholders in the company. The firm consisted of dozens of hand-selected high-profile lawyers and support staff. These groups handled criminal and civil cases for the most influential people in the Chicago area.

"What the hell! Iris, get in here!" J.D.'s door was slightly ajar.

Iris hurried into the office. "I'm sorry, Jacq. I'll get someone to clean up the coffee..."

"It's not the damn coffee! Look at this!"

The top surface of Jacq's desk was scarred with repeated slashes of a hunting knife. The steel blade was imbedded in the desktop and through an ad from the New Yorker magazine. The ad featured a bottle of Jack Daniels Tennessee Sour Mash Whiskey. On top of the ad was stuck a yellow sticky Post-it note that read: "YOU ARE NEXT."

For the first time today, Jacq was at a loss for words.

Daniels punched Rumm's extension. "Jarvis! Drop whatever the hell you're doing and get in here! Now!" He opened the door to his outer office and waved at Iris. "Get me a refill!"

"Right away, Jacq."

"Make sure it's hot this time!"

Jarvis Rumm, a man in his mid-sixties, tapped on the fluted glass door. He was slightly out of breath as he pulled the panel open. Unruly snow-white hair and bushy eyebrows contrasted sharply with his blue shirt and navy tie. Jarvis ran his fingers over his receding hairline.

"What's up, J.D.? We've got Amy handling..."

"To hell with Amy! Look at this damn mess."

"Your desk! I can't believe it! We'd better call the police." Jarvis turned to see Iris approaching with two cups of her special blend.

"Here you are." She handed a cup to Jarvis and added, "I'll call them immediately."

"Wait a minute," said Jacq. "I don't want any cops coming up here, especially when we're in the middle of this Colby project! The media is the last thing I want. Iris...no police." He threw a glance at Jarvis and said, "Don't you agree, Rumm?"

Jarvis stood next to the desk, looking at the gouges in the

mahogany, shaking his head. He was absorbed in the fine print of the New Yorker ad, fidgeting with his sleeves. "I guess you're right. No use stirring the pot." He looked up at Jacq. "But why would anyone want to do something like this? How did they get into your office? And when?"

"Yeah, Iris. When? A hell of a lot of good our new security cards are doing us."

"There has to be an explanation," said Iris, squeezing the coffee out of J.D.'s scarf. "We should warn the staff. I'm frightened." She walked to the door, her short, ash-blonde hair, combed to one side, prematurely showing signs of wilting. "Let me know what you decide, in case you need a memo for the ten o'clock meeting." Iris put J.D.'s cup on the Corian-topped coffee bar and left the room.

"She's right, Jacq," said Rumm, loosening his tie. "Most of the people will be here for the ten o'clock."

"I guess we could start with the memo." Jacq fingered the top of the desk. "What the hell have I done to deserve this? Rumm, you know me better than anybody." Daniels slumped into his leather Oval Office chair.

"I don't know." A long pause. Jarvis was staring at the knife, still dug into the desktop. "As Richard Port would say, 'you ain't no choir boy.'"

"Hey! That's it!" Jacq jumped to his feet and pointed to his head. "Not a bad idea. Let's get Richard in on this!"

"Why? Just because he was a detective once?" After the words came out, Jarvis sensed they were on to something.

"Sure," said Daniels. "He'd know how to handle this. Just like a normal police investigation...without the cops."

"Richard's one of our top attorneys," countered Jarvis. "He's up to his eyeballs with the Colby trial."

"No problem." Jacq was rubbing his hands together, smiling,

pacing. He threw off his wool suit jacket. "Let's pull him off the case. Put Mai in his place. She's worked hard for a shot. Besides, we don't have much choice."

"Okay. But, hey...how about considering Gina...or Amy. They've been here as long as Mai. Amy longer. I think..." Jarvis reached for the office door's latch.

"Nah! I don't like it. Gina's too green. I can't dump this high-profile case on her pretty shoulders. And besides, Richard is hot for Amy. I don't want them working as a team on Colby. I've known Nathan a long time." Daniels took a sip of coffee. "Get Richard lined up—right away—to work with Mai. It'll no doubt take him a week or so to bring her up to date."

"If they work night and day," said Rumm.

"So? They can work here—or at Richard's place for all I care!"

"All right, whatever you say." Jarvis opened the mahogany-clad door that led to the secretary's office. "Iris, we're all set for you. Come on in."

Jacq motioned to his secretary and said, "I want you to compose a memo, a copy to go to everyone in the firm. Tell them exactly what happened here last night and don't leave anything out."

Jarvis interrupted. "Make a point for all the staff to be especially careful in the parking garage. Please have the memo ready for the meeting at ten."

"Iris. One more thing," said Jacq. "Call that damn refinishing place in Wyandotte, Michigan. Right now! I want my desk as good as new. They're the best."

"It's a shame," said Rumm. "He didn't care if he completely ruined your desk. It's a disaster!"

Maybe it's not a 'he,' thought Iris. *It could be a woman!*

"Okay, people! I'm cutting the meeting short!" snapped Jacq. "We've got too many loose ends to finish up out there!"

The sixteen-foot Italian marble-top conference table was littered with coffee cups, pieces of pastry, and empty juice glasses. The 12x20 Tibetan carpet under the table was strewn with napkins, crumbs, and women's shoes. The yellow pads, pencils, and stacks of folders marked for the upcoming Colby trial were all neatly organized, carefully placed in front of each lawyer and their assistants.

Jacq continued. "We've gone over the desk fiasco. Iris' memo says it all. Good job, by the way."

"Yes, very succinctly executed, Iris," said Charles Cognac, one of the young senior associates working on the Colby case.

"Thank you, Charles." Iris flashed a faint smile. Charles appreciated the gesture.

"Before we break, folks, one last reminder." Jarvis walked to the center of the plush burgundy and navy carpeted room. "Well, actually, two things. First, let's be especially careful in the parking garage and on the Els. Probably a good idea for a while to leave work at the same time. Maybe carpool for a couple of weeks. Until we can get a handle on the situation."

"I agree," said Daniels. "We'll have this damn problem under control shortly. I don't want anyone getting hurt. That's it." J.D.

turned and whispered in Jarvis' ear. He nodded his head and pointed at Richard Port, one of the senior lawyers.

Small talk and paper shuffling ensued as the entourage commenced to leave. It had been mandatory for all the key personnel in the firm to attend the meeting. The exceptions were Sherry Weinstein, one of the premier lawyers, who had called in earlier with "car trouble," and Jackie Jr., Daniels' son, who was in Columbus, pursuing a lead concerning the Colby case.

"Oh yes, and secondly..." Jarvis motioned to Richard Port, a ten-year veteran of the firm, sitting on the opposite side of the table. "Richard, would you and Mai stop in to see J.D. and me right away?"

Richard was in his early forties, dark black hair with a touch of gray. His suit jacket was draped over the back of his side chair and his designer tie was loosened at the neck.

"Sure, no problem. Come on, Mai."

Mai Tai picked up some of the Colby folders.

"You won't need the files for this meeting, Mai." said Jarvis. "You can get them later."

Iris hailed the last person to leave the room. "Would you help me straighten up here before you go back to your office, Brandy?"

Brandy Jones was young, energetic, and one of the legal assistants with the least seniority. With her jet-black eyes, close-cropped hair, and soft bronze skin, she looked like a senior in high school. She lived in a run-down neighborhood on the south side of downtown Chicago.

It had taken her six years to become a paralegal. Since her start with the firm six months ago, Brandy had been working closely with Marcus Lambrusco, one of the firm's top litigators, on pro bono cases for low-income families.

"Sure, I've got time," said Brandy. "What I'm doin' can wait." She got on her knees and began to pick up the discarded napkins under the table. Her tight-knit tangerine pantsuit revealed her shapely figure.

"I didn't mean the floor," said Iris. "Just help me clear the table."

"Ooooh," said Brandy. "Hey, I found a shoe!"

X

Jacq was on the phone with Sherry when the three opened the door to his office. "Just a second, Sherry," said J.D. "Come on in, people. I'll be right with you."

"I'll be damned," whispered Richard when he saw the knife and desktop. "Look at this, Mai." She was visibly shaken. "Here...sit down."

"My knees turned to jelly all of a sudden," said Mai.

Jacq continued on the phone. "Sherry, Iris just left for lunch. Let me get this in her office." He turned to the group and said, "I'll be back in a minute. Hang on." J.D. picked up Iris' extension. "You know, you could have used a better excuse than car trouble. Where the hell's the creativity?"

"I DID have car trouble, sweetie," said Sherry. "My brand-new Miata was stolen. Sometime last night, I suspect."

"Ouch. I am sorry. You poor kid."

"And I wasn't about to take the train. You know me and trains." Sherry laughed, remembering the last and only time she rode the Illinois Central Commuter and got lost in southeast Chicago. No laughing matter.

"I could have sent Guinness to pick you up."

"Not really. Iris said he was on a very important errand for you. Top priority, as she put it."

"Oh, yeah. She was right. It was a priority."

"Never mind," Sherry interrupted. "You want to meet for lunch?"

"Sure. When and where?"

"Meet me in a half hour. Front of the Bismark. We can eat at that new place across the street. Ta-ta."

While J.D. was talking to Sherry, Richard Port had gone to his office and returned with his Canon Super-Scope and taken several shots of the evidence: the knife, the desktop, the Post-it note sheet, and the page from the New Yorker.

"Okay. This is what I need, Richard," said Jacq as he entered the room. "Bag the evidence. Get it down to your buddies at the lab. See what you can find out about the knife. You know the procedure better than I do." J.D. sat on the edge of his damaged desk, playing with the sharp crease of his trousers. "Maybe they can come up with a print. I don't know—anything to get a lead on this travesty."

"Why bring Mai into this?" asked Richard, shrugging his broad shoulders.

"It's completely unrelated to the Colby case, but just as important. I need you to turn all your files over to Mai regarding Colby." J.D. watched Mai smooth the pleats in her taupe-and-white Liz Claiborne suit. "I want her to be one of the attorneys in the Colby case."

"Mai can handle it," said Richard.

Jarvis, sitting in a corner of the office, stood and asked, "How do you feel about this, Mai?"

"A little scared. Not because of the Colby project." Mai looked at the desktop, then deeply into Richard's azure-blue eyes. She pursed her full red lips. "Just shocked by the violence in the note. He, or she, is out there somewhere."

"Don't worry, Mai. We're taking every precaution." Jarvis was very reassuring. "You and Richard can work together for the next few days. He'll brief you with every bit of information we have on Colby."

"We can start by getting together right after lunch," said Port, "but first, I'm going to drop these pieces of evidence off at the lab. Meet me in your office at two."

"Remember, no cops. Anything else?" asked Jacq.

"Yes," said Richard. "I suggest you line up a private investigator, for your personal protection. The sooner, the better."

"Good idea. I'll see what I can do."

"I've got some names if you need them."

"No, I can handle it," said Jacq.

"In the meantime, Jarvis," said Richard, "call security. Get me a copy of the video tapes from the corridor cameras. All of them, from this past weekend."

"I'll get right on it. I understand they're re-used every week. I hope it's not too late."

Mai was a beautiful young woman of Tahitian ancestry. Long raven-colored hair, dark eyes, and an elegantly sculpted nose. She had attended law school at night and weekends. Mai was so absorbed in work and school, she didn't have what was considered a "normal" social life.

"You're welcome to work here through the night, both of you," said Jacq.

"I'd like that," said Mai.

Besides...there are no classes on Mondays!

MONEY TALKS

"Now that I think of it, Dewars," said the tall burly man, "I ain't supposed to be doin' no breakin' and enterin'."

The black '85 Buick Riviera crept along the side street and stopped on the shoulder adjacent to the west entrance of the Col-Umbus Orphanage. The ancient structure was located south of the town of Mansfield, on Route 13, two miles from Interstate 71. The facility was located conveniently between Cleveland and Columbus, Ohio.

The red brick and sandstone orphanage looked stately in the dim moonlight, a sharp contrast to its appearance by day: broken and cracked windows, peeling paint on the window sills and sashes, dented gutters, and crumbling mortar. The three-story building had been planned to be home for seventy-five children years ago, although today nearly one hundred pre-teens were crammed into its tiny rooms.

Built in the 1930s, the "Prototype of Child Development" had been a model of the future. Child psychologists and nutritional experts had been on its highly-touted staff. Physical exercise, emotional and mental health programs were considered paramount by the home. But as fiscal responsibility took precedent, the orphanage began deteriorating and was eventually sold at auction.

"Especially into a orphanage, at 2:30 in the mornin', fer cryin' out loud!" continued Johnny Vodka, the burly man. Johnny wore dirty black denim Levis, black sweatshirt, and a dark green hooded jacket.

"Quit your whining. You get paid to work for me. Just do what I tell you!" said Dewars.

Dan Dewars was a short, wiry man with a slight limp. Years on the police force and a stray bullet led him to his current occupation: private investigator—ala Sam Spade. He wore his favorite old navy pin-striped Brooks Brothers suit, worn and shiny at the elbows and knees.

"Now you gonna tell me what the hell we're doin' here?" whined Johnny.

"Shut up and listen," said Dewars. "This Colby guy is hot right now. I mean HOT! I got ten Gs from that clown, Jackie Daniels last week. The guy from Daniels and Rumm." Dewars turned toward Johnny, put his elbow on the armrest and continued. "A five grand check, and another five, if we can drum up something here. I want to milk this Daniels guy for all I can get!"

"Why here? At Col-Umbus Orphanage? Colby's into nursing homes, ain't he?" asked Vodka. The two men could see the faint outline of the red brick and stone building.

"'Col' stands for Colby. I got that information from one of the gabby nurses at the home in Glenview," said Dewars. "Colby was administrator of this place for about ten years. This orphanage used to be a state-run agency. My connections paid off, man."

"You got connections everywhere, Dewars," piped Johnny.

"Because it was state-run, they never did have a computerized file system. All the records are in those manila folders, the same as in the nursing homes." Dewars turned in his seat and started the engine of the old Buick. The soft drone of the motor belied its years as he drove carefully off the shoulder onto the two-lane blacktop.

"That's a stupid name for an orphanage," blurted Johnny.

"Yeah, but it used to be called 'Mansfield', before Colby bought it."

Dewars edged along, without lights, then parked the car with the motor running behind a rusted chain-link fence. The fence was too high to climb, the gate chained and padlocked. Dewars opened the glove box and pushed the yellow button, popping the trunk lid open.

"Get the cutter out of the back. Come on. Hurry it up!" said Dewars in a low raspy voice.

"This place reminds me of my days in Boys Town," whispered Johnny. He went to the back of the Buick and struggled with a heavy cutting tool.

Dewars turned off the ignition. From the trunk, he removed a small black canvas totebag and shouldered the strap.

"What are you lookin' to get out of this, Dewars?"

"Frankly, I don't know. Will you keep your voice down? Now get moving!"

The men, crouching, crept to the tall gate near the side entrance of the three-story building. The burly man cut the twisted chain around the latch. Dewars caught the chain before it hit the ground and lowered the length of links to the gravel.

"Damn it! Be careful!"

"There better not be nobody in there sees us," warned Johnny. "We could get our butts kicked. My parole officer won't like me gettin'...'"

"You'll be out of a job if you don't shut up," cautioned Dewars.

Floodlights lit up the concrete near the side door. The lone bulb over the entrance was broken. The two men approached the building, walking in the shadows cast by the dim lights.

Dewars removed a small worn leather case from his jacket pocket and proceeded to pick the lock. In a matter of seconds, the door was open. The men eased inside.

"The offices are straight ahead," whispered Dewars. "Come on.

You carry the bag." Dewars handed Vodka his totebag after he removed a small orange flashlight.

To the right of a long hallway, Dewars saw the two doors designated on the architectural plans he had picked up from a source at the building department in Mansfield. The office door opened with a slight creak. The intruders froze...waiting.

"Man, that was close!" panted Dewars. "The files we're looking for should be in the back." Dewars' light waved across the perimeter of the small outer office. He could see another door outlined on the far wall.

"There it is!"

Dewars opened the second door slowly. It opened without a sound. "Ahh...we finally got a break."

Along one wall was a row of four-drawer cabinets. Even in the dark, he could see the faded olive paint with its years of accumulated dents in the metal.

"What a dump. And that pissy green," said Johnny hoarsely. He had both arms around the canvas bag, following Dewars toward the cabinets.

"Let's see what we can find on our ol' buddy Colby," whispered the skinny man.

Dewars slid a drawer open labeled 'ADMINISTRATION'.

"Good a place as any to start," he said in low tones. "You watch the door."

Dewars scanned the files, starting with the A's. Digging through the C file, he exclaimed, "Ahh...pay dirt! Colby...graduate of Ohio State." Dewars kept shuffling the files. "Humm." He started to mutter to himself. "Colby worked here...yep...for about ten years. First as a social worker, then as the head guy...before he bought it from the state, in 1987. Looks like the state was going to close the joint. Colby must have had a good reason to stick around so long."

"That don't sound like it's worth no dough to me," said Vodka hoarsely. Then, as an afterthought, he said, "Maybe he had a kid in here he wanted to take care of. Heh! Heh! Heh! Just a joke, Dewars." Johnny smirked and crinkled up his fighter's nose.

Dewars stopped rummaging through the C's in the personnel files and looked at Johnny. "I been a cop too long to let that one go by me. You may be right, hotshot."

"Me, right? Hot damn!"

"Shut up. Keep your voice down." Dewars flashed his small light over the remaining files. "I got an idea."

In the corner of the office was a black metal relic of a cabinet labeled 'ABANDONMENTS', 'ADOPTIONS', and 'DEATHS'.

"Boss! Someone's comin'down the hall!"

Dewars switched off the light. Both men crouched behind the protruding cabinet. Footsteps shuffled past the office, continued up the stairs and diminished on the second floor landing.

"Shhh. Don't breath." Dewars waited another minute.

When the footsteps died, Dewars slid the drawer open. He pried a faded manila folder apart, a dog-eared file that had seen years of wear. The label had been typed on an old Underwood. The stained file read 'ABANDONMENTS'.

"Nothing in the A's, B's-or C's. Maybe I'm not so smart after all," lamented Dewars.

"That means I ain't so smart neither, huh Dewars?"

"I'll go through a few more folders. Then we get the hell out of here."

"You mean we got to come back here, again?"

"Hold it!" said Dewars. "I've got it!"

"What!" panted Vodka. "What ya got?"

He spread the papers on the desk and photographed several pages of the file with his miniature Nikon camera. He worked quickly and didn't bother to answer Johnny.

Dewars folded the files and replaced them in the cabinet. "Let's go!" he said elatedly.

Johnny opened the door to the office, peered out and said, "All clear." The men retraced their steps to the car after looping the chain over the latch. Dewars threw the small bag and cutter into the trunk. They held the car doors open slightly while the Buick pulled away from the orphanage.

As the car approached Route 13, Dewars slowed and slammed his door. Vodka did the same.

"Well, you smart son of a gun!" said Dewars happily. "The Colby files are peanuts! These pictures are worth 100 grand!"

"To who?" asked Johnny.

"None of your business," said Dewars.

I've just earned myself a trip to Chicago!

THE CONDO

Richard Port's black marble and glass condominium was one of several that sprawled the perimeter of the Green Oaks Golf Course in Bloomfield Heights. The condos were two miles north of downtown Chicago, hidden discreetly behind the twists and turns of Lakeshore Drive.

Richard was proud of the interiors in his unit, designed by Jacob Rheinhold & Associates. He and Jacob had collaborated on many of the design features, such as the ten-foot bar to the right of the two-story Great Room and the centrally located circular fireplace constructed of black marble and smoked glass. The suspended stairway to the left led to a loft-style bedroom, overlooking the Great Room. Richard and Amy, his fiancee and a lawyer at the firm, had had some wild times up there, throwing wadded up socks and other stuff down into the fireplace.

"Oh, hell!" shouted Richard. "The market's down again. Damn!" He wore gray silk pajama bottoms and wool socks. He sat in the kitchen drinking a glass of papaya juice, watching the wall-mounted giant-screen television relay the bad news. "This I don't need."

Richard turned off the power and went upstairs to his workout room, with its mirrored walls, weights, and exercise machines. The room adjoined his private spa, hot tub, sunroom and mirrored show-

er and bath. He turned on the stereo. A tape began playing a soothing aria from his classical collection.

Richard finished his exercises. Working at the office three
nights in a row past midnight left him bushed. He cut out some of
the work on his abs and decided to spend the extra five minutes
relaxing in the shower. The stereo was playing a melody by Franz
Lehar, one of his favorite composers. Richard planned to meet Mai
at the office in an hour. The hot water felt great. He stepped in and
pulled the mirrored door closed.

Mai pulled her car into the visitor's parking area, a short walk
west of the Green Oaks Condos. Mai had been to Richard's Christmas
party a year ago but couldn't remember his apartment number. She
was aware that Richard and Amy were an "item" at the firm.

Mai went to the passenger side of her Accura. She was wearing
a dark wool wrap and a tighter than usual brown knit dress with a
seductively low neckline. Mai reached in and picked up a small grocery bag, then swung her brown Gucci bag onto one shoulder and
walked to the lobby.

"Would you please ring Richard Port's apartment," said Mai to
the woman behind the reception desk.

"Of course, Ma'am." Her nameplate on the counter read JULIE
CHAMPAGNE. Whom shall I say is calling?"

"His co-worker, Ms. Tai."

"Certainly." The woman connected Richard's line and let it ring
repeatedly. "I'm sorry, he's not answering. He must be out," said
Julie.

"No, I think his music may be turned up. He enjoys the classics
with tons of volume." Mai picked up her brown bag from the
counter. "I'll go up and surprise him. His apartment number is...?"

"1957. If you need security, let me know, Ma'am."

"Thank you." Mai took one of the bronze-colored glass elevators to the nineteenth floor. On nineteen, the carpeting was earth-toned, with a deep plush pile, complimented by subtle monocromatic colorings in the wallpaper.

Mai walked down a long hallway, admiring the recessed sconces along the way. She rapped on the door. No answer. She rapped louder. Still no answer. Amy had mentioned, jokingly, the potted palm in the corridor. The one with the key. Sure enough, a few feet from Richard's door was the large brass urn, and a cute brass rock with Richard's key under it. Mai unlocked the door.

"Richard." Mai walked into the Great Room with the music blaring something classical. "Richard!" She carried her brown paper bag into the kitchen and set it on one of the black leather stools. Richard's briefcase was on the granite counter. Mai took her .38 nickel-plated revolver out of the Gucci bag and started up the circular staircase.

At the top of the stairs, Mai could hear the water running, its sound competing with the classics. She walked the length of the loft, down the narrow hall toward the sound of the water.

"What th...!" Richard jumped backward and slid one of the mirrored doors in front of his body.

Mai pointed the gun at him and said, "BANG! BANG! You're dead!"

BREAKFAST

"Hand me a towel," said Richard. He peered around the mirrored door. It didn't take him long to regain his composure.

"Why should I?" said Mai. "I like you better the way you are!" Her face flushed.

"What are you doing with a gun? A classic I might add." He caught the towel Mai pitched at him.

"A gal needs protection, even in this part of town."

"Looks like something out of the Al Capone era."

"I didn't know that. It goes so well with my silver beaded handbag," said Mai.

"How did you get in? Don't tell me! Amy and the potted plant story."

"Right. I think everyone at the office knows." Mai had her back turned, facing the wall, although with all the mirrors on the walls, she was still able to see Richard toweling off. She closed her eyes. She resisted as long as she could. She opened one eye. "I suggest you find another hiding place for your key, Mr. Port."

"Okay, how about under the door mat?" Richard picked up a Bill Blass striped robe from a contoured chair. "I thought we were going to meet at the office at ten."

"Yes, I know. I wanted to surprise you with breakfast. Some of those famous croissants from Milos that Jacq loves so much."

"You certainly surprised me."

"It was a spur of the moment thing." Mai nervously fluffed a towel. "I'll see if I can find the coffee."

Richard turned the music down to barely audible. "Sounds good. I'll be down in ten minutes. There's juice in the fridge."

Through the small arched window in the kitchen, Mai was able to see her car parked forty yards away in the visitor's lot. Several other cars spotted the huge area. The sun reflected off the top of a shiny Miata behind a grove of oaks.

"I see you took Jarvis' suggestion and parked in the lot and not in the parking garage," said Richard. He was tying a black patterned tie.

The croissants were on the table, piping hot, with melting butter dripping down their sides. Mai carried the coffee pot and two cups. She stopped in front of Richard.

"I remembered what he and Tom Beers from Security said as I drove over here...but...quite frankly...it was the way you looked at me last Monday in Jacq's office...when I was so frightened."

He stopped in the middle of his tying. Mai put the coffee pot on the counter and with the cups in one hand, she leaned into Richard, gently kissing him. Richard continued to hold the tie.

"I...I'm sorry...I know you and Amy have been going together- for awhile..."

"Almost a year," said a tongue-tied Richard.

"I know...but yesterday, and last night..." Mai backed away, flustered and self-conscious. "I guess I've been out of the loop for so long, it just got to me. I read it wrong. Richard...I'm truly sorry. Forgive me?"

"Hey. Nothing to forgive." Richard gently tilted Mai's face up toward his. "It's a good thing I've got a picture of Amy tattooed to the side of my brain, otherwise..."

"Thanks for being so understanding. You really are a nice guy, Mr. Port."

"And you, Ms. Tai, can brighten up anybody's day."

Richard reached out and squeezed Mai's hand. She gazed into his eyes.

What do I have to do to deserve someone like you? she thought. *Maybe next time.*

"Listen," said Richard, "while we're here, why don't we pick up where we left off on the Colby case. Let's have breakfast and dive right in."

"Uhmm, I don't think so," chimed Mai. "I think I'd feel more comfortable at the office, under the circumstances. But breakfast still sounds good. Great, as a matter of fact."

Richard and Mai sat at opposite ends of a small glossy table. The idle chatter about croissants and raspberry jam relaxed them both enough to start a conversation concerning the upcoming Colby trial.

"Jackie returned from Columbus yesterday, Mai. Did you know?"

"Yes, I heard he was gone for a few days." Mai sat with her hand tucked under her chin, smiling at Richard. She glanced down her plunging neckline and immediately straightened her back, pulling her ribbed collar together slightly. Her face reddened. She caught Richard self-consciously looking down at her.

"Maybe I shouldn't tell you this, but some of us at the office, including Amy, have a difficult time with Jackie. Not aways. Just when no one else is around."

"A real jerk, eh?" Richard opened one of the file folders. "I heard stories. What's he doing that's so bad?"

"Oh, nothing so bad...yet. I've caught him looking down my blouse when I sit at my desk. You know, the taupe silk that's open at the neck."

"Yeah, I know the one. Can't say I blame him." Richard smiled sheepishly, running his fingers through his hair.

"Well, when you do it, it's nice." She glanced up at Richard and their eyes met. "When I see Jackie do it, it's creepy."

"I think he's harmless." Richard went over to his office, adjacent to the kitchen, and came back with a sheet of copier paper. "Jackie sent this E-mail last night. Might be something important. Though you can't believe anything Jackie says some of the time."

"What's he got to say...believable or not?"

"He may have information that could blow this case wide open. He's not sure yet, but he might have a strong lead. That's it."

"It would be great if he was more positive. We need more to go on, if we want to convince the jury of Colby's innocence."

Richard winked at Mai. "I think Jackie wants another expense-paid trip to Columbus."

"What's in Columbus?"

"I don't know," said Richard. "But the next time he goes, I'm going with him."

"We should be getting back to the office." Mai gathered the cups and small plates from the table and carried them to the sink. "It's getting late."

"Yeah, you're right." Richard collected the manila envelopes and files.

Mai threw the wool wrap around her shoulder, picked up her bag and some of the files, and unlatched the brass handle on the front door.

"Oh, Ms. Tai. Don't forget to leave the key under the rock on your way out. Amy might be needing it again some day," said Richard with a wry grin.

"Gottcha, boss!"

Mai took the elevator down to the first level, hurried past the reception desk and through the double glass doors to the visitor's lot, carrying the files and a small paper sack. Her Gucci swayed gently on her shoulder.

"Do you need some help, Ma'am?" said the guard sitting along the wall and out of the bright sunlight. He was stockily built, with a slight paunch. He made a faint effort to get out of his worn leather armchair.

"No, thank you," said Mai. "I don't have far to go."

"All right, Ma'am. Have a nice day," said the relieved guard.

Mai walked the remaining distance to her car, caught up in the events of the morning. Daydreaming.

It was nice. Could have been better...still, it's the most fun I've had in a long time.

Richard Port stayed at the arched window in the kitchen. When Mai came into view, he enjoyed seeing her sexy walk, her fringed wrap swaying in the cool October breeze as she neared her car. Still watching, he knew he had to make sure she got safely into the Accura. Strictly for Mai's own protection.

Yeah...sure!

As soon as he was satisfied she was safe in her car, Richard grabbed his briefcase, coat, and car keys from his Bela Lugosi chair in the hallway. He took one of the tenant elevators to the underground parking garage.

Mai opened her car door, threw her belongings into the back seat and locked the door. Mai was so engrossed in her fantasizing, she didn't notice the shiny Miata slowly circling the parking lot. Circling ever closer to her.

Jacq leaned against the window, staring out at the harbor. A gray mist shrouded the skyline. Even Iris' coffee mixed with scotch didn't help his depressed, frustrated feelings. He walked across the office and sank heavily into his familiar leather chair, frowning as his hand touched the edges of the contemporary Herman Miller concoction, a temporary desk brought in from one of the unoccupied offices down the hall. Iris had said it might be three months before his old desk was restored.

If I didn't have so many irons in the fire, I could be a major S.O.B. about this stupid-looking monstrosity!

Jacq's phone buzzed. "Yeah? I want nothin' but good news!"

"I don't think I can help you there. It's DeDe on line four," said Iris.

Jacq spun his chair around facing the wall. He sighed and walked to the coffee bar. He straightened one of his framed red and gold diplomas.

Thank you, Dad, for paying my way through law school!

"Yeah, DeDe, what is it?"

"I wanted to remind you, darling, well in advance," said DeDe coyly, "about the dinner party next weekend. Come home early...for a change. I mentioned it last week, also. Remember?" DeDe's voice was soft and sexual.

"What dinner party?"

"Oh, you know. John Coors, the museum administrator. He's retiring soon, that dear little man. I've been elected to throw this impromptu bash for him." DeDe was still sugary sweet. "Be a dear and show up on time."

"Hey," said Jacq, "if you want to play nursemaid on all these committees..."

Jarvis knocked on the door and pushed it open. "Whoops. Didn't mean to interrupt."

Jacq waved him off with his free hand.

"I can come back later. Not that important." Jarvis quietly closed the door.

"...do it yourself. I've got my own problems!"

"I can count on you, then? About sevenish? Jacq?"

Jacq looked at the ceiling, rolled his eyes, and said, "Oh, hell-you know I will!"

"Good! That will give you time to dress. I'll have your new Brioni waiting for you. Ta-ta," cooed DeDe.

"To hell with the Brioni," mumbled Jacq to himself.

Jarvis returned to his austere office set in a corner between Dearborn and Madison Avenues. On a clear day, he could see the Sun-Times building across the Chicago River. Today the building was a faint silhouette.

Jarvis was startled when Jacq pushed his door open. "You want to see me, Rumm?"

"Yes. I read Jackie's memo. Looks like the trip to Columbus paid off."

"How so," asked Jacq. It amazed him how Jarvis could get any work done in such a boring environment.

Where is your self-esteem, Rumm?

"Jackie says through his diligence and hard work, he found out that Colby not only owns the one nursing home in Glenview, but get this—he owns two others in Michigan and another in Indiana." Jarvis was genuinely excited.

"What's this got to do with the price of tea in Taiwan?" asked J.D.

"Each home was incorporated under a different name. Colby must be trying to hide that information from a lot of people. Maybe Uncle Sam. Our Jackie must have done a ton of digging."

"I love the kid like a son," said Jacq facetiously, "but I can't see him coming up with this kind of info...not without outside help."

"He said he did it alone. Also, I'd like to..."

"Bull! I'm meeting with Jackie as soon as I get back from lunch." Jacq walked down the long marble hallway to his office and slammed the door.

Jarvis sat down in his worn burgundy chair. He lit a half-smoked Bagatello. He had wanted to suggest, again, that perhaps Gina Collins, his favorite young lawyer, and not Mai, would be the better choice to work with Richard on the Colby case. Jacq was too busy. He was always too busy.

Go to your damn worthless parties. They may be your last!

SWEET EXCHANGE

Mai closed her large, expressive eyes for a moment. She let her raven hair cascade over the headrest. She pursed her full red lips, daydreaming for a few more seconds about what could have happened in the apartment.

She had parked her Accura at the end of the lot, facing a grove of dense maples and several tall oaks. Mai didn't see the red Miata pull quickly across the back of her car, blocking any chance of escape.

It had taken three days and nights...but today is it!

A slim shadowy figure casually walked up to the driver's side door, latex gloves cradling a short piece of lead pipe. The window was shattered with one blow. Glass pellets covered Mai's lap.

Mai Tai screamed. Her eyes filled with terror, then recognition. "YOU!" she said, trembling. "Why??"

The assailant hit Mai sharply across the bridge of her nose with the pipe. Blood splattered down her chin. Mai slumped back into the headrest.

Mai's beautiful full lips were duct-taped and her body carried and pushed into the back seat of the red Miata. Her wrists were taped behind her back, hurriedly yet efficiently. Mai's body was wedged down between the seat and floor.

Now...calm down...let's not get too excited and blow this production!

The slim figure walked confidently back to Mai's car, opened the passenger side door and removed all of the Colby files. The glove box with her cell phone and other personal items was left intact. The brown Gucci bag, containing Mai's nickel-plated protector, was thrown into the front seat of the red car.

Very good! The excitement lasted only...thirty seconds? Start to finish? Excellent!

The assailant covered Mai's body with a blanket, drove slowly out of the visitor's lot, and turned south on Lakeshore Drive. The car maintained the posted speed limit.

Don't want to get careless now!

The Miata continued south on Route 41, past the Navy Pier, then left, crossing the Chicago River north of the harbor. Mai was beginning to stir and moan under the blanket.

Can't have that, Mai...can we?

The driver exited on Monroe Street and turned left into Grant Park. The car stopped in a secluded area shielded by a row of tall hedges. The dark, smoked privacy glass on the Miata reflected peace and tranquility on the outside. The assailant, without opening the doors, climbed over the leather seat back, threw the blanket to the front of the car, and pulled Mai up onto the rear seat.

Her eyes were wild with fear. She began to shake her head from side to side. The blood above her taped mouth had dried to a deep, rich maroon. Mai pleaded in muffled tones. She was struck again with the pipe. The attacker pulled off her pantyhose and began to methodically wrap them around her neck.

Sorry, Mai. Hope your last tryst was worth it...but alas, no more Colby case for you!

No screams. Her body collapsed, head hanging over the edge of the seat. The killer pushed Mai back onto the floor, again covering her with the blanket. The slim figure crawled to the front, removed

Mai's driver's license from her handbag, and threw it on the passenger seat. Making sure nothing was left on the floor or seats, the figure locked both doors, then walked down the concrete sidewalk that ran parallel to the row of hedges. At the end of the row, parked on the opposite side of the high shrubbery, was a dark blue Minivan. The files were tossed into a box in the back of the van. The Gucci bag was placed onto the front seat. The figure jumped into the van, turned the key, and drove slowly out of the park, heading toward mid-town.

The van made a series of turns, eventually stopping in one of the lots at Children's Research Hospital a mile and a half from Grant Park. The driver rifled through Mai's brown bag, pocketing the money from her wallet. In the largest compartment of the Gucci bag were Mai's personal items. The figure tossed them into a black trash bag. Searching deeper, the killer felt cold steel, even through the latex gloves. It was the nickel-plated revolver.

This will come in oh-so-handy the next time!

All of Mai's belongings, except for the money and her gun, were shoved into the plastic bag. The bag was knotted. The slim figure stepped out of the van and walked to the truck bays at the end of the receiving dock, then flipped the bag into a dumpster behind the brick partition. The latex gloves were discarded at the foot of the dumpster, thrown in with several other gloves that littered the base.

How's THAT for research, Daniels!

The killer drove two blocks to the corner of Adams and Wells Street, turned right and headed east on Monroe.

Hi Ho, Hi Ho—It's off to work we go!

JACKIE BOY

CHAPTER IX

"You did what?" yelled Jacq. "Not with the receptionist!"

"Hey, you do it all the time," countered Jackie. "What's the big deal?"

"Not with the bimbo that wears the hair mascara?"

"Those rainbow bangs are outrageous, Pops. I love 'em!"

"I sent you to Columbus on business, to see what you could come up with on Nathan Colby. Not this damn monkey business!" The men sat down and stared at each other. Neither man spoke.

Jackie Daniels Jr. had worked for his father in various capacities since he was a teenager. Primarily because of his father's connections, Jackie eventually graduated from law school. He had no current title within the firm. Jackie was in his early thirties; close-cropped hair, a subtle hint of a mustache and goatee. His attitude, along with his piercing eyes and hand-tailored wardrobe, gave him the look he was after: a suave tough-looking womanizer. Just like Dad.

"Listen," said Jackie finally. "Rosie flew down Friday night. Nobody in the firm knows." Jackie walked to the window, pulled the drapery aside and squinted at the silent traffic below. "Hell, you know how it is on those damn trips. No reason to risk picking up some broad in a bar."

"Especially when we've got a stable here in the office. Is that what you mean?" said Jacq.

Jackie turned and faced his father. A smile crossed his lips. "You said it, Pops. Not me."

The men glared at each other. Jacq twisted his Rolex and wished he was somewhere in Jamaica on one of the pristine beaches. Jackie continued to smile.

"If you're going to mess around with someone, why pick our receptionist, of all people? You could have been a little more discreet."

"So what," replied Jackie. "It's nothing serious. We were having a little fun. You know Columbus."

"Yeah—fun. I spent a week in Columbus one day."

"At least you still have your sense of humor," said Jackie grinning.

"Let's drop it—for now. We've got something more serious to worry about." Jacq reached across his desk and picked up a red-tabbed file. "We've got a major problem. Look."

"Yeah—so?" said Jackie. "All I see is a pile of folders with red flags."

"Precisely. Nathan Colby is an S.O.B. He's probably guiltier than hell, but we're being paid to get him off...and that is exactly what we're going to do."

"It's good I dug up the evidence I did about those nursing homes. If the D.A. gets wind of it..."

"That's okay," said Jacq. "We'll find a way to suppress the information. Collins and Rumm are working on it right now."

"So what do you want me to do next?" Jackie shrugged his shoulders. "You want me to go to Glenview?"

"No." Jacq picked up an expense reimbursement form from a pile of clutter on his desk. "I've got one more sore spot I want to clear up. Sit down."

"Now what'd I do?" Jackie plodded to the opposite side of the desk and sank into a bentwood sidechair.

"Explain this," said the elder Daniels. "Iris tells me you spent five grand. A check paid to some P.I. in Columbus. I thought you told Rumm you did all the leg work."

"Hey, I wasn't trying to hide anything," said Jackie. "Information costs money. I figured that was the quickest way to go." Jackie brushed his lapels. "Besides, they'll keep whatever they found out privileged."

"Yeah, right!" Jacq supressed his anger, shuffling the papers in one of the folders. "According to your memo, a secondary piece of information we got on Colby is that he started out as an administrator of an orphanage about thirty years ago." He examined the two photocopies. "A few minor violations. Nothing suspicious or pertinent to this case." Jacq paused, then stated flatly, "We can rule out all this orphanage nonsense."

"But the fact he got into the nursing home racket, first as executive director, and now as owner of three of them in Illinois, now that's enough to perk up your ears," said Jackie. "And why did he change the name of every home he bought? I mean, why didn't he name them like he did here in Illinois, plain old Colby Nursing Home?"

"I don't think it's worth five thousand dollars," said Jacq. He walked across the room and poured himself a scotch and water at the coffee bar.

Jackie stretched his legs and went to the door. "If you need me, Pops, I'll be in my office."

"One more item. I want you and Richard to go back to Columbus, and keep digging into the nursing home angle. We're bound to come up with something more that'll help this case."

"Okay, you're the boss," said Jackie. He shook his head,

grabbed the chrome doorlatch and pushed the fluted glass panel. "If you ever had a magic wand, now's the time to use it. This guy Colby was suspected of arson in Michigan. Even though the case was dropped, he was guilty as hell. Now, you and I both know he's probably guilty of the murder at the home in Glenview." Jackie continued as he left the office. "I don't know why you took this case, Pops. I really don't." Jackie slammed the door.

Jacq twisted in his Oval Office chair.

And for your own good, you never will, kid!

ROSIE

"Going up. Step to the rear, please," said Bass, the elevator operator. "Hi, Rosie. Have a nice lunch?"

"Yes, I did. Thanks for asking. Kristie and I ate at the new place across from the Bismark. Great food."

Kristie and Rosie backed into the elevator, crowded with luncheon passengers. Pushing farther back, the way Bass told her to do, was one of Rosie's favorite daytime activities. She enjoyed the attention, the closeness, and especially the subtle groping. She wore a multi-colored mohair shawl wrapped around her shoulder, protection against the chill of the late October weather. Her tight-fitting knit pants were easy prey for the young financial advisers from the tenth floor. Rosie's auburn hair was closely cropped, with a slight curl. Very conservative. No rainbow bangs today, although her eyes were dramatically outlined.

"I forgot to ask. Where were you last Friday night? I called—no answer," said Kristie Claret, a young secretary who worked between four lawyers at Daniels and Rumm. Kristie looked more like a college freshman than a career woman. She wore her hair in a casual wind-blown style that complimented her pixie personality. Her blouse was loose-fitting. Black leather pants two sizes too tight. Her accessories were well coordinated, yet inexpensive.

"I took Mom to a movie," replied Rosie. "Once a month I try to get her out of the house." Rosie backed a bit more into one of the adviser's hands. "Ohh...ah...we went to see that Anthony Hopkins movie."

Kristie turned to see Rosie's flushed face and said, "I tried to call you again for Saturday. We planned to go to the Liquid Kitty, remember?"

"Yeah," said Rosie. A slight pause. "I thought I heard the phone. I had to leave the machine on. Mother didn't feel too good after her night on the town."

The express elevator came to a stop on ten. Rosie and Kristie stepped aside for the group of financial people. One of the group was a tall red-headed woman.

There is progress being made in this country after all, thought Rosie.

"Is it anything serious?"

"No. You know how she is." The two women got off the elevator on the nineteenth floor and proceeded down a marble-tiled corridor. Adjacent to the law library, Kristie and Rosie stopped at the sign-in office and made their required notations on their time cards. "She spends more and more time in that damn wheelchair. Her being a major pain doesn't help either."

"Your mother is a major pain?" Kristie smiled as she glanced at Rosie.

"As if you didn't know."

They walked back toward the elevators, Rosie stopping at the reception desk fronting a large curved glass-block wall. The words 'DANIELS AND RUMM' were sand-blasted in twelve-inch-high letters across an enormous mirrored panel. She threw her rust suede carryall bag behind the counter.

"Well, anyway," said Kristie, "I was going to borrow my brother's Mercedes. We could've gone in style."

Rosie shook her head. "Yeah, it would have been better than

taking my van with the handicapped sticker and the wheelchair lift!"
The girls laughed at Rosie's attempt at hilarity.

"He told me about another hot spot. Narcisse. They even give
you a fake—FAUX—string of pearls to take home."

"No way!"

"I'm not kidding!"

"That's awesome!" Rosie's lips formed a circle of bright red.
She looked down at the appointment book on her gray Corian
counter. "I'm really sorry, Kris. Maybe we can do it this coming
week, okay?"

"All right. We can hit one of those cigar bars, too! See ya."

Kristie hurried down the hall, took the elevator up to twenty-one
to her small unpretentious office opposite the corporate conference
room. As she neared her desk, Kristie Claret unbuttoned the top button of her white satin blouse.

Rosie returned from the restroom after touching up her makeup
and applying fresh lipstick with a touch of silk. She sat on the edge
of her burgundy stool and stared for a moment, deep in thought, at
the computer screen twinkling the afternoon appointments.

Kristie is so sweet. I'm sorry I had to keep lying to her, she said
to herself.

At least it's good practice when I have to start lying to Jackie!

REVELATION

Iris buzzed the CEO's office. "Jacq, you wanted me to remind you. There's a meeting scheduled with Richard."

"Yeah, I know." Jacq hung his navy trenchcoat in the walk-in closet. He took a minute to freshen up in his bathroom, then chewed two Tums. The veal scaloppini from lunch wasn't going down without a fight. He sat and spun his chair toward the desk and pushed the intercom button. "Who's office are he and Mai using today?"

"They should be in Richard's office, since ten or eleven this morning," replied Iris.

Jacq straightened his silk tie and brushed a speck off his charcoal-colored wool jacket. He walked hurriedly down the marbled corridor, then rode the elevator to the floor below.

On the twentieth floor were the offices of various 'B' lawyers. Richard Port occupied a corner office at the end of a black and white tiled hallway. His office was eclectic, very relaxed in nature. On the walls were photographs of police officers with their arms around Richard's shoulders. Citations, diplomas from the Police Academy and other related mementos adorned the walls.

Jacq walked past several offices, greeting Gina and Marcus Lambrusco as they conversed in the hallway.

The mailboy was pushing his cart toward the elevators. "Good morning, Mr. Daniels," said the bespectacled Harry Heineken.

Harry also worked in the print shop and kept track of the supplies for Iris. He was thirty-one, frail and pasty-faced, with long dirty-blonde hair. Daniels walked past without acknowledging the young man.

Jacq shoved the office door open. "Hey, Richard, how's it going?" He was smiling when he looked around the room. Then he frowned and said, "Where's Mai?"

Richard stood up abruptly. "Oh, it's you. I thought it might be Mai." A worried look etched his face. "I haven't seen her since around nine-thirty this morning."

"Where was that?"

"She stopped off at my place for breakfast."

"And...?"

"Then we agreed to meet here around ten. I tried to call her cell phone, but it's not connected." Richard crossed over to his small conference table and opened his chestnut calfskin business bag. "It's not like Mai to turn off her phone."

"Hummm. Well, I'm sure she'll show up any minute." Jacq sat on the bullnose of the marble table top, brushing an imaginary spot off his Italian loafers. "I wanted to see if you've uncovered anything in your investigation regarding the damage to my father's desk. You know, MY desk."

"The lab should be getting back to me before the end of the week. I'm hoping we can get at least a partial print off the knife. I'm waiting for a videotape of last weekend from Security, too. I told them I want the original tapes, not copies, of all the top three hall-ways. I might have those by the end of the day. That's all I've got."

"Sounds good."

Richard slumped back in his chair. He pulled a top drawer open and stared at some markers and felt-tip pens. "I'd like to know how someone could get access to the twenty-first floor on a weekend."

"Anything else?"

"You'll be the first to know." Richard stacked some folders on the table, lining up two of the fattest files facing Mai's empty chair. "I've got to wind up the Colby files with her today. So far, we've got an abundance of circumstantial evidence. Mai will know as much about Nathan Colby as I do by the end of the day."

"Good! Mai's a smart kid. A beauty, too," said Jacq. He walked to the large corner window, peering out toward the Times Building through the swirling fog. "You say Mai left your apartment around, what, nine-thirty? She had her own car, I presume?"

"Yes," said Richard. "She drove her own car. I saw her drive away." Richard looked up from the stack of files. A troubled frown crossed his rugged face. "Well, now that I think about it...I didn't actually see her drive away. But I DID see her get into her car."

"So hell, you figured she was on her way. That was in your lot at Green Oaks?"

"Yes. When I saw Mai get into her car, I grabbed my bag and took off. I knew she'd be okay in the parking lot. I'll be damned! Maybe I was wrong."

"Aww, don't sweat it," said Jacq. Trying to change the subject, he stood up, arms waving in a circular motion and said good-humoredly, "At least they tell me my desk will be as good as new when I get it back from the refinishers."

"Funny you should mention the desk," said Richard. "The other day during lunch, Mai said she thought there might be a link between the damage to your desk, and of all things, the Colby trial."

"Hell! At this point I wouldn't be surprised. Call me if you hear from Mai." Jacq slammed the door, rode the elevator to the top floor, and marched to his office. Iris came running down the hall to meet him.

"I called Richard's office!" she said excitedly. "I couldn't tell him! God! It's terrible!..." Iris began sobbing, her arms around

Jacq's shoulders.

"What is it? Tell me!"

Iris started crying hysterically. She pulled away slightly from Jacq, her face ashen. "We just received a telephone call from the Chicago police." Iris twitched nervously. "The police found Sherry's car."

Jacq self-consciously took Iris' arms from around his neck, pulling them down to her sides. Then, as he held her hands, he said, "Hell, that sounds like good news to me."

She looked up into his eyes through her tears. "Mai's body was found in the back seat of Sherry's car."

Richard Port ran from the elevator, down the hall toward Jacq and Iris. "What's wrong, Iris? Jacq?"

Iris grabbed Richard's lapel and sobbed, "Mai's dead! Strangled!"

"MY GOD! How? When?"

"The police are on the way."

Richard put his arm around Iris and hugged her. He held her tenderly, gave her his pocket handkerchief, then led her into Jacq's office.

"Iris," said Jacq. "Send a memo to Rumm. I want to start interviewing for a replacement immediately."

Iris wiped her eyes. Her sobbing subsided. She looked at Jacq and said, "Right away...your majesty."

You S.O.B! I'm so thankful we never married!

"I'm Lieutenant Miller. This is my partner, Detective Sergeant Dos Equis. We're from the Central Precinct, Homicide Division."

Iris, still shaken, ushered the men into Jacq's office. Sitting at one end of the conference table were Jarvis, Richard, and Jackie. Jacq was sitting in his black leather chair, stroking the padded arm, staring at Chicago's darkening skyline. He stood, acknowledged their I.D. cards, and extended his hand as Miller and Sergeant Dos entered the room.

Miller bore a striking resemblance to a young Humphrey Bogart. His companion Donny, affectionately referred to as "Dog," stopped at the doorway. Donny's build and mannerisms fit his nickname perfectly.

"Hello, gentlemen. I'm Jacq Daniels." Jacq shook hands with Miller. "This is Jarvis Rumm, my partner. My son Jackie. And this is..."

"Hey, Richie!" said Miller. He glanced back at Jacq. "Richie and I go way back. How you doin', man?"

"Richie! Ha! That's rich," said Jackie.

Richard stood, grabbed Miller's hand, and shook it. "I've had better days, Mike. This is a shocker."

Miller gave Richard a pat on the back. The two plain-clothesmen moved into the office. Miller sat across from Richard while

Sergeant Dos remained standing, both men removing notepads from their jacket pockets.

"Gentlemen," began Miller. "So far, this is all we've got. Numero uno. About two-thirty this afternoon, a couple of twelve-year-olds were rollerblading in Grant Park, south of the fountain."

"The two kids skipped school, if yer wondering why they were messin' around at that time," interjected the sergeant.

"The kids were skating around the fountain. Down by those tall hedges. You know, next to the parking lots." Miller flipped a page in his pad.

Sergeant Dos backed up slightly and bumped into DeDe's pear-wood cabinet, knocking over a Baccarat vase.

"Oops," was all he said.

Miller continued. "One of the boys, a Bud Porter, lost his balance coming around the corner and landed in the hedges, head first. He was the first to see the red Miata. About an hour later, the boys saw the car still parked in the same spot. Nobody around it. They got nosey and took a closer look. They saw a woman's shoe sticking out from under a blanket. The kids said it was hard to see anything else because of the dark windows on the Miata."

"They panicked," said Dos, still looking at the broken crystal. "They got the attention of a jogger, a woman who called 911."

"Donny and I got to the crime scene from central about the same time those jokers from EMS arrived," added Miller. "I'd hate like hell to be bleedin' somewhere having to wait for..."

"How did she die?" asked Richard.

"Looks like death by strangulation. She was hit with a blunt, probably metal, object. Hammer, maybe a pipe. Above the bridge of her nose. The blow most likely rendered her unconscious...at least for a while. She was strangled with what they presume to be her own pantyhose," said Miller.

"My God!" said Jarvis. He was twiddling his fingers, head bowed, looking at his hands.

"You'll most likely find Mai's car in the Green Oaks visitor's lot," said Richard. He was staring vacantly at a Dali print hanging over the Corian coffee bar.

"We'll get on it right away, Mr. Port," said Dos.

"Richie, as soon as I get the photos back from the lab, I'll send them over to you." Miller thumbed his notepad again. "According to the examiner, this didn't seem to be a sexual assault. No indication of any kind. The autopsy will verify his assumption. Because of that information, the killer MIGHT be female."

"She was quite a looker," said Donny.

"She was a beautiful person," said Richard. He turned away from the group, gazed out the window for a brief moment, then dropped his head in his hands. Rain began to splatter on the giant glass panels. Rivulets flowed downward.

"Hang in there, Richie."

"We were working on a special project together," said Richard hesitantly.

"Yes, Mai and Richard were working on the Colby case, for over a week," said Jacq. He put his hand on Richard's shoulder, then said to Miller, "They spent twelve-fourteen hours together almost every day."

"Whoever killed her must have been frustrated—waiting for the right moment," said Miller. Looking Richard in the eye, he announced, "Gentlemen, all indications point to a cleverly planned, premeditated crime. I'd bet my shield on it. Someone took the time to plan very carefully. This was not a crime of passion."

"Mai had a .38 nickel-plated revolver in a brown Gucci bag. Did you find those?" asked Richard.

"No," said Miller. "There was nothing in the car, except her body, a driver's license, and a blanket."

Dos chimed in, "We'll check to see if she had the gun registered. Maybe it's still in her car, but I doubt it."

"Can you guys put a lid on this?" asked Jacq. "The publicity would..."

"It's too late for that now, Mr. Daniels," said Miller. "The press is panting out in the hallway."

"She was probably being tailed for days," lamented Richard. "You know, Mike...I was the last person to see Mai alive."

Dos' elbow hit the side of the cabinet again.

Richard paused, then sighed, "If I wouldn't have been in such a hurry, she might be alive today."

Now I know Nathan Colby is involved in Mai's death...somehow!

MANSFIELD

CHAPTER XIII

SEPTEMBER 14, 1979

The basement, in the west end of the orphanage, was creepy, cold, and damp. The electrical systems, boilers, and heating equipment were all located on the far side of the lower level. A chilling wind moaned through a cracked pane of glass across a dimly lit hall. Patterned shadows cast an eerie design on the wooden stairway from the single fifty watt bulb hanging from the cob-webbed ceiling. The asbestos tile floor was dull and worn with age.

A trail of dirt and mud led to a small enclosure at the opposite side of the stairs. The structure was barren and windowless. The tiny "room" was an old obsolete utility area, with warped pine shelving on one wall. On the opposite side of the floor, in a corner, was a stained crib mattress. A brown plastic tray, food half-eaten, was on the floor near the locked door. Nailed to the remaining corner of the eight-foot-square room was a wooden home-made device with a hole cut into the seat. The room was called THE CLOSET.

"What did that damn juvenile delinquent do this time?" demanded Nathan Colby.

"Nothin' too bad," said Schlitz, the aging social worker. Schlitz was bald, tired, and ready for retirement. "All the kid did was sass

Miss Bordeaux."

"And what else! I know there's more!"

"Oh...and Johnny Walker got his face pushed into the mashed potatoes...during a small food fight. No big deal." said Schlitz.

"Into the closet!" ordered Colby.

"Not again, Nathan. That poor kid's been in that closet at least once a week for as long as I can remember."

"Into the damn closet. Now! That brat's going to learn to shape up, or suffer the consequences. Nobody starts a food fight in my cafeteria and gets away with it."

Schlitz, half-heartedly, shuffled out of Colby's musty office with the keys.

X

All I did was stick out my tongue. So I elbowed Johnny. The food fight was a blast! I don't deserve this. I swear I'll get you some day, Mr. Colby.

A large hairy rat skittered across the closet floor.

WORKING IT OFF

"Hey, Richard. Wait up!" Amy ran down the tiled corridor toward the employee's workout facility. Her black clunky-heeled shoes echoed through the long hallway. Amy's beautiful dark brown eyes were partially hidden by her dishevelled shoulder-length tresses as she hurried to meet Richard. The hem of her Max Mara skirt was barely a foot off the floor, causing her to take abbreviated, choppy steps.

Richard Port turned toward the familiar voice. "Oh, hi, Amy." He reached out to her. She put her hands in his and gave him a short tender kiss. "I need to blow off some steam. Want to join me?"

She tilted her head back, hair flying. Amy's olive complexion looked darker in the dim light of the hall. She balanced her business bag and a dozen file folders. "No, I can't. I've got a meeting with Sherry in ten minutes."

"We can get together tonight?"

"I hope so. We'll see. Call me." Amy fastened a button under the collar of her jacket and went echoing down the hall.

Even though the exercise equipment was "state-of-the-art," it was sheer torture for Richard. With every rep, he was reminded of every step Mai took as she walked away from his window to her car.

From my window!

Richard was pumping iron, perspiration soaking his sweatshirt.

Suddenly, the large double doors opened on the other side of the room. Gina Collins, looking as gorgeous as ever, approached with several manila folders cradled in her arms. Gina's brown high-lighted hair was combed straight back in a boyish style. Her high cheekbones, piercing green eyes, and swan-like neck helped underscore the fact she was potentially one of the top young litigators at Daniels and Rumm. Gina wore a gray pantsuit, cinched by a black patent belt with double uniform-style buckles.

"Richard, there you are! I've got good news."

A loud 'clang' reverberated through the room when Richard released the fifty-pound barbell. "Gina," panted Richard, "what brings you here? Looks like you've got quite a load." Richard pointed at the files. "What gives?"

"Jarvis worked it out with J.D."

"What?"

"I'm taking over Mai's workload on the Colby Case."

"I don't think that's such a good idea." Richard wiped his face and neck with a terrycloth towel. He sank into a small leather bench.

"At this point, I don't care what you say." She placed her folders on a metal rack that held rows of progressive weights. "Besides, I volunteered, unofficially, to help you."

"I don't want you getting hurt."

"Mai was a very good friend. I won't change my mind," said Gina firmly. She folded her arms and faced Richard.

"You don't know what you're getting into."

"Meet me in your office right after lunch." Gina picked up her files off the rack.

"Damn Jacq and Jarvis!"

"Flattery will get you nowhere," said Gina as she closed the tempered glass door. A small hallway led to the burgundy and wheat tiled showers. Richard spent five minutes under a pulsating shower massage, then crossed the interior hall and dressed in the austere locker room.

His office was down the hall at the end of the corridor on the twentieth floor. Richard quickened his pace as he pushed in the door. He could hear the phone ringing.

"This is Richard."

"It's Lieutenant Miller for you," said Rosie.

"Good. Put him through. Hello, Mike?"

"Richie. How's it hangin'? Just wanted to let you know..."

"Yeah, what?"

"I'll be bringing the pictures of Mai Tai's body, and pictures of the car, to you on Monday. If I sent it by messenger, the press might grab hold of it. You know how that works. The longer we stall, the better our chances of coming up with a lead."

"I appreciate it."

"Man, this case sucks. We haven't come up with one solid lead. How about you?"

Richard was staring out of the window at the Marshall Fields store.

"How about you? Richard? Are you there?" asked Miller.

"Yeah, I'm here." A slight pause. "I may have something for you by Monday, too."

"Great."

"Try to make it around two or three. Thanks." Richard placed the receiver on his telephone gently. He sat down in his nondescript chair and continued to stare out at the darkening sky.

From my window! If I could see Mai through my window, perhaps there was someone in the building who saw her, too!

BRANDY

"GOOD MORNING, CHICAGO! IT'S 6:30 A.M. SATUR-DAY, OCTOBER 24. IT'S CLEAR AND 45 DEGREES," blared the Bose Wave tabletop radio. "THIS IS YOUR BIG, BAD, AND BEAUTIFUL D.J., BOBBY BOMBAY, BLASTIN' AT YOU WITH THE LATEST 'FLIED LICE' VERSION OF..."

"OH, MAN!" whined Brandy as she reached for the off button and slammed it with a vengence. She fell back into bed and stared at the ceiling, tracing the hairline crack across the plaster, all the way to the edge of the closet. Brandy was wearing her hospital scrub top and pants.

If I had my head on straight, this wouldn't have happened!

KNOCK-KNOCK!

Brandy's mother pushed the door open with her knee. She had on a faded chenille bathrobe, tied at her ample waist. Mother Jones wore her blue plastic glasses at the end of her nose. She peeked into Brandy's room, smiled and said, "What's all the yellin' in there so early in the mornin', baby? I thought you were gonna sleep in."

"I was, Mom. I forgot."

"It's a wonder that racket didn't wake your brother. He's sleepin' at the kitchen table again."

"Working late and trying to study will do that to you," said Brandy. She stretched toward the hairline crack.

Brandy lived in a small two-bedroom bungalow on 36th Street and Parnell on Chicago's south side. Most of the houses were gray-sided, with peeling paint and rotted wooden steps that led up to the steel gratings covering the front doors. Councilwoman Johnson will tell you how the area has changed since Darin's version of "Mack the Knife". Don't ask the residents on 36th Street.

"Better get your shower while you can," said Mother Jones.

"Nah, I'm up now, Mom." She threw her blanket aside. "I'm gonna go for a run. Well...at least for a walk."

Brandy pulled on white cotton socks and her Fila jogging shoes. She made a quick trip to the bathroom, the door of which opened into the kitchen. Walking across the creaky floor, Brandy opened the refrigerator, poured a glass of orange juice and closed the door with a loud thud.

"Oops!"

Brandy's brother, Colada, grunted and sat upright. He stared at the walls, trying to get his bearings. He finally focused on his sister. "Hey, baby."

"Welcome to the world, Cole."

"What time is it? Feels like I just got home."

"You probably did." Brandy walked to the tiny closet and slipped on a red nylon hooded jacket. "Too tired for a walk? I could use a sounding board."

"Gimme a few. I'll be right up." Cole collected his books and disappeared down the rickety basement steps.

Cole was in his third year at the University of Illinois. He was twenty, non-athletic, slightly obese, but had a raging ambition to become a lawyer someday, every bit as good as his older sister. His tuition was being paid through a scholarship for low-income families, with the balance financed by Brandy. Cole worked the late-night shift at a local McDonalds in his limited spare time.

X

The house on the left was boarded up. Across the street, an elderly man was rummaging through a dumpster. Farther down the block were the remains of an arsonist's prank. Brandy and Cole walked past the house that had had parts of its aluminum siding stolen last year.

"I don't know how you did it, babe," said Cole. "College and McDonalds. Man! It's eatin' me up."

"Well, you wanted to move up the food chain, didn't ya?"

Cole looked at Brandy and smiled. "I got one more long year to go."

"I know. Daddy would have been so proud of you."

"We can do it. You've helped me so much. Man! I hate to see you livin' here. Not havin' a chance to get a place of your own."

"Hey. If I was able to do it, so can you. I got lots of time to get what I want."

"Someday I'll be walkin' down Michigan Avenue, with a woman on each arm. Sittin' courtside at the Bulls game. That'll be so sweet, sister."

Cole reached for Brandy's hand. They continued walking down the sidewalk, hand in hand, swinging their arms like two young children, oblivious to the drones of the cars on the I-90 and 94 Expressways. The elevated train in the distance, with its unique rumblings, added a lower octave to the muted sounds.

The pair walked east to the Pennsylvania Railroad tracks. Brandy kicked at the oil-stained gravel. She tip-toed on the ties and tried to walk the rails. Cole waited.

"He's doin' it with Rosie. Maybe Wanda. Now he wants me," said Brandy finally.

"Who? Tell me!" She got his attention.

"Jackie. At work."

"What did that slime-ball do? What'd he say?"

"He brushes up against me all the time. He peeks down my blouse. I'm getting paranoid. Now I think he wants to go out...to dinner. You know what that means."

"I can take care of him...REAL QUICK!"

"It's not that simple," said Brandy. She sat down on an old wooden crate near the tracks. "I've worked too hard over the last years to let this job slip away, just because of one creep."

"Yeah. The boss' son."

"I need this job, Cole. WE need it."

"Yeah, but at what cost?" Cole sat on the rusted track next to his sister. "Let me talk to him, baby. Please."

"No, you can't."

"You sure?"

"I'll handle it my own way," said Brandy. "I'll talk to him."

"Okay. You do that."

But I'll do more than talk, Sister!

THE INTERVIEW

The two men were sitting in Charles Cognac's small office on the nineteenth floor. Charles had been an associate with Daniels and Rumm for two years. Because of Mai's death, and the pressures of the up-coming Colby trial, today, on a hectic Saturday morning, October 24th, Charles was embarking on his first order of business as a full-fledged, newly-appointed lawyer. Charles was thirty-six and extremely handsome. His blonde hair and hazel eyes brought James Dean to mind. He was wearing a beige cableknit turtleneck with dark brown wool trousers.

"Humm," said Charles, "I see you're a graduate of I.U. Law School. Magna Cum Laude no less." He was going through Tony Martini's resume and a leather-bound booklet that contained a multitude of Tony's accomplishments since he graduated from law school three years ago.

"Yes," said Tony, "and as you can see on page seven, I also have my legal assistant certification." Tony wore a navy Italian wool suit, gray shirt, and a bold tri-colored silk tie. He was in his mid-thirties. His black hair, flecked with gray, was slightly receding at the temples. Tony nervously fluffed his pocket handkerchief.

Charles set the packet on the desk and said, "Your resume and credentials are great, Mr. Martini..."

"Call me Tony."

"Right, Tony. One question." Charles flipped through the last page of Tony's booklet. "I see no paperwork here with regard to your bar exam. Is that an oversight?"

"I haven't had a chance to take the bar." Tony fluffed his hand-kerchief again.

"Humm. Three years." Charles shuffled the papers. "You mean you haven't attempted to take the bar exam yet? Is that correct?"

"There were problems. Family illness. One thing after another. That's behind me now. I'm ready. I'll be taking the next available exam."

Charles nodded. "I'm sure you understand that we do a thorough investigation to confirm documentation of..."

"I wouldn't have it any other way, Mr. Cognac," said Tony.

"Now, you can call me Charles." He looked at Tony and smiled. "I'm very impressed with this entire package, Tony."

"Thank you. I might also mention I've had offers from Seagram and Sons. They're located in Philadelphia. And another from Macallan and Macallan out in L.A. I was seriously considering both positions...until now."

"The position I'm trying to fill for Daniels and Rumm, I hope you understand, is for a legal assistant. With your background, perhaps..."

"No, I understand completely. This firm is exactly what I've been looking for. And I hope you feel the same about me."

"This is an excellent firm in which to launch your career." Charles leaned back, tugging on the collar of his turtleneck. "They expect a lot, but they have so much more to offer."

"Seems like a wonderful place to work. The history, the warmth," said Tony. Footsteps hurriedly diminished in the hallway. "I hear quite a bit of activity for a Saturday morning. Is it always like this?"

"Not really. The people that are in today are working gung-ho on the Colby case. Maybe you've heard of it."

"Yes, somewhat. It sounds like a fantastic case."

"Richard Port is our chief counsel for the Colby trial. At least I think he was. Sherry Weinstein is our specialist in criminal law. She's a good friend of Mr. Daniels. The others are listed in the brochure."

"I'm very impressed."

"A person can grow, continuously, in a firm such as Daniels and Rumm." Charles turned his chair to the photos behind him. "They were boyhood pals, by the way."

"I know," said Tony. "I read something about that in the firm's brochure. 'One big happy family', it says."

"Uh...yeah." Charles pointed to a framed photograph on the wall of Jacq and Jarvis, shaking hands and smiling, in front of the firm's logo.

"They do seem like buddies, don't they," said Tony. He stood to take a closer look at the picture.

"Jarvis Rumm worked his way through law school. He's from the 'old gray line'. Reserved, very formal. He treats all of us as equals. Always fair. Now Jacq Daniels...he's something else." Charles stretched his arms toward the ceiling, arched his back and said, not too convincingly, "He's a good guy. Once you get to know him."

"I'm looking forward to that meeting, too."

"J.D.'s father had money. Money made, or so the story goes, during the Great Depression."

"During Prohibition? I read about that," said Martini.

"Even though Jacq's education came easier, he's still a hell of a litigator. He and Jarvis share controlling interest in the firm. As far as I know, they have an equal amount of shares in the company."

"I suppose it'll be a while before I get an opportunity to work with people like them, but I'm looking forward to the possibility," said Tony eagerly.

"Sometimes we work in teams. It may not take as long as you think." Charles tapped a key on his computer. "We've got a mock trial coming up within two weeks. The Colby thing. Sometimes the lawyers don't want to come in on a weekend just for that. Some of them think it's a waste of time. I think it's great experience. There are times we have to use people from the law library, or one of the secretaries, just to fill the mock jury."

"I'd love doing that! Count me in."

"We need a minimum of a forty-hour week. Most of the time, it's closer to sixty."

"That's fine," said Tony.

"That'll include salary, a small expense allowance, and a gas card. Later, there'll be the standard retirement plans, and as a special perk, free tickets to see the Bears play on the Sunday before Thanksgiving. Also—and a lot of firms don't do this—you can select furnishings for your office to suit your tastes. Within reason of course."

"That seems fair," said Tony. "Are there any stock options?" He was standing, very business-like, next to Cognac's desk, with his hands in his pockets.

"I'd rather you discuss that proposal with Jarvis. The firm is very liberal-minded." Charles straightened the papers on his desk and clicked off his computer screen. "If you like, we can take a tour of the three floors. I can show you our facilities. The exercise room, and so on. Then we can continue the interview during lunch. How about it?"

Tony went to the oak coat rack near the door and removed his gray London Fog raincoat. He put the coat over his shoulders and said, "There's nothing I would enjoy more!"

"Great. The men's room is around the corner. Meet me in front of the elevators in five minutes. I have a quick call to make."

"I know I'm going to enjoy working with you, Charles...a lot," said Tony Martini before he closed the oak door.

Charles leaned across his blank monitor and speed-dialed a number. The phone continued buzzing as he reached for his brown suede jacket.

"Hello."

"Hi, Alex, it's me. I'm at the office."

"I'm glad you called," said Alex.

"I still have to do lunch, but it'll be quick."

"Did you hire him?" asked Alex.

"Yeah, I did. It was quite an experience."

"I'm happy you're happy," said Alex.

"Are we still on for tonight?" Charles said coyly.

"Yes. Eight sharp. See you then." Alex hung up.

Tony stood next to the deserted reception desk with an elbow leaning on the countertop, waiting for Charles. He had his back to the elevators, looking up at the large D & R logo, visualizing a giant "M" on the mirrored wall.

I pray this will be better than Philadelphia.

THE FUNERAL

The black hearse, heading north on Lakeshore Drive, exited at Irving Park Boulevard. The motorcade proceeded past the U.S. Public Health Service Hospital on the right, then, several blocks east, turned into the Rosehill Cemetery. J.D.'s black BMW limo, with Guinness at the wheel, followed closely behind the shiny black and chrome Lincoln.

Mai's parents and grandparents shared the stretch limo, courtesy of the Daniels and Rumm Firm. Jacq rode with Jackie in his red Mercedes as the third car. The rest of the procession consisted of other family members and part of the staff from the law firm. A mandatory function, per J.D., this Saturday afternoon, October 24. The press was forbidden.

The workload at the office, because of the Colby case, was becoming extremely hectic. Consequently, J.D. had wanted to have the funeral on Sunday. Since he was paying for Mai's expenses, because 'it made good press', he decided he might as well have his way, but his decision was vetoed by Sherry and Jarvis. Even with all the security efforts of the firm and the Perrier Funeral Home, the last car, with the two little flags fluttering in the cool breeze, was actually a rental driven by a member of station WLLZ Chicago.

The car entered at the main gate. A high iron fence encircled the perimeter of Rosehill. The cars passed several ponds alive with wildlife. Green pines stood tall and foreboding, accentuated by yellow, rust and orange maples at their peak of color. The motorcade wove slowly through the winding blacktop roads, coming to a stop a half mile from the entrance, at the gravesite, overlooking Rosehill Pond.

X

"Come unto me, all ye that labor and are heavy laden..." The minister droned on. Small groups of black and navy forms were standing circled around the casket, huddled close together because of the chilling wind blowing over the pond and the bordering hill.

Kristie was wearing a stunning lemon-yellow coat with a shawl collar curled about her neck. She looked fabulous.

Rosie elbowed her. "What the hell you doing wearing yellow," she whispered.

"Yellow was Mai's favorite color," Kristie said tearfully.

The lid of the ornate bronze casket glistened in the late afternoon sun. A half-dozen grave-site workers, four men and two women garbed in denim cotton dungarees, were standing behind a large oak, heads hanging and feet shuffling, waiting to lower the casket as soon as the rites were over. The sun was playing peek-a-boo with a large smoke-gray cloud.

"The peace of God, which passeth all understanding, keep your hearts and minds in the knowledge and love..." The minister concluded the service, shook hands with the grieving parents, and hurried to the hearse. A light rain began to fall.

Umbrellas popped open as the rain's intensity increased. Groups of people ran toward the rows of expensive automobiles. Brandy ran to her '79 Olds Cutlass.

Richard approached the casket. He placed a rose on the top of the coffin. Amy went to his side and put her arm around his shoulder and held him tight. Tears were streaming down his face.

I'll find whoever did this to you Mai. I promise!

The grave-site workers, with a rose and a hill patch over their breast pockets, began lowering the casket, unaware that the killer was only a few yards away.

AMYABLE

Richard was soaked. He didn't care. He stood under the large oak, watching the uniformed staff as they performed the final raking of the ground surrounding the gravesite, picked up debris, and threw wilted floral arrangements into the back of a pickup.

"Hey, mister," yelled one of the girls. "Show's over. Ain't you got no ride?" The girl jumped into one of the trucks.

"Oh...Yeah, I'm okay. That's my car over there." Richard motioned toward his Chrysler Sebring Coupe parked at the bend of the road. The pickup lurched toward the chapel.

Richard jogged to his car, removed his soaked raincoat and slid into the glove-soft leather seat. He folded his coat and laid it on the floor mat, remembering to remove the car keys from its pocket. Richard drove full circle and exited at Ravenswood, then turned east to Lakeshore Drive.

The same highway the killer drove!

Richard headed south on Lakeshore, a stone's throw from his condo in Green Oaks. He reached across his console and pushed the speed-dial on his cell phone. Amy's phone kept buzzing on the other end. The rain was letting up.

"Hello," said Amy, out of breath.

"Hey, it's me. You don't know how glad I am to hear your voice."

"Just got in. I'm standing in a pool of water."

"Sorry about that, sweetheart."

Amy laughed. "You know I'm kidding. I hear road noises. Aren't you home yet?"

Richard was fast approaching Belmont Harbor Drive, the exit he used when he visits Amy. This time he was driving in the opposite direction.

"I feel kind of bummed." He paused, listening to the static. "How would it be if I stopped over to see you for a couple of hours. I"ll try not to be a bother."

"That will be the day."

"I'm passing the golf course. I can be there in ten minutes. Around four thirty."

"Wonderful. I'll have hot cream of mushroom soup waiting for you. I'll be waiting for you, too."

"YOU are wonderful, gorgeous. See you."

Richard took the ramp to Belmont Harbor Drive. On the left, he passed the tennis courts, the field house, and the archery building. In the distance he could make out the faint outline of the majestic lighthouse at the entrance to the harbor.

Amy's apartment was nestled into a hillside with a beautiful panoramic view of the Chicago Yacht Club. She loved sports and all the other outdoor activities available near Belmont Harbor. Amy worked out at the field house, playing basketball two or three times each week.

Her two-car garage door was open. Richard swung his Chrysler into the extra-wide opening. The laser beam unit activated and the door slowly dropped.

He hung his coat in the closet at the right of the entry hall and stepped into Amy's enormous living room, with its high brick walls and vaulted ceiling. Flames flickered in the gas fireplace.

"Honey, I'm home!" said Richard, trying to do his best Rickie Ricardo impression.

Amy, from the bedroom, said, "I"ll be right there."

He tossed his suit jacket on a leather loveseat, then warmed his hands by the fire which was flanked on both sides by natural oak cabinets. Each cabinet was eight feet high with horizontally-raised glass doors. Displayed behind the glass were basketball and soccer awards, ribbons, and other mementos of high school and college exploits. On top of the cabinets, leaning into the brick wall, were photographs of Amy and her uniformed teams, dating back to Junior High.

Richard turned to look out the arched windows behind him at the magnificent view of the harbor. Instead, he saw Amy standing under a dimmed ceiling fixture. She was wearing a blue velvet slip gown. No shoes—no jewelry.

"You look positively exquisite."

"Not bad, coming from an old cop. It must be the lighting."

Richard walked quickly to her. They embraced and kissed passionately, he needing her now more than ever.

"I love you," said Richard. He buried his face in her cheek.

"And you know I love you...madly." They kissed again.

Richard's hands were entwined in Amy's auburn tresses. Their bodies were silhouetted against the windows by a lone spotlight shining in from the patio deck.

Amy, still holding his hand, glided to one of the glass-doored cabinets and pushed the play button on the Sony. A CD began playing a haunting aria of "Le Tue Parole," sung by one of her favorite singers, Andrea Bocelli, a world-renowned tenor.

"Dance?" asked Amy.

"Love to." Richard put his arm around Amy and drew her close. "What happened to Michael Bolton?"

"I thought this would fit your mood just a teeny bit more. Michael can wait 'til later." She pushed her body closer to him.

They swayed gently to the music, moving circle after circle around the glass-topped book table in the center of the room. Amy's arm brushed against an arrangement of golden foliage cascading from a large crystal urn on the table. She paused, still swaying, then looked up into Richard's eyes and said, "Soup's getting cold."

He kissed Amy on the tip of her nose. The stereo was in the middle of Bocelli's version of "Romanza."

"E lo chiamano amore."

"And they call it love," whispered Richard.

"Do you want to spend the night?"

He held Amy tighter, looking deeply into her almond-shaped eyes. "Maybe I better go."

The haunting strains of "Con Te Tartiro" filled the room. Amy clutched Richard's shirt and kissed him.

"Yes...'I'll go with you,'" she whispered. "'I with you.'"

"Find my killer," whispered Mai in Richard's ear.

R AND REVENGE

A foghorn echoed in the distance. Richard wheeled his beige coupe up the ramps into the parking garage of his condo. The rain had subsided and the sun was mostly hidden by the late afternoon storm clouds. The short drive from Amy's, with the window partially rolled down, helped clear his mind.

Richard ascended the spiral ramp. His reserved space, with the numbers 1957 neatly stenciled on the blue-gray concrete walls was near a short hallway on one of the upper levels leading to the tenant elevators. His Chrysler screeched to a halt, barely missing a concrete column.

"I should have stayed with Amy." He shook his head.

Get your act together, Rich!

Richard entered the hallway and pushed his way through a steel firedoor. The security guard was sitting on her stool in the corner, drinking something from a Styrofoam cup. It was 4:45 P.M. on the wall clock. She waved when she saw Richard.

"Good afternoon, Mr. Port." The guard hid her cup in a cubbie under the counter.

"Hi, Henny. Any action on the poster?"

Jean Hennessy, the condo's newest security person, said, "No sir! No one's come to me, so far. I don't see any names on the sheet you gave us to use." Jean was young, tall and attractive, with a lean, lithe body. She pulled out her masonite clipboard that held sheets of yellow lined paper from underneath the counter. The sheets were blank. "Nothing from the other guards, either."

"Just thought I'd check."

Next to the elevators, Richard had thumb-tacked a white computer-aided poster on the bulletin board. The red-lettered sign had been posted since Friday night. The sign read:

I NEED YOUR HELP

THIS IS NOT AN OFFICIAL INVESTIGATION

IF YOU SAW ANYTHING OUT OF THE

ORDINARY ON THE MORNING OF OCT. 22

NEAR THE VISITOR'S PARKING LOT B,

CALL RICHARD PORT—562-3548

"You know, Mr. Port. I've been thinking about that sign. Maybe if you..."

"Not now, Henny. I just got back from a funeral."

"Oh, sorry."

"I haven't eaten all day. Whatever you've been thinking can wait until tomorrow. Okay?"

"Sure, Mr. Port. No problem."

Richard rode the elevator to nineteen. Two young women were chattering noisily in a foreign language in the room next to his. The housekeepers had the door open wide with their supply cart blocking the hallway. Richard squeezed past the cart. The girls giggled while he searched for his keys.

One of those girls resembles Mai.

Richard kicked off his shoes, hung his coat in the hall closet, tossed his Harry Rosen tie on the computer counter and turned up the stereo.

Two days mail was stacked on the Corian counter top next to the kitchen. He ignored it again.

Nothing there that can't wait until tomorrow, Mai.

Richard removed the bottle of Ecco Domani from the wine rack and poured the remaining contents into his morning coffee cup. He sank into the softness of the leather loveseat in the Great Room, listening to a Lehar rhapsody, head bobbing gently to the strains of a Gypsy violin. Richard leaned his head back into the headrest and tried to sleep. Sleep didn't come. Thoughts of Mai did.

Richard drank the last of the Italian vintage, savoring the wine as much as the music. He went to the entry hall closet and took down an old corrugated box with its lid taped to the sides. He put the box on the counter and lifted the top. Carefully, he removed his old .38 Smith and Wesson revolver, blued and gray, with its snubnosed barrel. He fondled the grip. He stretched out both arms, in his familiar shooting position, and aimed the gun at the imaginary killer. After loading it, Richard put the gun, holster, and handcuffs on the desk next to his business bag.

This is for you, Mai!

He turned off the stereo. The Herman Miller clock above the kitchen range ticked, in an agonizingly slow motion, to half past seven.

Richard opened a can of cream of mushroom soup.

SHERRY

Sherry's 2,500-square-foot condominium was tucked away behind the clubhouse at the fork of a secluded blacktop on Chicago's north side. The sun, barely visible above the horizon, cast deepening shadows on the beige Normandy brick of the units. Antique ivory and almond colors, in vinyl and aluminum siding accentuated the muted exterior. Arched windows in a muted color reflected the black BMW stretch limousine parked in the private drive.

"You know I can't stay." Jacq was sitting on a crushed-velvet sofa, facing a black and gray marble fireplace, nursing a drink.

"I understand," pouted Sherry. "DeDe has her dinner party tonight, right?"

"Yeah, and Guinness is outside, waiting for me. He's got his orders from DeDe."

"And?" Sherry sat on the sofa, cuddling up next to him. She wore a tiger-striped gown by Melinda Eng. Pearl and diamond floret earrings were her only accessory. The silver burnout gown and the dark mascara outlining her eyes gave her silver-blonde hair a more seductive look than ever.

"And he only takes orders from me." Jacq leaned into Sherry, his hand behind her short-cropped hair, and kissed her tenderly. He pulled her closer.

"You know how much I love you," whispered Sherry.

"I love you, too, Sher." Jacq bit off one of the dangling diamond earrings. The earring fell into her plunging neckline.

"That is a piece of Tiffanys you're playing with," toyed Sherry.

"I can be careful. Real careful." Jacq extracted the earring and held it up to the light. Rainbow hues reflected in the facets. He balanced the small piece of jewelry in his hand, gently placing the earring back into the vee of the gown. He kissed her again, this time more vigorously.

"Shouldn't we be working on the opening statements for the Colby trial?" said Sherry.

Jacq knew she was joking. "The papers are right there on your desk." He pointed to his initialed calfskin case next to the newspaper. "I've got my coat off, ready to work." He grinned at Sherry. "You got anything you want to take off? Nice dress, by the way."

Sherry reached out and put her arms around Jacq's shoulders, drew him close, and looked longingly into his dark brown eyes. Jacq put his drink down.

"Tell me again...how it's going to be," said Sherry, purring in his ear.

"You smell great!" Jacq rubbed his nose in her platinum blonde waves.

"Can I put it on the expense account, too? It's called 'CHER.'"

"Yep! It's well worth the price." He kissed her, more aroused than before.

The doorbell chimed. It's loud DING-DONG penetrated the stillness of the moment.

"Oh, my God! Who could that be?" whispered Sherry. She stood up quickly, smoothing out the wrinkles in her gown.

Jacq sauntered to the wet bar and poured himself another scotch and water. "I'll be in the kitchen." He grabbed his suit jacket, closed the black cafe doors, and staggered to the other room.

Sherry stepped down into the vestibule and looked through the small quarter-sized hole in the door. "Oh, hell," she said, then opened the door. Guinness was standing on the porch, the bright light of the brass fixture illuminating the sheepish grin on his face.

"Sorry to bother you, Ms. Weinstein."

"Hello, Guinness. Looking for Jacq?" Sherry knew the answer to her own question.

"I'm not looking for him, Ms. Weinstein, but Mrs. Daniels is. She called a minute ago to remind Mr. Daniels about the party tonight. For that Mr. Coors, from the museum. He knows about it." This was the most fun Guinness had all week.

"We're still working on a couple of briefs. We're almost done."

Poor choice of words, thought Sherry, after she said them.

"The party started a few minutes ago, at 7:30. I'll need twenty minutes to drive to the Daniels' home." Guinness stood tall, with his black cap tucked under his arm, wondering how Jacq was going to handle this stroke of bad luck.

"Jacq is in the bathroom. I'll see to it that he gets your message, Guinness. Now if you'll excuse me..."

Sherry reached to close the door, and as she did her upper body turned ever so slightly, enough for Guinness to catch a glimpse of a pearl and diamond earring, hanging precariously from Sherry's bustline.

"I'll be waiting in the limo, Ms. Weinstein."

Is this a great job—or what!

X

The antique clock on the mantel chimed faintly at eight o'clock. Jacq was nursing his fourth or fifth scotch. He'd lost count. Sherry was sitting on the sofa with Jacq, the slit of her gown showing her silky-smooth legs. He was stroking her knee.

"I know you have to leave soon, honey. Let me get rid of this heavy dress."

"Let ME get rid of these heavy trousers. Don't forget those heavy earrings." Jacq grinned at Sherry.

"I'll meet you in the tub in five minutes."

Sherry, shoeless, daintily picked up the hem of her dress with both hands and tip-toed up the stairway to her bedroom.

Jacq had his own walk-in closet in what used to be a sewing room before Sherry moved into the condo. He had the upstairs room converted into a work area. He and Sherry spent many evenings working on pre-trial procedures, closing arguments, and other legal issues. At least that was the way it began. The bathroom, with the twenty-one-jet tub, was through the adjoining door.

Jacq found it difficult to climb the stairs. He stumbled on the carpet as he worked his way up to his room at the end of the hall. Jacq stripped off his clothes, folding them neatly on the bed. His burgundy silk robe was hanging at the end of the closet, exactly where he hung it the last time.

Jacq opened the door to the bathroom. Sherry was waiting for him at the edge of the tub, sitting on the wide cove, one leg dangling in the bubbling water. "Be My Love" by Billy Eckstine was playing on the stereo. She wore a short see-through nude gown, the front plunging to her navel.

"Oh, my Papa!" was all Jacq could muster.

X

Guinness was in one of the back seats of the limo. His feet were up on the leather of the opposite side. He was lying comfortably in the heavily padded seats, watching an X-rated cable movie. Candy wrappers, popcorn, and other snacks littered the floor and seats.

Every fifteen minutes the phone would ring.

I know who that is!

Guinness had orders not to answer the phone. Although it disturbed his concentration while he was watching the movie, he began to get used to the routine. DeDe called continuously for three hours. Then once an hour. Finally, around midnight, the phone stopped ringing.

Thank goodness! The XXX rated movie is about to start!

"Jacq. Wake up." Sherry's voice wasn't exactly excited. She shook him again gently. "Jacq."

"OH, hell! What time is it?" said Jacq groggily.

"It's past one. You better get home." Sherry relished these moments, just as much as the sex.

Jacq sat on the edge of the bed, running his fingers through his silver-gray hair. "My ass is in a sling now anyway." He looked at Sherry, sitting next to him, shyly holding a printed satin sheet in front of her like a shield. "But it's been worth it...every time."

"Get dressed. I'll alert your faithful companion, Tonto."

X

The black limo sped south on the Edens Expressway. Guinness turned west at the interchange, then into the sparsely populated areas of the Forest Preserve. Once on the domed blacktop of Grand Mariner Drive, it was a matter of minutes before the gates to the sprawling mansion would come into view. Guinness glanced at the LED lights on the digital display panel, twinkling among the other gauges. The time was 1:55 A.M.

The witching hour, thought Guinness.

He enjoyed these midnight diversions. On occasion, Jackie

would take his turn by entertaining one of the young ladies working for him. It was part of Guinness' job to stock the mobile bar, keep the hors d'oeuvres hot, and to clean up after every "session."

Guinness pushed the remote as the BMW approached the circular brick driveway. The stone and brick quad-level structure had all its outside lights burning and all the four doors to the garage open. J.D.'s Jaguar, barely broken in, was parked in the last bay. His second-favorite toy, a royal blue '35 Ford coupe, was parked in the middle two bays, along with DeDe's Lincoln. A Hyundai Tiburon, custom-painted to match her fiery red hair, was still parked outside, glistening in the moonlight. DeDe enjoyed showing off her latest acquisitions.

Whoa! Madam is upset tonight!

"Swing around to the back," yelled Jacq into the intercom. "Make sure to kill those lights..."

"Yes, sir. I'll be sure to re-park Madam's car and secure all the doors."

"Yeah, yeah. It's too early in the morning to start sucking up," drawled Jacq.

Guinness swung the car behind the brick-paved patio and stopped next to the rear entry door. Jacq staggered on the narrow concrete walk, ignoring a large clay urn, broken, with its dirt scattered and fronds bent, in the center of the brick lanai. He used his keypad and boldly pushed the back door open. Guinness drove the limo down a one lane road that led to a maintenance building and his small quarters near the edge of the property.

DeDe was sitting in a bright gold velvet stuffed chair, reading a James Patterson novel. Her eyes were tired. She took off her gold-rimmed glasses, ran a hand through her boyish short hair and put the book down when she heard the familiar gait on the stairs. She stood and faced the door, her arms folded across her breasts. She had on

Jacq's favorite black and white Intimo silk robe. She was prepared.

It's days like this when I wish I was plain Debrah Bacardi again!

"Well, it's about time!" began DeDe.

"We had a ton of work to do," countered Jacq.

"Colby, no doubt." DeDe didn't move from her spot.

"As a matter of fact, yes. Plus some other pressing matters." Jacq began undressing near his triple dresser. He threw his shirt and tie on the chaise lounge, then realized DeDe was wearing his robe.

"You have my pajamas on, under my robe?"

"Don't change the subject!" DeDe stomped across the huge bedroom. "I'm SO angry at you! How many times do you expect me to be humiliated in front of my friends—and the people at the club—and the museum!"

"And don't forget your charity snobs!" Jacq took out a pair of gray silk pajamas from its plastic wrapper and pulled on the bottoms. "And those damn garden club crones of yours."

DeDe stared menacingly at Jacq. The robe swirled and swished as she hurried to block Jacq's path to the bathroom. DeDe put both hands on the jambs, very dramatically.

"Get the hell out of the way," said Jacq in an irritated, but controlled, tone.

"I swear! One of these days, I WILL divorce you!" shouted DeDe.

"It'll never happen, baby."

"It WILL! You've made me look like a fool in front of all my friends!"

"What—two or three people? Besides, if you go, you'll go with nothin'." Jacq was getting testy. "I'll see to that."

DeDe put her hands on her hips. She faced him squarely and said, "You are THE meanest person I have ever known!"

"Aww, shut up and go to bed." Jacq raised his hand as if to strike her. She backed away instinctively, frightened at first, slow to react.

"Go ahead! Hit me!" she screamed.

"I said go to bed."

"Hit me! I'll sue you for everyth..."

"My old man would've knocked you and your boob job clear across the room." Jacq slammed the bathroom door.

DeDe stood near her nightstand, looking at the floor, digging her toes into the plush carpet, like she had done so many nights before. She threw Jacq's satin print pillow against the bathroom door.

Christmas is coming. I'll make sure you get EXACTLY what you deserve!

SUNDAY FUN

Sunday morning, like clockwork, Richard took a late leisurely run through the picturesque paths behind his condo. The nature trail was in full color; deep reds, multiple shades of yellow, orange, and rust. The blacktop path, heavy with fallen leaves, wound around the outskirts of the golf course. Today Richard took the short route back to the clubhouse. He was barely winded.

Sunday was a "catch up" day: reviewing mail, tending to legal matters, and making up schedules for the coming week's workload. Not today.

"Hi, sweetie. I miss you," said Richard into the speaker phone. The toast was browning in the toaster oven while he whipped eggs in a skillet. The counter in the kitchen was littered with felt markers, posterboard, a Lucite ruler, and legal pads.

"Hi, Richard! I miss you, too," said Amy. "How did you sleep?"

"Sleep? What's that?"

"Oh, you know what you get to do when you come over," said Amy.

"I can't today. Come over, that is."

"Oh—sorry." Amy was all business. "Is anything wrong?"

"No, but I got a great idea during my run. I've started making a chart, with a possible seventy-six witnesses who may have seen something last Friday in the parking lot."

"You're talking about Mai."

"Yeah." Richard scraped the eggs onto his plate and buttered the wheat toast. "It's a complicated procedure, but its worked for me in the past."

"No need to explain," said Amy. "If there's anything I can do, let me know. I love you."

"Love you, too. I'll call you tonight. 'Bye."

X

Richard was in the shower when the phone began to ring. The answering machine picked up the call:

"Hello, Mr. Port? This is Jean Hennessy calling. You know, Henny...the part-time security guard." Henny paused, waiting for Richard to pick up the phone.

Richard stepped out of the shower and began wiping off in the exercise room. Questions relating to what any witnesses may have observed ran through his mind.

"Well, anyway, Mr. Port. I was thinking, you know...what I was trying to tell you yesterday...during my shift?" Hennessy cleared her throat and continued. "I was thinking about your sign. You know, if you were looking for..." Jean Hennessy was silent for a second. "Oh, oh. My boss is coming! I'll call you after my shift."

Richard changed from his black Chicago Bears sweats to a gray Ralph Lauren casual shirt and charcoal denim trousers. He bounded down the circular stairway, two steps at a time. He took a minute to clear off the breakfast plates from the long Corian countertop, then spread the art supplies next to the posterboard.

On a standard 22"x28" piece of cardboard, Richard divided the board into seventy-six equal rectangles using his ruler and marker. The seventy-six blocks represented the apartment units on the Parking

Lot B's side, four units per floor. He began filling in the rectangles with the apartment numbers, starting with 157 on the first floor.

I've got 76 potential witnesses. That's the only way to look at it!

Richard speed-dialed the building manager. He hung up immediately when he saw the red light flashing on his answering machine. He listened to Hennessy's aborted message before redialing.

"Yeah, Stout here," said the gruff building manager.

"Paul, this is Richard Port in 1957."

"Yeah, Richard. What's the problem? That shower valve screwed up again? I hope not." Paul Stout had just opened a can of Red Dog, waiting for the pre-game show to began.

"No, nothing like that. I have a question for you. Maybe you can help me."

"Like how?"

"Can you make up a list of people for me, from the apartments facing Visitor's Lot B, who might have been home last Friday morning? It's important."

"This about your lawyer friend? You doin' some homework, Rich?" The gruffness left his voice. "I can tell you right now. There's forty, maybe fifty apartments on your side of the building where the tenants have gone to work by that time. I know, 'cause we gotta do our repairs early in the day in those units."

Richard sighed. "If you could get me that list, it would save me a ton of legwork."

"It's as good as done." Stout scribbled a reminder on his yellow pad. "Oh, and Rich. There's four units that are unoccupied on your east side. I'll include those numbers, too. It could save you time."

"You've been a great help, Paul. Thanks a lot."

"Remember me at Christmas."

Richard pushed the doorbell of apartment 359 shortly after lunch. After two hours of methodically working his way up from number 157, he had nothing to show for his efforts except a sore index finger.

"Hello. I'm Richard Port. I..."

"Whatever your're selling, I'm not buying!" said the thin pale man. "I'm busy." He started to close the door.

"I have some questions I'd like to ask you, if you don't mind."

"I've told you people the first time. I didn't see anything last Monday." The thin man in gray sweats swung the door open and peered at Richard. A yellow parakeet in the corner squawked, "COME ON IN! COME ON IN!"

"Shut up, Malty!" The man turned toward Richard and said, "You ARE the police, aren't you?"

"No. I live upstairs on nineteen. I'm a...private investigator, trying to assist the police with a case."

"The dead girl in the red car?"

"How did you know about the...?"

"The papers and TV. It's all over."

"Then you told the police you saw nothing, Mr..."

"Molson. Ricky Molson. I told the police, yes, I was home. I was busy, watching my early morning talk show."

"Then you left for work, Mr. Molson?"

"No. I didn't feel well. I spent most of the time in bed. I saw nothing."

"Thank you for your time, Mr. Molson. Here is my card, if you think of anything that might help. Or call Lieutenant Miller. You have his..."

"Yes. I have his card." He watched Richard until the elevator doors closed. Molson closed his door.

The parakeet squawked again.

CHAPTER XXIII

Richard canvassed two more apartments before he gave up for the day. He had too many unanswered questions churning inside his head. Perhaps some of those forty or fifty tenants that Stout was talking about might have stayed home with a cold or flu—or taken a day off for personal business. He made a mental note to personally check every apartment he didn't canvas today. Was anyone he talked to afraid of coming forward?

Richard thought he could help Miller, but so far he had nothing. He went back to his apartment, ate a light dinner, and began preparing for the meeting with J.D., Miller, and Jarvis.

The phone rang, breaking his concentration. He could see it was Amy on the caller I.D.

"Hi, sweetie. I was about to call you," said Richard.

"Beat you to it. How did your idea pan out?"

"Not as great as I figured. I'll tell you all about it tomorrow. I'm working on my morning meeting with J.D. and Mike right now."

The doorbell chimed.

"Oh, oh," said Amy. "I can hear the bell. I'll talk to you at the office. Love you."

Richard hung up the receiver and opened the dark oak-stained door.

"Hello, Mr. Port."

"Hello, Ms....?" said Richard. A beautiful young woman was standing in the doorway.

"I'm Jean Hennessy. Henny...the security guard."

A startled look crossed Richard's face. "Henny...the security guard?"

Henny was dressed in a black tailored suit. Her long dark brown hair cascaded down on her shoulders in soft curls, accentuated by her dramatic makeup. She was carrying a small black leather hand-bag and a bottle of sparkling water.

"Forgive me for staring, please."

"We're not allowed to wear much makeup on our shift," she said self-consciously.

"My compliments to Max Factor."

"I'm sorry to bother you so late in the day. I tried calling you a while ago, but the line was busy."

"Yes, here, come on in." Richard opened the door wider and led Henny to a sidechair near the entrance. "I got your message." He kept staring at her.

Henny sat on the edge of the padded seat, legs crossed, back straight, her small handbag on her lap. She smiled at Richard and finally said, "Well, what?"

"I'm sorry, Henny." Richard smiled back while he pulled his black computer chair across the carpet and sat down facing Henny. "I can't get over the metamorphosis—for want of a better word."

"You pass by my station almost every day."

"It's a crime what a uniform will do. Again...forgive me."

"Consider yourself forgiven," said Henny shyly.

"Yesterday, you mentioned you had something to tell me about the sign in the hallway. Did I misspell a word or two? I never was good at spelling."

"No, the spelling is fine." Henny cleared her throat. "I was staring at your sign the other day—actually, for a few hours—and I got a crazy idea. Maybe it will help you."

"What's your crazy idea, Ms. Hennessy?"

"In Parking Lot B, all along the edges of the lot, are all kinds of bird feeders. I know, because I've helped carry packages out to the cars in that lot on occasion. There must be a couple of dozen feeders."

"And the feeders might lead to...?"

"Bird watchers!" said Henny proudly. "There HAS to be some bird watchers on that side of the building." She flashed her biggest smile yet.

"And the bird watchers have cameras..."

"Focused on the feeders!" said Henny excitedly.

"With telephoto lenses, hopefully. This is great!"

"With the progress being made in the image enhancement field, you may find a clue to help you in your investigation." Henny stood up. "I'd better go. I've taken up too much of your time. I see you're busy." She reached out to shake his hand.

"Ms. Hennessy," said Richard, "do you mind if I give you a great big hug?"

"No. No, not at all." They shared a brief, friendly, self-conscious hug.

"Thanks again, Henny. If you decide to continue your career in law enforcement, let me know. I've got a couple of friends in quote 'high places.'"

As soon as Jean Hennessy left his apartment, Richard began making another sign for the bulletin board:

ATTENTION BIRD WATCHERS

LUCRATIVE OPPORTUNITY GREAT POTENTIAL

CALL 571-4992 FOR INFORMATION

On the sign, he listed his office number at the firm. He didn't want the same phone numbers on two different signs. Soon after finishing his notes for the meeting, Richard took the elevator to the parking garage hallway and tacked the sign on the bulletin board. It was almost midnight.

This can't miss!

MARCUS

Marcus took the concrete steps, two at a time, to the waiting cab. He squinted as the morning sun's rays glanced off the giant steel casement windows of his elegant loft, a converted factory on Wabash and 8th.

"First National Bank Building," said Marcus.

"Hang on," said the driver. He made a sharp U-turn and headed north.

Marcus Lambrusco, with his piercing gaze and perpetual frown, sat in the back of the cab, taking the precious minutes he had, reading the headlines in the *Sun-Times*. The traffic was light for a Monday morning. The freshly-washed taxi sped past the Federal Courthouse on the left, site of the upcoming Colby trial.

Marcus, a top litigator for Daniels and Rumm, was wearing a brown Armani suit the color of his eyes and a burgundy and white pin-striped shirt with a putty-colored tie. His calfskin business case on the seat matched his hand-sewn shoes.

Marcus had a full day's work planned with Margarita and Brandy in the law library. Hopefully, they would be there waiting for him. The pro bono cases could wait. Colby and the impending trial had become the top priority, according to Jacq.

The driver turned left on Madison in midtown Chicago.

"Drop me by the Clark," said Marcus to the portly cabbie. The

driver squealed to a halt in front of the Clark Theatre, across the
street from the First National Bank.

X

"Good morning, Ms. Rosé," said Marcus, as the elevator doors
opened on nineteen.

Rosie was checking her eye makeup, squinting in her tiny gold-
plated compact. "Oh! Good morning, Mr. Lambrusco. Brandy and
Rita are waiting for you in the law library office." Her voice lacked
the usual exuberance.

"Thanks." Marcus walked quickly down the hall. He passed
Charles Cognac's deserted office. Two men in overalls were stacking flat cardboard cartons against the walls next to his vacant office.
Marcus hurried past the print shop on his left, then approached his
corner office, located across the hall from the law library.

One of the girls had a hot cup of coffee waiting for him on his
desk. He tossed his coat on a chair, grabbed a handful of manila
folders along with the coffee, and walked down the hall through the
massive double doors that led to the library.

"Good morning, ladies. Are you ready for a grueling day?"
Marcus entered the library smiling. Volumes of reference materi-
als and books, floor to ceiling, covered most of the perimeter of
three walls. The remaining east wall was all glass, with a partial
view of the Chicago Harbor. Brandy was on a wooden ladder,
removing some heavy books from one of the top shelves.
Margarita had one hand on the ladder. She was nursing a cup of
coffee with the other.

"Ooops," said Brandy. "I forgot, Mr. Lambrusco." Her short
skirt revealed her curvacious legs more than she intended. "I don't
usually work in the library." Brandy stepped down a rung and

handed the books to Rita.

Margarita Lopez, affectionately known as Rita, had been a part-time employee in the law library for the past six months. She was in her early twenties, conservatively dressed in a white silk blouse and navy wool pants. She, like Brandy, was planning a career in law.

"Hi, Mr. Lambrusco," sparkled Rita. She put the tomes on an oak table, looked at Brandy and said, "Let ME get up on the ladder, Brand." She slid the ladder toward the window wall.

"According to the list I gave you last night," said Marcus, "most of the reference material of cases similar to Colby's is in this section." Marcus motioned to the shelving near the young women.

"Look at those big fat ones up there," pointed Rita.

"Many of those were written by Jarvis Rumm, years ago," said Marcus. "Most of them on criminal law. That's his specialty." Marcus thumbed through one of the books on the table.

"We've got some of the books on the list pulled, Mr. Lambrusco," said Brandy. "We have to find the volumes dealing with motions for summary judgment and dismissal."

"Ms. Lopez," said Marcus, "Ms. Jones here is an excellent person to introduce you to the importance of research. Many a case has been won because of dilligent behind-the-scenes effort."

"Thanks for saying that, Mr. Lambrusco," said Brandy as she glanced at her young helper. "Rita understands the importance of our job."

Rita hopped up on the ladder and began checking the numbers on each spine. "Here's another one, Brand!"

"We've got one week before the pre-trial proceedings," said Marcus. "They're set for 10:00 A.M., November 3rd. We're counting on you."

"We won't let you down, sir!"

Marcus pushed one of the huge oak doors open. "Richard and

Gina will be in after their meetings, probably this afternoon. Have the material ready for them. If more research is required, it's perfectly fine to work past your normal working hours. This is top priority." Marcus began dialing his cell phone as he left the library.

"He's such a nice guy," said Brandy.

"Yeah, he does seem nice. I love his hair. And he's SO handsome."

"There are a lot of handsome guys around here," said Brandy innocently.

"You're right. I met the new legal assistant this morning in the hallway. Tony Martini. He is SWEET!"

"Did you talk to him?"

"No, I didn't have to. He reminds me of Tom—you know, Tom..."

"Cruise?"

"Yeah, that's him."

"I'll be watching for him, girl," said Brandy.

X

Marcus sat in his office, staring at the neatly stacked folders on his desk. The computer screen cursor was blinking, reminding him of his next meeting. He looked at his hands.

Trembling more each day, he thought.

Marcus unlocked the bottom drawer of a metal cabinet. He removed a bottle of Jim Beam and placed it on the desk next to the picture of his ex-wife. He sat in his chair, staring at the full, unopened bottle.

It was barely ten in the morning.

PICTURES AND TAPES

"Right this way, Lieutenant Miller," said Iris. "They're waiting for you." She opened the door to Richard's office. "Can I get either of you a cup of coffee?"

"Yeah," said Miller. "Cream, no sugar."

"Black, two sugars," mumbled Donny.

The men entered the office, exchanged greetings, and commented about the change in the weather.

Jacq sat in a maroon leather sidechair, facing away from the window. Iris had pulled the blinds partially closed for the ten o'clock meeting. Jarvis was sitting next to him, cutting one of Jacq's special croissants brought in for the occasion. Richard stood near his desk, organizing video cassettes into small piles.

Richard walked around the desk and joined the other men at the table. Dos took his customary stance near the door.

"You have the pictures, Mike?"

Lieutenant Miller took the black and white glossy photos of Mai out of the manila envelope and pushed them across the table. No one said a word as the pictures were passed around. Richard winced at the last shot of Mai: a vivid photo of her broken nose and bruised neck. A repressed, yet lingering, memory.

"No leads yet," said Miller. "The photos don't give us much to go on." He collected the pictures and handed them to Donny. Jarvis and Jacq were fidgeting at the far end of the table.

"Anything new about the sticky note...or the knife?" asked Jarvis. He looked at his Lacroix watch first and then at Richard.

Jacq glanced at the wall clock and stood up. "Rumm and I have other meetings to attend. What's the status to this point, gentlemen?"

"No prints on the knife, according to the lab," said Richard. "The sticky note is the exact kind used here in the office and a million other places."

"I still don't understand the contents of the note," said Jacq. "But I did take your suggestion. I've hired a man, a private investigator, to watch my back."

"Good. It won't hurt."

The partners excused themselves. Richard pointed to the stacks of video cassettes on his desk. "As you can see, guys, I've been doing some homework, too." He picked up four of the cassettes.

"Something for the brain-dead?" said Miller.

"Mike, I've gone through four videos so far. I got these from our building security guy. No one in these films has appeared in any of the hallways on the twenty-first floor who didn't belong there." Richard handed the cassettes to Donny. "You guys can have these copies. Go over them and see if you can come up with something new. I can't."

"Rich, it's a good thing we're buddies. Holding back like this..."

"I know. I wouldn't like it either. But I've got a major stake in this one."

"All right," said Miller. "We'll follow it up, but while you're at it, check the tapes on nineteen and twenty. Maybe someone, besides security, has a key to the stairwell doors. It's worth a shot."

"Now I know why you made Lieutenant." Richard opened his business case and removed a legal pad. "Mike, I have a list of questions here, pertaining to our firm's Colby case. I was hoping you could help me find some answers."

"Donny," said Miller. "Turn on your recorder. Go ahead, Rich."

"No one has spent enough time checking into Colby's taxes and various bank accounts. Not as thoroughly as we should. From what I've seen, the figures don't add up. We need to keep digging."

"Not a problem. What else?"

"We know Jacq Daniels and Colby are both graduates of Ohio State. Probably buddies from way back. Logic tells me Colby and Mai's killing may be linked."

"You're starting to make sense, Rich. Keep going."

"Get me all the names of his classmates. Kids he hung with. Names of his professors, and Colby's, too." Richard flicked the pages of his yellow pad. "Names of the personnel—mostly nurses and aides, at the orphanages and nursing homes, especially within the last year or two."

"Uh...in case you've forgotten...I handle ten cases at a time. Some in my spare time." Mike smiled at Richard. Dos looked as dour as ever.

"And if you guys give me a reason for somebody screwing up Jacq's desk," said Richard, "I'd sure as hell appreciate it."

"That ain't our job," said Donny.

"I've got one more thing, Mike. It looks promising."

"The Lieutenant said you might have something for us," said Donny. He flipped through the last page of his notes.

"Yeah. One of the security guards at the condo gave me a great tip. She pointed out the bird feeders along the back edge of the parking lot. Lots of them."

"Right. One of my boys brought that to my attention," said Miller. "We went back and canvassed the apartments on that side one more time but we struck out...so far."

"I did my own canvassing yesterday. Like old times."

"Any luck?" asked Donny.

"No, but I've developed a system, and I'm going to continue knocking on doors until somebody cracks. I posted a sign in the garage hallway."

"Yeah, we know," said Donny. He gave Miller a look and a shrug of his shoulders.

"We've still got the yellow tape cordoning off the crime scene," said Miller. "My men have gone over the area several times, but no dice. We'll keep looking. The bird-watcher might have seen a car or something. Anything would help."

"By the way," said Donny, "the dead girl had a permit to carry the missing .38."

X

The new gray carpeting in Tony Martini's office was being trimmed by a workman. Tony was tightening the last bolt on a black laminated piece of office furniture. The Atelier desk, with its shiny metal legs, curved gracefully toward a tall computer unit. Black frames with animation art were leaning against the far wall, ready for hanging. A black metal Richard Sapper table lamp was sticking out of a cardboard box.

Jacq stuck his head through the open door. "You must be Tony Martini. I'm Jacq Daniels." Jacq extended his hand as Tony got up off his knees. "And this is my partner, Jarvis Rumm. Welcome."

Tony wiped his hands on his Canali wool trousers. "Good morning, sir. Mr. Rumm. I'm so happy to meet you both." He eagerly shook their hands. "Charles has told me so much about the firm and its original founders."

"Charles is a good man," said Jarvis.

"Yes," said Jacq. "I see someone helped you with directions to the freight elevators, for your furniture and decor."

"Charles showed me where the back elevators were last Saturday," said Tony. "I wanted to get started as soon as I could. I contacted a friend in the interior design field. He had the perfect carpet remnant. And the wonderful modular desk is a piece of do-it-yourself furniture."

"This is all you have coming?" asked Jarvis.

"No. A gray sectional is on order, along with a black laquered coffee table. I have some other accessories coming later."

"Good job, young man," said Jarvis. He worked his way past the kneeling carpet man. "Jacq, it's getting late. Don't you have a meeting scheduled?" He glanced at his wrist again.

"Yeah, I do. Some person by the name of Dewars. Know him?"

"Humm...can't say I do," said Rumm. He stopped at the open door with Jacq. "I've got a meeting with Gina myself in ten minutes."

"It's been a pleasure meeting you both." Tony vigorously shook their hands once more. As soon as the men left, he opened a small wooden crate and unpacked the bubble wrap around a B-17 airplane model. He carefully removed the plane's metal base and set it on the desk. He suddenly had a feeling someone was watching.

Rita was standing in the open doorway.

In her most provocative voice she said, "It's cute!"

And I don't mean the plane, honey!

THE MONSTERS

CHAPTER XXVI

JULY 9, 1984

The concrete closet was damp. Musty odors permeated the tiny cubicle. Large blackish-brown roaches were feasting on a snack near the locked door. A young skinny figure lay on the moldy stained mattress, staring, wide-eyed, at the dirty bare bulb in the porcelain ceiling fixture. Spiderwebs, interwoven between the rafters, swayed serenely to and fro. It was difficult to sleep.

Maybe they're putting drugs in my food.

The hideous monster had stayed longer than usual tonight. It wouldn't go away for a long time. And when it finally did, the images came back with a vengeance. The veins in its giant hulk of a body bulged more each time: light and dark blue veins, the colors of death. Its one head, with three identical faces, was grotesque beyond belief. Wild deep-set pairs of eyes that pervaded the soul no matter which way the monster turned its ugly head. The only way to keep it out of the closet was to stay awake.

What's wrong with me?

The nights were getting longer and longer. Less and less sleep.

Why haven't I been adopted after all these years?

The rage within was becoming more difficult to control with each passing season.

X

At 2:00 A.M., the security guard yelled, "Hey! You in there?"

The young skinny figure, reading a worn comic book, yelled back, "Yeah!"

The guard jiggled the lock. Once he was satisfied the padlock on the "closet" door was secure, he went upstairs to his post and another coffee.

The skinny fifteen year old sat upright, listening intently until the sounds of the footsteps ceased on the landing. Silence, except for the starving rat in the corner. The small figure rolled off the crib mattress, crawled to the wooden shelf unit on the opposite wall, and slowly pulled it away from the wall, revealing a small hole in the concrete block. A hole big enough for a slim figure to squeeze through its opening. The opening led into the boiler room, with all its eerie hissing and dripping sounds.

The hole was painstakingly dug over the years, thanks in part to Schlitz, the aging social worker, who provided spoons, knives, sharp utensils, and other pieces of metal available for digging. Tonight, the final scrapings were being done with a large stainless ladle. In the smelly dampness, the concrete seemed to crumble more easily.

There were no mementos or clothes to take, only a small brown sack with a journal made from scraps of toilet tissue. A journal with names never to be forgotten.

When the air conditioning system kicked on, the skinny body wedged itself through the opening into the boiler room, tip-toed up the stairs without breathing, pushed the side door open and ran into the night.

I'm free, Mr. Colby! I'm FREE!

"Hey!" shouted Jackie, "what time do I have to be back for my meeting with Brandy Jones?" He turned the water off in his office's small bathroom and adjusted his Zenga tie. Both doors were wide open.

Kristie looked at the Monday planner on her computer screen. "You've got her scheduled for two." She was wearing a tight leather "nuclear-waste green" suit with matching shoes. The short skirt made it difficult for Kristie to sit at her desk.

"Do you know why Ms. Jones wants to see me?"

"No. I saw her in the cafeteria during break. She looked kinda bummed." Kristie squirmed in her chair.

Jackie pulled on his pin-striped suit jacket and grabbed the door knob. "I may be late getting back from lunch. I'm meeting with a client."

Kristie looked studiously at the monitor's screen.

"It's not on there," said Jackie. "I'll call if I'm going to be late."

X

Jackie walked west on Washington Boulevard for several blocks to Riverside Plaza. He passed groups of sidewalk vendors peddling their wares. A chilling breeze off the river blew the wide collar of his trenchcoat up around his face. He quickened his pace, hurrying to the center of the Plaza, near the arched bridge.

She was waiting at their usual spot, watching the diving gulls, facing the basin of the river. She was wearing a tailored beige suit, white open-collared shirt, and a wool scarf. Small pearl earrings completed her conservative look.

"Thanks for meeting me, away from the office on such short notice," said Rosie. She instinctively reached for Jackie's hand.

"You're the only one I'd do this for." Jackie pulled Rosie close, shielding her from the wind with his body. They kissed, playfully.

"You told me once...if I ever needed anything..."

Jackie laughed. "I paid for your gorgeous nose job, remember?" He laughed again. "Are you hungry?"

"This is serious."

A girl's gotta do what a girl's gotta do!

"Okay, no more laughing." Jackie tried to look serious, but he was still smiling, still holding her hand.

"I need a hundred thousand dollars." Her cheeks flushed.

"WHAT!" Jackie backed away from her. He started laughing again, not quite as hard as before. "You're kidding...right?"

"I need an abortion."

He stopped laughing.

"You're the father of my baby. I found out a few days ago."

Jackie couldn't laugh, talk or think.

"I need to have it done...like soon."

"I'll take care of it," said Jackie finally. "I need some time to get that kind of money."

"It can be done on a weekend. I know someone."

"You...you don't want the baby?"

"No. No, I don't."

Jackie turned his head toward the mouth of the river and stared at the gray-green water. "I'll get you the money."

"I don't know what else to do...where to turn."

Rosie's acting lessons paid off handsomely as tears fell gently down her cheeks, melting into the blue eye shadow.

"I'll take care of it, Rosie. You have my word." Jackie held her hands in his and said, "Right now, I've got to get back to the office. Another meeting."

"I hope it'll be more pleasant."

He stepped off the curb and hailed a taxi. "You want a ride back? I'm not hungry either."

"No. I'll walk."

"Give me a couple of days. We can work this out."

"Thanks, Jackie."

Pack your bags, Momma. This is going to be easier than I ever dreamed it would be!

Jacq was scribbling notes on his legal pad, penciling in the changes in the weekly schedule, when Iris buzzed him.

"Yeah, what is it?"

"A Mr. Dewars here to see you."

"Tell him to wait." Jacq rummaged through some papers on his desk, muttering under his breath. "Iris, come in here for a minute." He found the magazine ad under a menu.

Iris pushed the door open, steno pad and pencil in hand.

"I need you to go out this week and buy a watch for DeDe. You know what she'd like. Something flashy."

"And expensive."

"It's a make-up gift. I screwed up her little party last Saturday." Jacq shoved the ad in Iris' hand.

"I know," said Iris. "She called earlier, looking for you. I put a note on your desk." Iris pointed to a pile of pink memo slips. "DeDe mentioned you worked late and missed her party."

"Yeah, well, now I've got to pay for it."

"I know exactly what she wants."

"Okay, go." He motioned to Iris. "Send in the Dewars guy." Jacq got up, brushed an eraser crumb off his trousers, and extended a hand toward his visitor. "I'm Jacq Daniels."

"Danny Dewars, Private Investigator. I'm from Columbus,

Ohio. Glad to meet you." Dewars was wearing a new tie with his old faded pin-striped Brooks Brothers suit.

"Time is money, Mr. Dewars..."

"You can say that again."

"Now that we understand each other, what brings you to Chicago?"

"Your son, Jackie, hired me to dig up what I could on a guy named Colby."

"Oh, so you're the P.I. on that report." Jacq thumbed through a stack of folders and pulled out a crisp file. "Here it is. Fairly comprehensive, as I recall."

"Worth the money."

"If it's the fee you're after, I'm sure the check has been issued." Jacq scanned the papers. "It was for five thousand dollars."

"And another five Gs if I come up with more. Your son is aware of that."

Jacq hunched back in his chair, folded his arms and stared at Dewars. "Perhaps you'd like to speak with Jackie?"

"No. My business is with you." Dewars took a ragged folder out of his briefcase and tossed it on the desk. "You might be interested in this," he said innocently. A faint smile crossed his lips.

Jacq's face flushed beet-red. The dirty folder in front of him was labeled 'JEANETTE DOYLE.'

"Where did you get this?"

"Never mind. The important thing is, I have it." Dewars leaned back into the sidechair, smiling.

"These are copies," said Jacq gruffly.

"No kidding."

"Where are the originals?"

"Never mind." A wider smile.

"Where is the rest of the file?" Jacq's mind was racing.

"Never mind the questions. Do you want to hear what I want?" His voice turned venomous.

"What?"

"That half of the file is worth, easy, $150,000. That's what I want. In cash."

"Preposterous!" yelled Jacq. "I don't have that kind of money." He composed himself. "Besides, that little scrap of information is not worth $150,000."

"Then make me an offer I can't refuse."

If looks could kill, Dewars was a dead man. "$150,000.—for this and the rest of the files, including the originals."

"Make it $200,000. and we've got a deal."

"Done," said Jacq. "I want the files on my desk by Friday. You'll get your money then."

Dewars grabbed his coat off a bentwood rack and waved at Jacq as he left the office. "A pleasure doing business with you, Mr. Daniels." As he limped out, Iris couldn't help but notice his Cheshire cat-like grin.

X

Jacq picked up his cell phone and punched at it with an unsteady hand. The phone buzzed a half-dozen times before it was answered.

"Yeah, it's me. Go."

"Labatt, get your ass up here fast! We gotta talk. Now!"

Labatt, Jacq's personal private investigator, hired to protect him, hurriedly left his '88 Plymouth parked at the curb and was in the office in five minutes.

"What's up, Mr. Daniels?" asked Labatt. He was a carbon copy of Dewars, with one exception; his clothes were more expensive.

"I've got a special job for you."

"That'll mean an extra fee, right?"

"Yeah, yeah, no problem." Jacq put his arm on Labatt's shoulder. "Ever been to Columbus?"

"Sure, lots of times," said Labatt. "What's goin' on?"

"Plenty. Let's take a walk. I can think better when I walk." Jacq opened the door to Iris' outer office.

"Hello again, Ms. Whiskey," said Labatt.

"Mr. Labatt and I have some important business to discuss. We'll be gone for an hour or so."

"Fine. I can pick up the gift for DeDe while you're out," said Iris. She clicked off her computer.

Jacq and Labatt walked quickly to the elevators. "I want you in Columbus in the morning. Ready to move the minute I call you."

"I'm on it. Sounds like top priority."

"I've got a meeting with Colby tomorrow morning. Seems he and I have some unfinished business."

"Whoa! That IS top priority," said Labatt.

"Now this is what I want you to do..."

X

An hour later, Iris returned from the small exclusive boutique shop on Washington Boulevard with DeDe's gift. She had selected, with the help of a pompous salesman, an eighteen-carat gold watch in a signature quilted design by Chanel. The watch was boxed and wrapped with an equally elegant foil paper. Iris filed the sales slip, and the gold-foiled price tag of $4,266., including tax, into a folder marked 'EXPENSE ACCOUNT, J.D.'

DeDe has earned this—and more!

Iris walked around to the pencil drawer of Jacq's temporary Formica-clad desk.

I'll put this in the top drawer. He can't miss it.

Iris pulled the narrow drawer open and placed the gift next to Jacq's Cross pens. She noticed the manila folder with Jacq's familiar scribblings: several figures scratched out, from $100,000. to a circled amount of $200,000. Iris couldn't resist the temptation.

To hell with secretarial confidentiality!

Iris opened the crinkled folder labeled 'JEANETTE DOYLE' and began reading the two photocopies enclosed. She began to shake violently, then collapsed in Jacq's Oval Office chair. When she caught her breath, she quickly put the folder back in the drawer and went to her outer office. She decided to leave early.

I need time to think!

GINA'S TURN

Jarvis' impromptu meeting with Gina was in the corner of the law library. Brandy, Rita, and two law students were busy with their research on the far side of the room.

"I wonder if those two kids could help Saturday with the Colby mock trial," said Gina, pointing at the group near the window.

"Good idea. We need more bodies to fill the various roles, according to Sherry."

"I'll ask them before we leave," said Gina. She and Jarvis spread folders and legal pads on the table. Gina checked the first item on her list. "Let's see. While we're on the subject, do we have enough jurors for the mock trial?"

"Sherry's notes list a dozen interviewed and selected, with at least six alternates. I think we're okay," said Jarvis, checking his file.

"Are we still paying sixty dollars a day to these people? That sounds like a lot for a mock trial."

"I'm concerned about the costs, too," said Jarvis, "but in this case, we've got to pull out all the stops."

"Who's keeping track of the billable hours?"

"Sherry and I. Well...Iris does the actual tabulating, but Sherry and I spot-check the timecards for any Colby-related projects."

"Sounds like a major undertaking," said Gina.

"It is. We're billing anywhere from $60 an hour for the rank and file, up to $500 an hour for our top people."

"What more can I do to help?"

"I'd like you to take over the billing on the Colby trial. We're looking at about 2.5 million dollars. Maybe more." Jarvis reached out and touched Gina's hand. Gina smiled at him and didn't pull away.

"That's a humongous responsibility."

"I know you can handle it. I want Jacq and Sherry to know, too." Jarvis settled back in the oak chair. "Since your recruitment, you've been my favorite protegé."

"I want to thank you again. It's been wonderful of you."

"I'd like to see you move up the ladder, ultimately make partner. I can see it coming."

"You've been a terrific mentor," said Gina softly.

"You know I'll be retiring soon. If anything goes wrong with this Colby trial and we can't get him off, all hell's going to pop. The reputation of the firm will certainly suffer. Sherry will most likely go down with Jacq. I have a feeling Colby's hiding something from us. Or perhaps it's Colby AND Jacq."

"I fear for you at times, Jarvis. I get the feeling you're being eased out."

"No. Don't think that way. I've had a great thirty years here-with Jacq. It was fun in the beginning." Jarvis waved at the young women across the room. "The last ten or fifteen years have been anything BUT fun. I'm honestly looking forward to fishing and painting."

"You don't look like the type to settle down. You need people around you."

"That reminds me," said Jarvis. "We need to line up one or two more people for overtime. I know of at least one secretary who wouldn't mind the extra income."

"And I know one or two L.A.'s that are far short of their twelve hundred hours," said Gina. "I'm sure I can twist their arms."

Brandy and Rita carried their research books across the room and set them on the table near Jarvis' elbow. Both girls wore pants and loose-fitting sweatshirts.

"Hi, Mr. Rumm," said Brandy. "Rita, Kristie, and I have been at these books for days."

"And doing quite well, according to Marcus."

"We've got an outline from Mr. Lambrusco we're trying to follow. Rita came across some fantastic research material about pretrial discovery. Like when each side is obligated to turn over all their documents to the other side, so there's no more surprise ambushes, like on the old Perry Mason shows."

"Very well articulated, Ms. Jones."

Brandy blushed and looked at Rita.

"We got so excited," said Rita. "One way to avoid turning something over is if the document is considered to be 'work product.' Sometimes the attorney can write notes on his folders, so they can call it a 'work product' and not have to turn the information over to the other side. Isn't that cool, Mr. Rumm?"

"I love this job!" said Brandy.

"I don't mean to burst your bubble, gals," said Gina, "but if you'll look closely, you'll see that Mr. Rumm co-authored that text."

"Yes, it is 'cool,' Ms. Lopez," said Jarvis. "And I love being around you young people...filled with enthusiasm. Reminds me of when Mr. Daniels and I were boyhood chums, during the Depression." Jarvis' voice choked up for a second. He pulled himself up from his chair. "Now if you'll excuse us, Gina and I have another meeting upstairs."

"Mr. Rumm?"

"Yes, Ms. Lopez?"

"I heard stories about underground tunnels being used during Prohibition, around the Chicago area. Is that true?"

"Yes, it's true. But most of the Canadian whiskey coming into the states was through Michigan. There were dozens of tunnels dug along the Detroit River. That's how my father and Mr. Daniels' father met—unloading whiskey from a boat to a truck in downtown Detroit. Again, excuse us."

"You are SO cool, Mr. Rumm," said Rita.

Jarvis and Gina took the elevator to her office on the twentieth floor, across the hall from the employees lounge.

"I won't come in," said Jarvis. "I've got a meeting with Richard. You be careful, honey." Jarvis gave Gina a gentle hug and a kiss on the cheek.

J.D. Daniels exited the elevator on twenty and hurried past the reception counter toward Richard's office. He gave Rosie an obligatory wave.

"Oh, Mr. Daniels," shouted Rosie. Jacq didn't stop or look back. "Iris went home early. She said she was sick."

What the hell! Iris never gets sick!

In the middle of the long hallway, Jacq stopped dead in his tracks. He couldn't believe his eyes. Jarvis was kissing Gina. He had one arm around her shoulder. She and Jarvis were smiling like two lovebirds.

Rumm, you dog! I'm finally beginning to respect you!

JACK OF HEARTS

CHAPTER XXX

"Your office looks great," said Brandy. "I love the picture of Betty Boop."

"It's my favorite, too," said Tony. A recessed pin-spot illuminated the animation art. He was organizing his canvas binders into a low bookcase. It was past seven in the evening and most of the offices on the floor were still occupied. Tony had no intention of leaving before Charles or the others.

"My office is two doors down, next to the print shop."

"Yes, I know," said Tony.

"Are you working on Colby, too?"

"No. A special assignment from Charles. Am I the only one NOT working on that case?" Tony got up off his knees and sat down in his black molded chair. "That's all I've been hearing about since I arrived."

"The Colby trial will be over before Christmas," said Brandy. "Don't worry. There'll be lots of work, A.C.—AFTER COLBY. Gotta go, Tony. See 'ya."

"Love your sense of humor, Brandy. Good night."

Brandy walked to the end of the corridor, past her small office and the print shop. She passed Harry's cubicle. His door was ajar. She could see him hunched over a pile of copy paper, stacking sheets into a collating machine.

Getting ready for the mock trial Saturday, huh?

Brandy went around the corner and took the stairs, two flights up, to Jackie's office. She could see the glow of his light through the frosted glass panel. Brandy knocked softly and pushed the door open.

"Mr. Daniels? You still here?"

Jackie was sitting at his desk, feet propped up on a stack of folders, hands behind his head, staring at the ceiling. She startled him.

"Hey!" Jackie sat up in his chair. "I'm sorry about cancelling our meeting. I had too much on my mind."

"That's okay."

"You working late, too?"

"Just trying to get caught up," said Brandy.

"I'm doing a little brain-storming myself." Jackie had a pleasant smile on his face.

A nice, normal smile, thought Brandy.

She stood in front of Jackie's desk with her arms folded. "My daddy always said to get straight to the point. Here goes. I have a very serious problem I'd like to discuss with you, Mr. Daniels. I wish we..."

"Call me Jackie, okay."

"Yeah. Sure." Brandy began rubbing her palms together and fidgeting with her drop earrings. "I know I've only been here for a little over six months..."

"Six good months, I hope."

"I'm kinda low on the totem pole, I know..."

"What the hell are you trying to tell me," said Jackie in his best Nicholson voice. "Go ahead. I won't bite."

"Okay. Here it is." Brandy took a wavering breath. "I need this job. I'm trying to support my mother, put my brother through law school, keep my '79 Olds running..."

"Where do I fit in?"

"You hired me. You could let me go on a whim!"

"Why would I do that?"

Brandy looked at their shadows playing out the scene on the textured wall. "If I didn't go out with you." She looked down at the burgundy carpeting. "If I didn't sleep with you."

"Is that what you're thinking? MY G..."

"I wanted to tell you before my brother got involved," said Brandy. "He has an awfully short fuse."

"Honestly," said Jackie, "I had no idea I was putting that kind of pressure on you. Most of the time I'm kidding. Believe me."

"So what you're saying is, it's okay if I don't go out with you? I'll still have my job?" Brandy sighed and wiped at her mascara.

"You have my word." Jackie left his chair and offered his hand. "I'm truly sorry for the pain I've put you through."

"Pardon me, Jackie," said Brandy, "but are you feeling all right?" She broke out in a broad smile.

"I've been sitting in the dark for a couple of hours. Years, really, thinking. Thinking if I have a crush on somebody, and finally came to the realization..."

"And...?"

"I think I'm in love."

X

Brandy threw her papers into a black leather carryall and buzzed the security guard. He escorted her to the parking lot and her beige '79 Olds. Brandy squealed out of the garage. She headed south on Canal.

"Whee!" said Brandy, shouting out loud. "This is how it feels to be free!"

I better let Cole know before he does something stupid!

X

Jackie left shortly after eight o'clock. Jacq and Richard stayed at the office finalizing the paperwork for the next day's meeting with Colby. He waved good night to them, declined the services of the security guard and headed north on the John F. Kennedy Expressway.

The top was up on his Mercedes. The red 300SL purred through the patches of fog, the stereo blaring. Jackie was oblivious to the tailgating dark van, with its lights off, slowly closing in on his rear bumper.

The Montrose ramp was under construction. Barricades divided the two-lane exit. Jackie turned up the ramp. The van sped up and forced his car into one of the concrete barriers. Jackie's car spun out of control, bouncing into orange plastic drums, amber flashing lights and striped barricades. The impact sheared off all the chrome strips from one side of the car, throwing debris and auto parts over the side of the ramp onto the curved lane below. Jackie's left fender rammed and wedged itself into a metal guardrail. The car's front wheel hung precariously over the edge. Jackie's experience handling sports cars enabled him to keep the car from crashing to the lane below.

It all happened so fast. A dark blur!

Jackie sat in his car, contemplating his good fortune. He got out and surveyed the damages. The Mercedes' body was severely dented on both sides, the front and back bumpers twisted and hanging from their mounting bolts.

Jackie called 911 on the car phone and waited.

Brandy's brother? A random accident? Or Mai's assailant?

CHAPTER XXXI

Jacq and Richard sat in the back of the limo comparing notes on Nathan Colby. The obscure glass on the BMW hid the passengers from the outside world. Guinness turned into a one-way street and drove to the rear entrance of the county courthouse, near two adjacent limestone structures. Somewhere in the maze of buildings and cubicles, Colby was being held in a retention cell for the murder of Mrs. Sarah La Grande.

"That was one hell of an accident," said Jacq. "I saw Jackie's car this morning. It's a pile of garbage. DeDe gave it to him for his birthday a couple of months ago."

"How is Jackie?"

"He's okay. The car's totaled."

"Maybe the fog contributed in some way to the accident."

"It was no accident, not according to Jackie. Someone tried to run him off the road." Jacq slammed his leather binder shut. "He's good with cars. Better than he is with law."

"There is a possibility the accident was related to the damaged desk. Maybe whoever forced Jackie's car off the road thought it was you."

"Nah, you're wrong. If someone was following me, they would've known I was still at the office."

"Whoever did it, then, was after Jackie. The question is, why?"

"The same reason they want to get rid of me? Forget it! I got Colby to think about right now. That's enough."

Jacq buzzed Guinness on the intercom. "Turn here. At Building C. Pull over by that no-parking zone."

X

Sheriff Jim Malt escorted the two men into the ancient labyrinths of the building. They followed him through each dimly lit corridor, the rusted iron gates of the sections clanging shut, resounding in the damp dungeons.

"Colby is in R-Cell 23," said Sheriff Jim. His stomach hung precariously over his wide belt. His tan uniform was spotlessly clean and starched. "Right around the corner."

Colby stood in the middle of the cell, silhouetted by the bright light streaming in from the small window behind him, waiting for the men. His gray-blonde hair was neatly combed. He wore faded green fatigues. No belt.

"Happy Halloween, you old S.O.B.," yelled Jacq before the Sheriff opened the cell door.

"Have I got anything to be happy about?" said Colby. "You tell me."

The Sheriff opened the cell. Jacq and Richard filed into the cramped quarters. "Nathan. Good to see you again. How long has it been?" Jacq extended his hand.

"Close to thirty years...but who's counting?" Colby acknowledged Richard with a nod and shook his hand. "And this is the high-priced lawyer you've got defending me?" Colby smiled one of his rare smiles.

"Nathan, this is Richard Port. He's one of the top people in my firm. If you are innocent, and we both agree you are, Richard and Sherry Weinstein, our specialist in criminal law, will be the two most important people in your life for a while."

"Mr. Port," said Colby, "are you as eloquent as your boss, here?" Colby was still smiling.

"Not really, Mr. Colby. Jacq's legal talents are to be admired. He's in his own special league. I wouldn't want to be against him."

"Well put, kid. You got my attention."

The two men sat down at a small table. Colby sat on the edge of the bed. Richard stacked his yellow pads on the plastic slab next to the sink. The men opened their cases and removed the folders.

"Go ahead, Richard. Nathan has assured me that whatever is said here will be the truth."

"We've got numerous holes to fill," said Richard. "This is one of the most complicated cases I've ever encountered."

"Ask me whatever turns you on."

"Mr. Colby, we've got the pre-trial proceedings set for Tuesday at three. I'm not sure we have all the facts we need to defend you properly. That's my gut speaking. We've got to be told everything, exactly as you remember it."

Colby stood and faced the window. The sunlight cut his body in half. He ran his fingers through his thinning hair, blinked his beady blue eyes, sighed, and rubbed his stubble of a beard. "I went into her room around 11:45 P.M., just before the nurses change shifts. I thought I heard her buzzing for help."

"'Her' being Mrs. La Grande," interrupted Richard.

"Yes. I went into her room. She was gasping for air. I went over to the bed to help her. I reached under her head, to see if she was choking. That's when the afternoon shift nurse, O'Doul..."

"That's Jennifer O'Doul?"

"Yes. That's when she came into the room from the nurse's station. What she saw was me trying to help Mrs. La Grande, not kill her."

"Jennifer's deposition states you were shoving a pillow over La

Grande's face. 'He was holding her head, pushing up into the pil-low.'" Richard closed the O'Doul file. "She says Mrs. La Grande was struggling."

"She's lying," said Colby.

"I've got my people checking into her background," said Jacq. "Her habits, whatever. We can most likely discredit her testimony."

"She's a hot-head," volunteered Colby.

"Why would she lie?" asked Richard.

"She's trying to get back at me for reprimanding her. I gave her a poor rating on her evaluation."

"Did she deserve the rating?"

"You're damn right! That's no reason for her to lie!" Colby started pacing. "It's my job, as Director, to keep these women in line. They have very limited experience."

"What were you doing in her room at that time of night?"

"Friday night, I usually worked late," muttered Colby. "I make my own rounds every once in a while, just to keep the broads on their toes."

"The fact she signed over 1.3 million dollars to your nursing home, payable upon her demise, have any bearing on her death?" asked Richard.

"We all know she signed those papers over three years ago. Why would I risk my reputation and do a stupid-ass stunt like..."

"You look as if you've lost some weight," said Jacq.

"Yeah. About ten pounds. I can't afford it." Colby dragged a wooden stool to the table and sat down, facing Richard. "That's all I can tell you. Exactly as it happened."

"I've known Nathan for over thirty years," said Jacq. He looked intently into Richard's eyes. "He's never lied to me."

Until now!

"Okay, we're done. I'll buzz Sheriff Malt." Richard collected his files and slid them neatly into a black leather case. "You ready to go, Jacq?"

"Tell Guinness to run you back to the office. Nathan and I have some reminiscing to do about the good old days at Ohio State." Jacq removed his suit jacket and pulled a chair up to the table.

Another iron gate clanged shut in one of the cubicles. The sound of Richard's footsteps diminished as he walked down the narrow hall. Colby held his breath, listening.

"You fool!" said Jacq finally. "You didn't destroy the files!"

"Those files have been my insurance policy, all these years!" whispered Colby. "Would you have continued paying me the fifty grand a year if I would've destroyed them?" Colby's eyes grew beadier. "I don't think so."

"I'm sending a man to Columbus to get rid of all the files!"

"Quiet down. Don't worry about it."

"I hope it's not too late."

"Listen," said Colby, "there's no way anyone can find the originals."

"What makes you so sure?" asked Jacq, his brown eyes straining in the dim light.

"All of the files on you and the kid are under an assumed name."

"I know. Under 'JEANETTE DOYLE.'"

Colby's head jerked back. "How did you know?"

"I'm being black-mailed by a private investigator. He says he got the Doyle file from Mansfield. I saw the copies. He says he's got the originals."

"Look, Jacq. The only thing the Doyle file tells him is that you had a kid, and it died. Simple. You're off the hook."

Colby sat in the spindled chair and smiled.

"He says he has other files."

"Impossible!" Colby leaned forward and put one hand on Jacq's knee. "Nobody would be smart enough to check my personal files. And even if they did, the only thing they'd find is a file labeled 'JANE DOE'.

"Meaning?"

"Jane Doe is your file. It's another code name for J.D....you- Jacq Daniels. I'm the only person, besides you, who knows. Nobody would bother to look further."

"Sounds like a lot of bull to me," said Jacq. "I'm sending my man to Mansfield to destroy ALL those freakin' files!"

Colby sat up abruptly and in an irritated voice said, "I was going to burn the files one time. Before I wised up and decided against it. I started a small fire in the gym. Played hell with the insurance adjuster. Cost me three grand to shut him up. Jacq, believe me, you have nothing to worry about."

"I remember the incident. We heard you were suspected of arson. I helped get the insurance company off your back, in case you've forgotten."

"I'll be damned. You're right." Colby's beady eyes brightened. "You know, the place was a dump. But I'm glad old Schlitz doused my little fire. He saved my neck."

"Not to mention all the kids in the orphanage." Jacq didn't

remember his friend being so cruel and heartless in the old days.

"Just before my old man died, he and I bought the orphanage in Mansfield. We were close." Nathan glanced up at Jacq. "Were you close to your father?"

Jacq looked out of the small meshed window, wishing he had gone with Richard. "I thought I was. Jarvis' father and my dad were the real pals. Jarvis and I got along great, when we were younger. Something happened. It's not important."

"So what you're saying is, you and your old man didn't get along."

Jacq stood in the center of the cell, staring at the floor, frozen in time. Colby knew what was coming.

"Nathan, I was a smart-ass punk. Too young. No brains. My old man forced me to do what I did. She and I were going to get married and keep the kid. My father said he would disinherit me of a position with Daniels and Rumm. He kept harping about reputation. The illegitimate child. He was the one who wanted to keep the kid a secret."

"Yeah, George Washington," said Colby, "your father has been dead for years. Who's been paying me the fifty grand a year for keeping the secret from the kid's mother?"

"I'm so fortunate to have a pal like you."

"Oh, yeah," said Colby, "while we're in a confessional mood. The kid escaped from Mansfield in July of '84."

Jacq's jaw dropped a foot.

"You've got bigger problems then I have, Jacq old buddy," said Colby, grinning. "Your kid is out there...somewhere...looking for YOU!"

"Sheriff!" yelled Jacq. "Get me the hell out of here!"

Iris opened Jarvis' office door and threw the rumpled copies on his desk. She was tired and distraught.

"Heaven's sake, Iris! Sit. You look like you haven't slept a wink. What happened?" Jarvis helped her to one of his worn chairs.

"These are from a file I found in Jacq's desk last night. I made the copies this morning, when he and Richard left." Iris began sobbing softly. "I can't believe it."

Jarvis opened the folder and stared at the stark-white copy paper in disbelief. His jaw slackened. "Jacq had a child? Before Jackie?"

"The file says the baby died."

"Here's a copy of the death certificate. It has J.D.'s signature on it." Jarvis bit his upper lip. "The baby's name was Jeanette Doyle."

"I can't believe it!" repeated Iris.

"So that's the secret he's been carrying around. The J. Doyle file is some sort of code name for Jacq's child."

"There's more to it." Iris wiped her eyes with a handful of tissues. "I've been carrying around a much bigger burden. I'm more guilty than he is. I've got to tell someone."

"You could've come to me any time, Iris."

She hung her head and picked at her red painted nails. "I met Jacq during his last year at Ohio State. I was a sophomore—a starry-eyed ingenue. We fell madly in love. We were going to change the world."

"I recall days such as that."

"The day Jacq was accepted into law school, we decided to celebrate. We drank too much. Things got out of hand."

Jarvis leaned toward Iris and patted her hand.

"I became pregnant," said Iris. She began to breath normally. "A few months after Jacq graduated, I had a child."

"You've held this in...all these years?!"

Iris became more relaxed. "Jacq and I were thrilled. We moved into a small apartment on the east side of Detroit. He was going to school, working nights, while I took care of the baby and worked at the library on weekends. We were so happy. We were going to get married. That's what Jacq told me."

"Why move to Detroit? He could've gone to school here."

"Jacq said the schools were better. I found out later his father didn't want any part of the baby...or me. We never married."

"I can understand now where Jacq gets his ruthlessness. That must have been devastating." Jarvis shook his head and continued to hold her hands.

"There's more." Iris pulled away, leaned back and clenched her fists.

"Take your time."

"One evening, while I was at work, I got a call from Jacq. He sounded hysterical. He said he had taken the baby to the mall, just to get out of the apartment." Iris choked up again. "He said he was looking at some merchandise on the counter in one of the stores...then, when he turned around, the baby was gone!"

"Oh, my! What...?"

"Jacq said he called store security, but the baby was missing. No one remembered seeing the child."

"How about the police?"

"Jacq's father convinced us not to call the police. He said the adverse publicity would hurt his firm if word got out." Iris took a deep breath. "He said he'd hire a private investigator to help us find our baby." Iris paused again. "I don't know if he ever did."

"How did Jacq handle the kidnapping?"

"He seemed to throw himself into his studies even more. As the weeks and months went by and we didn't hear anything, I just gave up. Jacq and I drifted farther apart."

"How so?" asked Jarvis.

"Jacq's father offered him a part-time job in the firm. He told him he could finish his studies in Chicago. Jacq said he'd send for me once he got settled."

"Sounded like a good plan."

"I didn't hear from him for months," said Iris.

"That was unconscionable." Jarvis sighed and rubbed Iris' hand.

"Yet, that wasn't the worst of it. Jacq moved around. I had no way to reach him. When he finally called me the following year, he asked me to come to Chicago. I was still angry. I refused."

"Unbelievable," said Jarvis comfortingly.

"He said he was working for his father. It sounded like he wanted us to get back together. He said his father was retiring soon. I was stubborn. I told him no, again. I went on with my life."

"Then what happened?" Jarvis was listening intently.

"Years passed. I was a secretary at GM. One day, I was looking through the latest news bulletins and saw an article featuring the law firm of Daniels and Rumm. The article was vague, but it mentioned a new addition to the firm, Jackie Daniels, SON of Jacq Daniels. I felt my heart stop. Could this be our son?" Iris began trembling. Painful buried memories came gushing back.

"My God!" said Jarvis.

"For once in my life, I stood up for myself and called Jacq's office. I didn't mention Jackie. We talked. I told him what I was doing. Probably because he felt sorry for me, he offered me a job. At first I declined, but before we hung up, I accepted. I was hoping that if I stayed near Jacq..."

"...you might find out more about Jackie. If he was indeed your kidnapped child?" interrupted Jarvis.

"When I got to Chicago, I found out Jacq was married to DeDe. Jackie was THEIR son."

"What a shock that must have been. I don't know how Jacq sleeps at night." Jarvis waved his head from side to side, trying vainly to console Iris. "Does DeDe know about any of this?"

"To my knowledge, no. She's always been pleasant."

Jarvis motioned to the files on the desk. "After seeing those copies, it's still confusing. According to those signed papers, the baby died."

"Jacq told me our baby was kidnapped."

"It's time for you to confront him. It's WAY past due!"

"You're right," said Iris. "Died? Kidnapped? A girl child? Could there have been another woman?" Iris looked at Jarvis and said, " I have a feeling my child is still alive."

"So do I." Jarvis rolled his chair to his phone and lifted the receiver. "We'd better let Richard know. Mai's killing might be linked to this tangled mess. Colby could be involved." He punched Richard's extension.

For the first time in thirty years, thought Iris, *I will finally learn the truth!*

APARTMENT HUNTING

"Swing by the parking garage instead, Tommy," said Richard over the intercom. "I want to go over to Green Oaks and grab a lunch. I've got some 'bird watching' of my own to do."

"Your wish is my command," joked Guinness. Then seriously, he said, "I could drive you."

"No, thanks. Jacq's probably waiting for you by now. He has meetings all afternoon."

"Whatever you say." Guinness pulled over to the curb at the garage's entrance.

"Tell Iris I'll be back around three."

X

Richard drove to the condo and checked his answering machine pertaining to his bird watcher poster. Out of four messages, three callers were from his side of the building. One was on the opposite side, facing away from the parking lot.

Not much help here.

He made a list of the callers between bites of a vegetarian burger. He gulped his diet drink, grabbed his coat and writing pad, and was on his way out when he remembered Amy's interesting suggestion to try "bird watching" in the opposite direction, to see if any telescopes were visible through the windows from the parking lot.

Richard took his high-powered German binoculars out to Parking Lot B, to the site of Mai's attack and focused on the windows facing the crime scene. The afternoon glare of the sun off the panes of glass made his efforts futile.

Thanks anyway, Amy.

X

Richard knocked on doors the rest of the afternoon. He checked several apartments on his side of the building; two of the callers who left their names on his machine were not at home. The third had nothing new to reveal.

Richard went to the other side of the building and took the elevator to the third floor. He walked down the carpeted hallway and rapped on the last caller's door. A small Halloween wreath was pinned below the numbers.

"Yes—who is it?" said the woman behind the door.

"I'm Richard Port. I'd like to talk to you about the bird-watcher sign."

The door's chain jiggled and the deadbolt snapped. An elderly woman, with a dish towel in her hand, opened the door. "Come in, Mr. Port." She extended her wrinkly hand and said, "My name is Smirnoff. Sadie Smirnoff."

"Hello, Mrs. Smirnoff." Richard nodded, smiled and shook Sadie's hand. "I live upstairs on fifteen. I'm trying to help the police with an investigation. I was hoping I could find a bird watcher in the building, preferably on the other side, who might've seen something that could shed light on last week's attack in the parking lot."

"Oh! So that's what all those signs were about. No matter! I was going to call you again later." Sadie yanked her coat out of the hall closet. "I'm late already. My daughter's waiting for me downstairs."

"Wait! You called me, remember? You had some important information. About bird watchers?"

"Bird watchers? Me? Heavens, no," said Mrs. Smirnoff. "I don't know a thing about bird watchers. Never did. Now I really must go." Sadie slammed the door behind her.

"I'm sorry I bothered you, Mrs. Smirnoff," said Richard dejectedly. "Have a nice..."

"Oh, young man," said Sadie cheerfully as she limped down the hall, "I don't know squat about bird watching, but you might want to talk to Mr. Molson in 359. That nice man helps me with my groceries. He's always home. He goes on and on about all sorts of birds. It's boring, if you ask me."

"He's always home?" Richard followed her down the hall.

"No matter when I call for help, he's there. I don't know." Sadie shrugged her stooped shoulders. Richard helped her to the elevator. "He tells me he watches the birds every morning while he has breakfast.

EVERY MORNING?

X

"Mr. Molson. Remember me?"

"The police have been here twice. Now you again. I told you guys everything I know." Molson started to close the door. "I didn't see a thing." The parakeet flew across the room and landed on his head. "Damn it, Malty! Get the hell off me!"

Molson reached up and brushed the bird away with both hands. As he did, the door swung open, revealing several computers complete with printers, fax machines, e-mail and other technical pieces of equipment. All the monitors were connected, flashing charts and numbers.

"That's quite an array of electronic equipment you have, Mr. Molson."

"Everybody has computers nowadays."

"Four of them?"

"I'm a computer freak," said Ricky.

Malty, sitting on the top of the window casing, screeched "BUY! NO-SELL!"

"What do you do for a living, Mr. Molson, may I ask?" said Richard as he pushed the door open farther.

"I'm...a...investment counselor."

"You work downtown?"

"Yes. As a matter of fact, I'm leaving for the office in a few minutes," said Molson.

Malty was silent. He was pecking at a curtain rod.

Even I know you're lying, Ricky!

"Come on in," said Amy. She took Rosie's jacket. "I'm glad you guys could make it. Brandy and Kristie are in the kitchen."

"This was a fabulous idea!" said Rita. "Even if you didn't invite Tony!" The girls giggled. Rosie adjusted her makeup in the wall-hung mirror. Rita put her plastic bowl of salad on the hall table.

"A pizza party—on Halloween!" Rosie laughed. "Who came up with this concept?"

"Actually," said Amy, "it was Richard. He's had Mai on his mind. We haven't seen each other for days."

"A bummer," said Rita.

"That's not like him." Amy picked up the salad bowl and proceeded to the kitchen. "At least he says the Colby case is finally starting to come together. Whoa! No more shop talk! Brandy brought the beer!"

Kristie and Brandy were arranging napkins and paper plates on the Corian counter. Kristie was nursing a can of Miller Lite. Brandy sipped a diet coke as she tore the plastic off the orange plates.

"Hey, guys!" said Brandy, "Where's Iris and Gina?"

"Iris called," said Amy. "She has a cold coming on."

"She doesn't want to infect us," said Rita.

"Ha!" said Kristie. "That wouldn't stop you!" She pushed the sleeves up on her extra-large sweatshirt and plopped herself on the leather sofa.

"Look what I've got for everyone!" shouted Amy. She handed a comical orange mask to Brandy. "They're all alike. If we put them on, we won't know who is who!"

"How many beers have you had already?" yelled Rosie. The girls howled.

"Oh, before I forget," said Amy, "Gina had a late meeting scheduled with Jarvis. She won't be here."

"Her loss, our gain," said Rosie. "Who wants another beer!"

Kristie cranked up the stereo.

X

Two of the girls were sitting on a long gnarled piece of driftwood sipping from glass bottles. Amy sat in a striped canvas chair, stoking the yellow and orange flames of the bonfire. Sparklers floated upward into the ink-black sky. Rosie was a stone's throw down the beach, digging her toes into the fine-grained sand. Brandy was busy picking up the empty cans.

"I told you I knew what I was doing," said Amy above the crackling of the fire. "Yellow and orange fire. Yellow and orange masks."

"I don't think so!" yelled Rita. "It's hell trying to drink beer through this little hole!" The girls roared.

"Rosie!" squealed Kristie. "Rosie! Show us your new tattoo."

"Oh, my God!" said Amy. "You didn't!"

"I did! Look!" She pulled down the collar of her flannel shirt and revealed a small tattoo, discretely etched below her right shoulder.

"That is soooo cool!" said Brandy.

"I got angry at my mother again and I went right out and did it—the same day—before I changed my mind."

"It's pretty," said Kristie.

"It sort of back-fired on me, though," said Rosie. "When I got home, my mother was heaving. Throwing up bad. She looked awful. I thought she was having another attack, so I took her to the emergency room."

"MY gosh!" said Amy. "What happened?"

"While I sat in the waiting room for three hours, wondering if she was going to be okay, I realized just how much I'd miss her yelling and whining..."

"Mothers will do that to you," said Amy.

"Hey," said Brandy, "talking about surprises, has anybody noticed a distinct change in Jackie? I mean...a big change?"

"Yeah," said Kristie. "He wanted me to pick up some custom-made shirts for him on my lunch hour one day. Then he calls me into his office and tells me to forget it. He says he'll get Guinness to do it."

"People change," said Rosie.

"I need cake," yelled Rita. The girls screamed.

"I wanna marry a lawyer and live like DeDe!" chimed Kristie.

"Now that would be so NOT cool!" cautioned Brandy.

"Everyone around here is so squeaky clean!" said Rosie. She laughed and threw a handful of sand at Brandy.

"Is she gonna dump on me now, or what?" Brandy shook the sand off her black Levis.

"Follow me to the fridge!" They marched, single file, like three dwarfs, to the beach house.

"Brandy, come over here where it's warm," yelled Amy.

Brandy had a lightweight nylon jacket around her shoulders. "Wow! That's so much better."

"You want some coffee?"

"Hey, guys!" shouted Brandy at the girls. "Bring me back something HOT!"

The two women sat on the smooth driftwood, poking into the dying embers with long charred sticks.

"Jackie HAS changed," confided Brandy. "I was afraid he wouldn't let me alone. He was always hinting about me going out with him."

"I heard those stories."

"They were true. Then—all of a sudden—when he and I talked this week, he backed off. Just like Rosie said...people can change."

"This is OUR Jackie we're talking about?"

"It shocked me too, Amy." Brandy took her smiley-face mask and threw it into the fire. The flames licked the mask's edges, then shriveled into a black ball. "A fitting ending."

"I'll drink to that," said Amy as she raised her can of cola.

Brandy zipped her jacket and felt for her car keys. "Man, it's one o'clock! I've gotta be home in a half hour."

"Mom give you a curfew?" said Amy, laughing.

"Cole and I have some celebrating of our own to do. He gets off work around 1:30. I haven't seen him for a couple of days. I'm dying to tell him the good news."

Amy kicked sand on the smoldering ashes. She took off her mask and said, "I'm so glad you were able to come. I'll walk you to the car."

Brandy turned the key and her '79 Cutlass roared to life. "Thanks for everything. See you tomorrow."

She backed the car down the sandy driveway.

"Take it easy around the first bend!" yelled Amy. "See you!"

As Brandy's taillights disappeared in the fog, a Belmont Harbor Police Cruiser, with its red and blue lights flashing hysterically, turned into Amy's driveway.

This will be the last Halloween party I ever throw for this bunch!

X

Brandy drove south along the shoreline and exited at thirty-first. The fog followed her in from the beach. She drove under the I-94 freeway toward Parnell, unaware of a dark van with its lights turned off, trailing a half block behind. Brandy parked her car at the curb. It was 1:45 A.M.

The van pulled parallel to Brandy's car before she opened the driver's-side door.

"Hi, Brandy," said the slim figure. The passenger-side window was rolled down. The shadowy form slid across the bench seat toward Brandy. The figure wore a Halloween mask. Brandy tried to scream. It was a frightened, soundless cry.

"Relax, Brandy Braveheart." The slim figure took off the mask. "Surprise!"

"OH! It's you. What are you...lost or somethin'?" The terror left Brandy's eyes.

"Yeah, I am as a matter of fact," said the slim figure. "There's an all-nighter goin' on at McGuane Park. Can you show me where it is on this map?"

Brandy jumped into the front seat of the van. The dome light clicked on. . .

"Hey, what's with the rubber gloves!?"

. . .then immediately off.

Tag! You're IT!

THEY'RE BACK!

CHAPTER XXXVI

SEPTEMBER 26, 1989

"I mean it!" said the grocery store owner. "You short-change one more customer and yer otta here! You got me!"

The slim figure fidgeted and pulled down on the green produce apron. "Yeah—I hear you."

"How many times do we have to go over the same damn mistakes?" yelled the angry owner. "Break this! Screw that up! When the hell are you going to learn to...!"

"You know what!" shouted the skinny figure. "You can take this job and sh...!"

"Yer fired! Get the hell out! Now!"

"Shove it up...!"

"Out! And gimme that apron!"

"You owe me three day's pay," said the slight figure, throwing the apron into the face of a nearby employee who was stocking the shelves with homemade jellies and jams. The stockgirl, startled, fell backward into a free-standing metal displayer. Jam and jelly jars smashed onto the tiled floor. The store owner's wife came running from the back of the shop.

"There goes your three day's pay!" yelled the red-faced owner. "Out, damn you! I don't want to see your skinny ass in here again!"

"I'm otta here, you old fart!"
I'll get you...like I'll get Colby!

X

It became increasingly difficult to tell the good days from the bad. The recurrent nightmares persisted, lingering, with each passing day, farther into the lonely wee hours of the morning. The slim figure, unable to sleep, sat in a maple chair, rocking in time to the neon sign across the street. Forward: red. Back: white.

When the eyelids drooped, the hideous monster reared its veined body and beckoned to the slight form.

I can help you...if you'll let me.

The slim figure, bathed in perspiration, stood and opened the window of the apartment another notch. A smell of burning leaves filled the small room. The acrid odor was followed by the faint seafood aroma from the crumbling brick building next door. The figure paced the worn carpet. The neon sign stopped blinking. The sun forced itself between the steelwork of the elevated train and begrudgingly into a corner of the dingy apartment.

The slim figure began working at a makeshift desk, a converted bureau with the drawers removed. Scraps of notes on toilet tissue, wrinkled typing paper, Wonder Woman comics and torn phone books littered the surface of the desk. The double dose of little white pills was finally starting to kick in. The rage subsided. The monster gone.

Mr. Colby! You can run...but you can't hide!

RED AND YELLOW TAPE

Yellow tape swayed from a clump of birch, out over the sidewalk to the NO PARKING sign, then parallel to the curb and back around to a tall elm. Dos cut the engine on the faded blue Plymouth. He and Lieutenant Miller climbed out of the unmarked police car. Richard pushed the back door open and walked with them through the brush to the crime scene. A weary patrolman, ensuring the non-contamination of the scene, hopped out of his parked cruiser and greeted the men.

"Hell of a way to start a Friday morning," said Miller to no one in particular.

"At least it's the thirtieth, not the thirteenth," offered the patrolman. A swatch of powdered sugar was evident on his chin.

"How far away is this park from Brandy's house?" asked Richard. He was looking at the orange spray-painted outline behind a rotted log.

"McGuane Park is ten blocks from her house," volunteered Dos.

"Any significance?" said Miller to Richard.

"No. Just trying to get my bearings."

"The body was found by a man, out walking his dog, early this morning," said Dos.

"Actually," said Miller, "the dog sniffed it out. Some leaves were thrown over the body, right there." He pointed to the ragged orange lines in the dry grass.

"Your report mentioned she was shot with a .38. Did your guys have a chance to check it out?"

"Yeah, we did," offered Dos. "The gun registered to Ms. Mai Tai is the same weapon that was used to kill this girl."

"Nothing like rubbing our noses into it."

"Oh, yeah," said Miller. "The knife from your boss' office was clean."

"I figured that. Any more good news?"

"Here's a Polaroid of the Post-it note that was found in the victim's jacket," said Miller. He removed the plastic-bagged picture from the inside pocket of his trenchcoat and handed it to Richard.

"J.D. I CHANGED MY MIND—AGAIN—YOU'RE NEXT!" He looked at Miller, then back at the note.

"What?" said the Lieutenant.

"J.D.'s desk, Sherry's car, Mai and Jackie. Now Brandy." Richard paused and took a deep breath. "It all points to Colby."

"What's he got to do with the killings? He's in jail," said Miller.

"I think he's the missing link. Since we took on the Colby case, all hell's broken loose."

Dos contributed his two cents: "You find where Colby fits, you solve the murders."

"A man after my own heart," said Miller.

The only sure thing—this was no suicide!

X

Mother Jones was sitting on the edge of Brandy's bed, sobbing softly. Blue plastic glasses hung from a braided cord around her neck. Her crocheted handkerchief was wet with tears. She wiped her eyes and looked up as Cole entered the darkened room.

"Momma. There you are," said Colada.

Mother Jones began weeping uncontrollably. "Cole! Why?"

He sat on the bed and hugged his mother. She buried her face in his shoulder. "Let it out, Momma."

"Who could have done this to my baby?"

"I don't know, Momma."

Yes—I do!

"She was such a wonderful baby." Mother Jones wept and put her arms around her son.

"It'll be all right, Momma."

"What we gonna do, Cole?"

"We'll make it, Momma. I promise."

"You my wonderful baby now."

"I know, Momma."

Jackie's days are numbered!

X

Kristie hurried down the long corridor to her office, combing her mousey brown hair. She took off her black Armani jacket and threw it on the back of her chair. She sat down, opened her handbag, and removed a Nicorette patch. Kristie applied the patch to her arm.

Treat myself to Armani—give up cigarettes!

Anything for Marcus.

Kristie's door was ajar. She saw Jarvis, Richard, and Iris entering the conference room across the hall.

Jarvis poked his head into her office. "Where's Jacq?"

"I don't know. Still out to lunch, I suppose."

"We're meeting in here," said Jarvis, pointing at the double doors. "We're not to be disturbed."

Kristie buttoned her jacket and poured herself a cup of muddy coffee. Rosie rang her extension.

"It's Brandy's brother, Cole Jones," said Rosie. "He wants to talk to Jackie."

"Humm. I wonder why."

"He sounds REALLY upset."

"Put him through."

"Go ahead, sir," said Rosie.

"I want to talk to Jackie Daniels!" said Cole, his voice noticably quivering.

"I'm his personal secretary, Mr. Jones," said Kristie in her most professional manner. "Mr. Daniels has been out of town on business since yesterday morning. Can I help you?"

"You're sure he's out of town?"

"Absolutely, sir," said Kristie cheerfully. "Would you like to leave a message?"

"No. Forget it." Cole put the receiver down gently. He felt numb. His pent-up anger slowly began to subside. He needed to console his mother. To be consoled.

Maybe it WAS a random killing!

CHAPTER XXXVIII

"Jacq was so handsome...so forceful," said Iris. "We were so young."

"You were able to keep this a secret all these years?" said Richard. "It's mind-boggling."

"Jacq made me promise. I was afraid at first. I prayed someday our child would turn up, so I kept quiet." Iris sat at one end of the conference room, flanked by the two men. "Now you know the truth, too."

Richard held the photocopies in his hand. "Iris...is there anything else you may have come across since the last time we spoke? Anything suspicious in nature?"

"There ARE a couple of things I made notes on." She pulled out a slip of paper from the back of her steno pad. "At first, I didn't think it was important. Now, I'm not so sure."

"What are they? asked Jarvis.

"I've been keeping track of the billable hours for the Colby case. So far, Colby has not been billed, nor has he paid, for legal fees up to this date. That's not like Jacq."

"We know J.D. is a friend of Colby's. Maybe they worked out some sort of deal."

"That is strange, though," said Richard. "Anything else?"

"Yes. Jacq has donated $50,000. to the Mansfield Orphanage every year since I've been with the firm. I have no idea how long he was doing that before I got here."

"Seems innocent enough," said Jarvis.

"A sizable donation," said Richard. "Could've been blackmail. Or hush money."

Tears welled in Iris' eyes. She looked at Jarvis and said, "I never dreamed it wasn't ligitimate. For the longest time, I wanted to believe Jacq. And for the first few years, I did. Then..." Iris began sobbing again. "I became so disillusioned, I..."

"Stop trying to protect him," said Jarvis firmly.

"But if we confront Jacq, and discover the truth about the child," cried Iris, "the publicity will be devastating."

"I agree," said Richard. "Let's keep the lid on this at least 'til next week."

"Well...I think you're right," said Jarvis. "We've got to make the best possible decision for the good of the firm."

Richard collected his papers and shoved them into his briefcase. Jarvis was still holding Iris' hand.

"I'm flying to Columbus to meet with Jackie tonight," said Richard. "We're going to Mansfield. I want to get a close look at those files and the orphanage."

"Iris," said Jarvis, "no one else in the firm is to see any of these papers."

For the sake of MY firm!

X

Labatt pulled his '88 Plymouth off the road and onto the gravel and switched off the lights. His assistant, Tito Tequila, awoke with a start.

"We there already?" He sat up straight in the front seat of the car. "What time is it?"

"It's late. After three," said Labatt.

"We're lucky to find it at all in this damn soup." Tito looked out of the window toward the orphanage. The outline of the building was barely visible.

"Shut up!" said Labatt. "Get the cutters from the back and let's get this over with."

The men hurried to the gate at the side entrance of the building. The chain was wrapped around the gate. Labatt grabbed the chains and pulled them apart with his hands as Tito cut them. They fell to the ground in a twisted pile. A dog barked in the distance.

"Why would our client instruct us to destroy the files?" asked Tito. He and Labatt crept toward the building. "You said those files have been here for years. It's old news."

"I don't know," said Labatt. "I do as I'm told."

Labatt picked at the lock while Tito sprayed the hinges with WD-40. Once inside, they tip-toed down the long hallway toward the offices.

"I think we should keep the files," whispered Tito.

"That's risky. If anybody ever found out..."

"Give 'em to me," said Tito in hushed tones. "I'll take good care of 'em."

"No! We do as we're told. I don't need the aggravation."

They entered the rear offices. Labatt held his penlight in his mouth as he slid the file drawers open.

"What the hell!"

"What'sa matter?" whispered Tito hoarsely.

"The damn files aren't here!"

"No kiddin'!"

"J.Doyle—missing. J.D.—missing. No John Doe!" said the startled Labatt. "What the hell's going on?"

I'll call my old buddy, Dewars, and see what he knows!

HANKY PANKY

iii

HANKY PANKY

CHAPTER XXXIX

Tony's door was open. Rita peeked in and said, "Hi. How was it?"

"It was fabulous! I enjoy it more each time."

"It's been at the Schubert for three months," hinted Rita. "I haven't seen it...yet." An uncomfortable pause. "One of these days." She smiled at Tony and fluttered her eyes.

"Yes, you should go," said Tony. Another tortured pause. "My favorite musical of all time is 'Chicago'. I've seen it eleven times."

"That's nice."

Well ask me, already!

"You know, Rita..." Tony pulled on the bottom edge of his polka-dotted tie. "Uhh...from what I've seen, every one of the offices around here is dramatically different."

"Have you seen Richard Port's office?" Rita rolled her eyes.

"He's the exception!" Tony finished dusting one of his model airplanes.

Rita played with the belt of her Bill Blass suit. "Do you like basketball?"

"Not really."

"Amy gave me Bulls tickets for tonight." Rita took a deep breath and said, "Richard is out of town, so she's not going. You wanna go?" Rita crossed her fingers behind her back.

"No—I can't," said Tony. "I've got other plans."

"Well...okay," said Rita. She glanced around the room, then backed out the door. "I'll see you tomorrow at the mock trial."

"Right. See you then."

"Oh, I forgot," said Rita. "Charles and his friend, Alex, are going to the game, too." She walked out with a hint of a pout.

"Thanks for telling me, Rita."

I was right, thought Tony. *I wonder if Charles is busy tomorrow!*

Rita walked hurriedly down the corridor to the print shop. She glanced at her watch. "Oh, man..." she muttered under her breath. "I hope Harry's still here."

Harry turned off the copier machine and looked at Rita as she entered the room. He pushed his wire-rimmed glasses up on his nose. Stacks of folders and booklets were neatly arranged on a table near the door.

"Is all the material ready for the mock trial?" Rita opened one of the folders.

"Yeah, it's there," said Harry, motioning to the long table.

"Great. The trial is going to be across the hall in the law library. Are you coming in tomorrow?"

"Nah. Can't make it."

"You know, it's kinda peaceful and safe in here," confided Rita. "Everywhere I go in the building, there are guys ogling me...even the older men."

"Cool," said Harry.

"What do you think of the new guy, Tony?" Rita was looking at the piles of papers on the table. "He's always looking at me, too."

"You don't want to know what I think about the new guy," said Harry with a half-hearted smile.

X

"Hello, young man," said DeDe. "You must be Mr. Martini." She reached out with her gloved hand. "We haven't been formally introduced. I'm DeDe Daniels."

"A pleasure to meet you," said Tony. "I've heard so much about you." He shook her hand and smiled, showing his perfect white teeth.

"Not from that bore of a husband of mine, surely," said DeDe flirtatiously.

"Today has been hectic. I heard Mr. Daniels was in meetings all day." His tone sounded sincere.

"Yes, he's in one now!" said DeDe curtly. "With an obnoxious little person with a limp. Jacq and I have theater tickets for tonight. Do you mind if I wait for him here?" DeDe sat down in Tony's molded desk chair. "Ooohh! How nice."

"What show are you going to see?" asked Tony.

"We're going to see 'Ragtime.'"

"It's a wonderful cast. You'll love it!"

DeDe crossed her legs and removed her gloves. "And I LOVE what you've done with your office, Mr. Martini. Who is your decorator?"

"I have a friend. He's an interior designer. I helped." Tony rolled his sleeves down on his shirt and adjusted his cufflinks.

"You must give me his card...Tony. May I call you Tony." It was more of a statement than a question.

"Yes, of course."

"Tony—I am flying in to New York on Wednesday. I could use your expertise in selecting some pieces for our library." DeDe was very poised and businesslike. "I could arrange it with Jacq."

"I don't think I could fit it into my schedule, Mrs. Daniels."

DeDe looked up innocently, her green eyes shining. "We could catch an off-broadway play, too."

"Thanks for the offer. But I better not."

"Nonsense! I'll have Iris make the arrangements."

What a darling young man!

MOVIN' ON UP!

CHAPTER XL

Jacq closed the wall safe, spun the tumbler, and pushed the hinged frame of the Dali print against the textured wall. He shoved the four pre-packaged stacks of bills into a manila envelope, then hurriedly placed the small package in his desk drawer. He was reaching for the keys in his jacket pocket when Dewars knocked on the partially-opened door.

"Secretary gone home early?" said Dewars. He pushed in on the door panel and stood in front of Jacq's desk, resplendent in a new navy Brooks Brothers suit, with a blue tie that matched his button-down shirt. Dewars set his leather briefcase on the corner of the desk.

"You're early. Good!" snapped Jacq. "I've got a hell of a lot of work to finish up before I can get out of here."

"You got the money?"

"Right here." Jacq slid the drawer open. Next to the crisp envelope was his pearl-handled .22 caliber pistol. Jacq reached into the drawer. The sudden buzz of the telephone startled him. He pushed the drawer in and grabbed the receiver.

"Jacq, darling," said DeDe sweetly, "I'm waiting for you in that nice Mr. Martini's office. Do hurry."

Dewars made himself comfortable in a highback chair, flipping the pages of a Richard Nixon novel.

"I'll be right there."

"Reservations at Fredericks at six. Remember last Saturday?"

"See you in ten minutes," said Jacq.

"I love you, too," said DeDe at the other end.

Dewars stretched his gimpy leg and grimaced. He opened his case and tossed the folders on Jacq's desk.

"That's all of 'em. Including the pictures."

Jacq began examining the papers in the files. He flipped through the folders, nodded, and opened the desk drawer. He carefully slid the gun aside and picked up the stuffed envelope. "No need to count it."

"I trust you," said Dewars. He rippled some of the thousand dollar bills. "Green's my favorite color."

"Now get the hell out of here. And stay out!"

"No problem." Dewars locked the money in his briefcase and left, limping and grinning.

This is only the beginning, hotshot!

MOCK JUSTICE

"How did the mock jury vote?" asked Jarvis, closing his office door. Sherry and Marcus sat facing the tiers of law books behind his worn leather chair.

"Not guilty!" said Sherry. She smiled demurely.

"I know it wasn't the actual trial," said Marcus, "but Sherry did a marvelous job playing to the jury."

"Jacq's suggestion of discrediting the nurses' testimony helped," said Sherry.

"What did you think of the witnesses' responses, Mark?" Jarvis resurrected a half-smoked cigar from a ceramic ashtray. Stale aroma soon filled the air.

"As the trial wore on, much of the evidence seemed to turn up being circumstantial." Marcus' hands were trembling ever so slightly. "Perhaps due, in part, to Sherry's magical charms."

"There's a fine line between making testimony sound real, or rehearsed." She winked at Jarvis.

"You are the master of the fine line," said Marcus. "Congratulations." He patted Sherry's arm. A stunning gold Chanel watch adorned her delicate wrist.

Jarvis fanned at the circling smoke. "Then we're reasonably assured that the Colby trial will play out pretty much the same?" He leaned into his leather chair.

"Absolutely." The brown flecks in Sherry's pale green eyes

sparkled. "Colby, not guilty'!" She pounded Jarvis' gavel on a notepad. "He will be a free man soon."

"Good," said Jarvis. "Jacq will be pleased. He and I are meeting shortly."

Colby—not guilty! Jacq—guilty!

Marcus stroked his leathery chin, glanced at his watch and exclaimed, "Oh, my gosh, it's almost five. If you'll excuse me, I've got to get going." He gathered his files and hurried out of the office.

Marcus took the stairs down to his nineteenth floor office. Once inside, he locked the door, removed his jacket, and collapsed in his chair. His hands were shaking more than ever. He took the bottle of Jim Beam out of the metal cabinet and set it on the desk. His hands encompassed the neck of the bottle, perspiration beading his face. He sat in the darkening room, taking deep breaths, fighting his personal demon.

X

"I loved you so much, Iris," whispered Jacq. "I swear I never meant to hurt you."

Iris began sobbing. Jarvis tried to console her by offering his handkerchief. They sat in matching burgundy leather chairs facing Jacq. A small desk lamp, focused on an open file folder, was the only illumination in his office.

"We were so young. I was mixed up." Jacq looked down at Iris. "The pressure from my father...law school...then the baby." Jacq picked up a crystal tiger from his desk and began stroking it. "I didn't want you to think I was so cruel and heartless, as to give up our child."

"But you did!" Her voice cracked.

"The pressures from my father were unbearable."

"You're a lowly coward," said Jarvis.

"Maybe so." Jacq set the tiger down. The light reflected blues and greens on the tainted files. "It all sounds so cut and dried now. Can't you understand?"

"No," said Jarvis. Iris was shaking her head, staring at the design in the carpet.

"Thirty years ago, I had my whole life ahead of me. A wife and kid wasn't a part of it," whimpered Jacq. "My father threatened to disown me."

"You were gutless," grumbled Jarvis. "Why did you tell Iris the child was kidnapped, when according to these records, the baby, Jeanette Doyle, died when she was two months old?"

"I couldn't tell her the truth. For Iris to know, someday, that her child was out there, seemed a more decent way of handling a bad situation." Jacq bit his lower lip.

"You're talking decency? Hah!" Jarvis got up and walked across the room. He looked out the window on the miniature street below, its ant-size cars scurrying in the winding streets.

Iris said quietly, "No more lies. I need to know, once and for all...the REAL story about our child. Can you do that?"

Jacq rubbed his eyes, took several deep breaths and said haltingly, "I don't know why I kept these files. Maybe I thought if I didn't destroy them, the kid would seem more real to me. That never happened."

"The 'Jeanette Doyle' file says the baby died," said Jarvis. "Is that true?"

"The baby died," said Jacq softly.

"When?" asked Iris.

"Shortly after I told you it was kidnapped."

"Where?"

"In Colby's orphanage...in Mansfield."

"Is that when Colby became involved?" asked Jarvis.

"Yes. He and I were friends at Ohio State. We graduated together. I felt I could trust him."

"Enough to lie for you?" sobbed Iris.

"Yeah." Jacq's eyes narrowed. "If Nathan wouldn't have gotten into trouble himself, I could have spared you all this heartache."

"I still had feelings for you."

"You know I loved you."

"My love...has turned to hate." Iris looked defiantly into Jacq's eyes.

Jacq slammed the crystal tiger on top of the files.

"Does DeDe know anything about this?" asked Jarvis.

"No. I don't want her to know. It would kill her."

"The publicity would kill her," said Jarvis.

"Well...don't worry about it anymore," said a subdued Jacq. "I have all the files and photos in my possession now. They'll be destroyed."

"I want Richard to hear this." Jarvis walked to the wall switch next to the doorway. The three domed overhead lights lit up the desk area, highlighting the crystal tiger. "He'll be back Monday for Brandy's funeral. Maybe he'll be able to piece it together."

"It all started innocently enough with Sherry's stolen car," said Jacq. He was leaning back, slumped in his chair. "Now...the murders, Colby. My worthless life being threatened. There has to be a connection."

"My baby is dead!" sobbed Iris.

"Just for the record," said Jarvis. "Are we talking about a BOY or a GIRL in the 'Jeanette Doyle' file?"

THE PSYCHIATRIST

CHAPTER XLII

JANUARY 21, 1994

The slim figure was sitting on one of the chrome and blue padded chairs in the outer office, thumbing through a two-year-old People magazine when Dr. Amaretto said, "Good afternoon. Would you come in now, please?"

Dr. Amaretto's straight blonde hair was dishevelled, falling awkwardly around the collar of her beige tweed suit. She led the slim figure into her austere office, sat down in a brown leather chair and began shuffling papers and writing furiously without looking up from her paperwork.

"How you feelin', Doc?"

"Oh. How are YOU feeling?" asked Dr. Amaretto. She continued scribbling. A picture of three children was in a brass frame on the corner of her small desk.

"About the same."

"Increasing the milligrams hasn't helped?"

"Nah. Not really."

"Let's see." She flipped the file over. "You're on Buspar, right? And-uh, we've been juggling your medication for over a year..."

"I don't feel any better."

"And the nightmares? Do you still have the nightmares?"

"Yeah. I don't sleep so good, either," said the slim figure. "I get dizzy sometimes. And I get these pounding headaches..."

"I don't want you getting hooked on sleep medication. It's difficult to get off those things once you start."

"Maybe for just a little while?"

"We'll try something else." Dr. Amaretto thumbed at the corners of her medication journal. "Humm. Restoril, for sleep. Too habit-forming." She glanced at her marble desk clock. "Let's try Desyrel, 150 milligrams, but only at bedtime, okay? That way we can stop any time we need to."

"Sounds good to me."

The doctor sifted through the remainder of the papers. "Yes, now I see. You're the one we had on Paxil last year. You've recently completed a thorough physical. All results were negative."

"I still don't feel good."

"Why do you think that?" asked the doctor.

"Maybe it's the medication."

"Could it be your perceptions? Your attitudes?"

"Maybe it's you!" The slim figure laughed nervously.

"Could be," said Dr. Amaretto uncomfortably. She began writing furiously on her yellow pad. "Let's see. We can start you on Serzone, 225 milligrams. I'll prescribe the dosage in 75-milligram tablets. Take two in the morning and one in the evening, a half hour before bed. We'll increase the dosage each month if necessary. We can go as high as 500 or 600 milligrams a day."

"Anything to help me feel better."

"You're still living alone now, right?" Dr. Amaretto was scribbling on a prescription pad.

"Yeah. And I'm working and going to law school."

"Marvelous. When is the bar exam?" Dr. Amaretto looked at the slim figure for the first time with her doctoral smile.

"I just started law school."

"The headaches. Do they..." The doctor's extension buzzed. "Excuse me. I've been waiting for this call." Dr. Amaretto spoke to her babysitter. "Yes...I knew one of the twins threw up this morning." Then silence. "I'll be home as soon as I can."

She hung up the phone, shuffled more papers and stacked the files in a fat folder. She didn't look up from her papers.

"Is that it?"

"We'll have to cut our session a few minutes short," said the irritated Dr. Amaretto. "Here are your prescriptions. Get them filled today, and remember—no double dosing or mixing any of these medications. See me in a month."

"Thank you, doctor," said the slim figure.

You're on my list, doc—right after Colby and Schlitz.

COLE TO THE RESCUE

The small group of men and women were standing on the courthouse steps, doing their best to avoid the cameras and news media. A lunch crowd of city workers galloped past them, completely ignoring their impromptu meeting.

"We have no comment at this time," said Sherry in a high-pitched voice.

"Trial date set for November 30?" yelled a red-headed reporter.

"Yeah!" said Jacq. "Ten in the morning! Can you make it? Now get the hell out of here!"

When the members of the media dispersed, Jarvis asked, "Were there any surprises at the pre-trial?"

"No," said Sherry. "It's not complicated. Very few witnesses. We've turned over all the necessary documents to the other side. They did likewise."

"None of the witnesses have criminal records," said Marcus. "One less problem to deal with."

"We're finished with *voir dire*." Sherry smiled at her co-workers. "Everyone is happy."

"Anything related to 'work product'?" asked Gina. She was standing next to Jarvis, holding her briefcase with both hands, looking as gorgeous as ever.

"No, Gina," said Jarvis. "Everything in this case was discoverable. We're all in agreement on that."

"It was a good question, though," said Marcus. He smiled and gave Gina a fleeting wink. "Kristie and I have been helping Sherry with a work-up, regarding the probable nature of the witnesses' testimony."

"And Sherry's been working hard on the psychological points of view of the witnesses. Their strengths and weaknesses," said Jacq. He used up his smile for the day.

Sherry smiled back. "No problems with subpoena lists, or witnesses. Naturally, the determining issue is the cause of death."

Jacq hailed his limo. Guinness pulled to the curb, the group scurrying down the concrete steps and into the extra-wide seats.

"I spoke to the police," said Sherry, "to be sure their testimony is consistent with the reports they've filed."

"Good." Jarvis was looking out the window at the bundled pedestrians on Madison Avenue. "We need their credibility as police professionals."

"Not to change the subject," said Sherry, "but that was a very touching funeral yesterday." Jacq looked at Jarvis. Neither said a word.

"It was wonderful of the firm to contribute to Brandy's estate," said Marcus. "All she had was a small insurance policy."

"Iris handles all that kind of paperwork" said Jacq.

"It was still good of you to do it," said Jarvis.

"Shut up. What's done is done," said Jacq. He wiped the side of his face and turned to Sherry. "Let's dump these guys at the office and grab a lunch, okay?"

Where is DeDe when I need her?

X

Colada Jones was pacing the floor at the end of the corridor near Richard's office. He walked briskly around the corner of the hallway and extended his hand.

"Thanks for volunteering," said Richard.

"I want to help. I gotta do somethin'."

"Come on in. I've been doing some thinking about what you could do since we spoke at Brandy's service." Richard settled in behind his desk and offered Cole a seat, then glanced at his watch. "Three o'clock. Where the hell does the time go?" Richard tore the date, November 2, off his desk calendar and tossed it into the basket.

Cole held back his tears. "I thought Jackie Daniels was responsible for Brandy's death. Then when I found out he was in Columbus with you..."

"Jackie was almost killed himself. Did you know that?"

"Man, no! I didn't."

"I think the killings are linked to Colby and Jacq somehow. How, I don't know...yet. My gut tells me it's someone who knows the both of them. Right now, I don't know of anyone who fits the bill."

"Why would anybody want to hurt Brandy and the other girl, just to get back at Mr. Daniels?" asked Cole.

"Some sicko, I guess.."

"What can I do? I need to do SOMETHING to help my Momma. Tell me how I can help."

Richard removed a shopping bag from a wall cabinet behind him and dumped several videos on the desk. The tapes clattered, one falling on the floor.

"I've got seventy-two hours of boring videos," said Richard. "I made copies of the originals I gave to the police. They're reviewing them too. I've gone over the tapes twice. So far...nothing."

"I'll go over them with a fine-tooth comb," vowed Cole. "What am I supposed to be looking for?"

"I don't know. I wish I could tell you. All I know is I need a fresh pair of eyes to view these videos."

Richard stacked and taped the cassettes together, marking the floor numbers on each tape. He handed the bag to Cole. "Also, here's an envelope of all the employees in our firm. It has their photos in it, too. Along with that, I've got a list of people—visitors, other lawyers, etcetera—on a yellow pad, and where they appear on the tapes. Those people you can rule out. Some parts you can fast-forward."

"I'll figure out some systematic way of looking at 'em," said Cole. His voice was filled with enthusiasm.

"The films run three days, from Friday morning, the 16th of October, through Sunday. Mr. Daniels' desk was ruined sometime between Friday afternoon, when he left, and before Monday morning when he got back to his office."

"I can get one of my buddies' VCR and hook up two videos at the same time," said Cole excitedly.

"Sounds good," said Richard. "I haven't seen anyone on 19, 20, or 21 that didn't belong there."

"That's the problem. I'm afraid the killer of my sister is someone who BELONGS there."

X

Richard sat at his desk, doodling, drawing Xs and Os, making lists of people in the firm that might possibly have a motive to discredit Jacq. Richard scribbled several names off his list. Jacq didn't have, according to his final tabulation, many friends in the firm.

"I can cut out these seventeen names," he muttered to himself, "put them on a dart board, throw the damn dart, and find the killer. Nothing ELSE has worked so far."

Richard started to make an alphabetical list of key personnel in the firm: Amontillado, Cognac. He stopped and stared at the two names. A & C. AC-air conditioning. He started to laugh. "I need a vacation!" he said to a framed picture of himself and Lieutenant Miller.

Richard dialed the number to the building's security division.

"Yeah. This is the security manager."

"Mr. Royal, this is Richard Port, from the law firm of Daniels and Rumm. I would..."

"Yeah, I know you," said the manager. "You're working with the cops on the videos I sent up to you."

"Right. Thanks for your cooperation. I need another favor, Mr. Royal."

"Shoot."

"Would you send me a copy of the architectural plans of the three floors taken up by Daniels and Rumm? I'm mainly concerned about the HVAC system."

"You got it."

"Thanks, again," said Richard.

Just another dead end?

"Thanks for coming on such short notice," said Jacq. Jarvis ushered Iris into the conference room. Richard closed the oak door behind them. The small informal group sat down at one end of the huge table. No legal pads, no folders, no coffee cups.

"What's this all about?" asked Jarvis, his face gaunt.

Jacq took a long look at Iris. He took an equally long breath. "I've done a hell of a lot in my life that I'm not proud of. Things I thought I could live with." Jacq's nose reddened. His eyes were swollen.

"We all have secrets," said Richard.

"Guinness knows me better than anyone. He convinced me to come forward with the truth."

"The truth?" said Iris, startled.

"If I would've told you the truth, you'd hate me forever." Jacq reached out for her hand.

Iris pulled away. "How do you think I feel at this very moment?"

"Are you still hiding something from Iris?" said Jarvis angrily. His face flushed.

Jacq took another deep, anguished breath. "Two women have been murdered...because of me."

"How do you know that?" asked Richard.

"I know. There is no other explanation."

"Is Colby involved?" Richard took a small notebook from his jacket. "I think he is."

"I thought fate smiled on us when we got the Colby case. I figured I could pay him off, once and for all, for helping me all these years."

"For helping you hide the truth, you mean!" Jarvis swung his chair around, away from the table and stared at the Dali print behind Jacq. An eternity went by.

"You said the baby died." Iris looked up at Jacq. "Was that another lie?"

"Our child is alive. Our BOY is alive."

"You are despicable!" shouted Iris. She stood and pushed her sidechair backward. The chair fell silently into the plush carpet. Iris stormed out of the room.

"Iris, wait!" Jarvis hurried behind her.

"You're somethin' else!" said Richard finally.

"I didn't take Colby seriously enough."

"You've been a fool!"

Jacq sat back, his face contorted. "Right now, the key problem is for the jury to find Colby 'not guilty.'"

"That's your priority?" Richard was stunned.

"If they don't, he swears he'll go to the press regarding my illegitimate son."

"It IS yours, AND Iris', right?"

"Yes. She's the only one I fooled around with...until I met DeDe." He twisted nervously in his seat.

"Didn't you think of the firm's reputation then? How it might be tarnished beyond..."

"Now I've got problems with blackmailers."

Richard was taken aback. "Why didn't you mention that earlier? I could have helped."

"It's a P.I. named Dewars."

"His reputation precedes him," said Richard.

"He's got all the files...on the kid."

"I'll make some calls. He's history."

X

Back at his Green Oaks condo, Richard inserted his Colby disc into the computer. As the computer was searching for the file, Richard organized all the paperwork he and Lieutenant Miller had accumulated on the case. He began typing in additional information on the gray keyboard:

Colby: Verified graduation from Ohio State.

Degree in Business Administration.

His father ran the orphanage in Mansfield, Ohio in the '70s.

Nathan Colby bought the orphanage from the state, after the death of the senior Colby.

Mansfield Orphanage—still operating.

Colby bought a nursing home in Northbrook.

Colby bought a nursing home in Glenview.

Colby accused of suffocating a patient in the Glenview Nursing Home (July 1, 1998)

Richard was studying the data, staring into the bright screen of the monitor. The shrill ring of the desk phone made him jump. He pushed the speaker button.

"Thanks for bringing me back to reality. This is Richard."

"Rich, this is Mike."

"Great! What's new?"

"I got a hold of an old professor—used to teach at OSU. He knew Colby—AND Jacq Daniels."

"Yeah...so?"

"According to the professor, they were close. Like flies on ..."

"You got a point?"

"Yeah," said Miller. "At one of the class reunions, this old professor introduces a friend of his. A guy by the name of Schlitz, to Colby and Daniels. This guy was in social work at the time."

"And the point being?"

"The point being," said Miller triumphantly, "when Colby took over his father's orphanage in Mansfield, he hired this guy Schlitz. Schlitz could be a key player."

"He's still alive?"

"Far as I know, he is," said the Lieutenant.

"Where is he?"

"Dos is digging as we speak. One other thing. We've checked every known baby broker on the computer and came up empty."

"I thought you might," said Richard. "Jacq's father was a very influential man. Any luck on the tapes?"

"Nah. I think that's a lost cause," said Miller bluntly.

"I'm still working on that angle, Mike. I'm hoping it'll pay off. Anything else?"

"Nada. No prints on the gun at the Jones scene. Nothing in either one of the cars. We need a witness, Richie."

"So far, we've been losing the battles," said Richard boldy, "but we're going to win the war."

"Hell," said Miller, "it's almost eight. I'll get out of your hair. Let me know if somethin' changes."

"You got it." Richard hung up the phone and resumed scanning the lines on the computer:

Daniels: We know Iris had a baby—a boy.

No social security number available.

Birth record: N/A.

Age—29.

Baby born, July, 1969 (per Iris)

Orphanage files—gone.

(Stolen or Destroyed)

Richard stared at the screen for several minutes, then began typing furiously: COLBY AND DANIELS: INVOLVED TOGETHER IN A SCHEME OF SOME SORT.

His mind began racing. He turned off the computer and began scribbling in his leather binder. He spun his chair around, his back facing away from the desk. He caught the first glimpse of the red flashing light on the answering machine.

"I need some good news."

Richard tossed his pencil on the desk, hurried to the table, and pushed the button.

"Hello, Mr. Port." Richard recognized the voice immediately. "This is Mr. Molson in apartment 359. Ricky. Remember? I tried calling you all day, but couldn't get you. I'll be out of town until the 6th. A major convention. I can't miss it. I have some pictures you will find very interesting. I just had them developed. What a shock. I'll try to call you Saturday morning."

"My birdwatcher buddy!" yelled Richard. "Wahooo!"

He jumped over the table behind the love seat, flopped into the cushions, and breathed a sigh of relief.

The pieces of the puzzle are starting to fit together!

BUDDIES?

CHAPTER XLV

The red neon sign flickered weakly high above the dirt road off Route 34 in Northlake, Illinois. "Lisa's Open-All-Night Diner" was deserted, with the exception of a large corner booth jammed with pimply-faced teenagers. Labatt and Dewars sat near the windows overlooking the parking lot. Dewars' '85 Riviera was parked at the far end of the lot under a floodlight, isolated from the other vehicles. Labatt's Plymouth abutted the concrete curb just outside the diner's windows. The juke box was playing a rap tune.

Dewars was nursing a black coffee. Labatt sipped a diet drink. The ground rounds were barely picked over. Both men sported pin-striped suits.

"What else you got on this guy?" asked Labatt, his eyes fixed on Dewars.

"Nothing much, except I know he's got a wife who would cough up a lot of dough for this info."

"He told you to get lost. Maybe you should do like he says."

"Hey," said Dewars sharply, "there's too much money involved. She's ripe for the pickin', too."

"I think you're pushin' it, man," said Labatt between clenched teeth. "Why don't you disappear...quietly...before someone gets hurt."

"Like who? Me? You're kiddin'." Dewars' gimpy leg started to ache.

"No. I'm not," said Labatt icily. "You got copies of the files?"

"What's it to ya?" said Dewars. Labatt stared fiercely into his eyes. "Yeah! I got pictures, too. Listen! This is too good to pass up."

"Dewars, you and I are going to get the files...right now."

"Now you're talkin'! You want a piece of the action, right?"

"No! The show's over. You're getting too old to play. I want the files."

"What the hell! said Dewars savagely. Then his words became brisk, business-like. "You're workin' for Daniels, right?"

"Yeah, Einstein. Now move!"

Dewars sneered across the table, "I can't tonight."

"Why?"

"They're in a safe deposit box."

"Where?"

Dewars hesitated. "At the C & N Station. The place is closed 'til morning."

"We'll wait there. Get movin'!" Labatt pulled a 9 mm pistol from his shoulder holster, out far enough for Dewars to see it.

"You'll be sorry...PAL."

"Shut up. By the way," said Labatt caustically, "you're buyin'."

And you'll be coughin' up the 200 Gs, before the night is over!

X

Tony took the back stairwell up one flight to the twentieth floor. He carried his Nike canvas bag by its shoulder strap and dropped it in the hall at the entrance to the exercise room.

Charles Cognac's office was on the opposite side of the corridor. His door was open. He was filling his briefcase with pads and folders, preparing for a long night of research in the law library. It was almost 6:00 P.M. The other floors were silent, although most of the personnel at Daniels and Rumm were working late.

"Hi, Charles," said Tony cheerfully. "Want to join me in a little workout?"

"No—I can't today. Thanks, anyway. Gina and I are helping Marcus with the Colby case."

"I've been working on the case a bit with Rita. When does it go to trial?"

"The thirtieth of this month."

"That's the day after the big game."

"The big game?"

"Yes," said Tony eagerly, "at Soldier's Field. The Bears against the Indians. No...it's the Cowboys, I think. Anyway, I've got tickets. Would you like to go?" Tony swallowed hard, his eyes avoiding Charles' gaze.

"You and me?" Charles' voice climbed an octave.

"Uhh, sure, why not?" Tony unbuttoned his navy blazer and brushed the toe of his shoe with his hand.

"I'd really like to..."

"You would!?" Tony smiled broadly.

"I'd really like to, but I can't. I have a previous commitment...with a good friend."

Tony stiffened. "Anyone I know?"

"With Alex. You've heard me speak of Alex." Charles closed his leather case and glanced at his watch, pulling on his suit jacket at the same time.

"Yes," said Tony, a disappointed look on his face. "I've heard you speak of him."

"Tony, you've got the wrong idea. My friend Alex is..."

KNOCK! KNOCK!

"Six o'clock, on the dot!" said the beautiful raven-haired woman as she peeked into the office. Her cream-colored Bill Blass suit was tied at the waist, the neckline plunging provocatively. "Hi, sweetie. Am I interrupting? Who's your friend?"

"Hi, honey. Alex, this is Tony."

"Hello, Alex," said Tony nervously.

"You're the Mr. Martini C.C. hired a couple of weeks ago. He speaks very highly of you," said Alex demurely.

"Alex and I have a dinner date, Tony."

"Six sharp!" said Alex.

"But then I'm coming back to burn some midnight oil." Charles looked longingly at Alex. "The weekends are coming..."

"Don't worry about me. I'm a big girl."

"Alex," said Charles, "would you please wait for me by the elevators. I want to finish up here with Tony. Give me five minutes."

"Sure. Take your time." She looked pleasantly at Tony and pushed the door open. "Nice to have met you."

"I'm sorry, Tony. I hope to marry Alex someday...soon. I wasn't aware I was sending messages to the contrary."

"It's not your fault," said Tony pensively. "I guess I misinterpreted our first meeting, at the interview."

"You didn't think I was...gay or something?"

"Or something?"

"I'm sorry. You know what I mean." Charles tapped the top of his briefcase repeatedly before he said, "Does Rita know?"

"Know what?"

"That you're gay."

"No. No one but you. Why?"

"Rita has a crush on you." Charles' face brightened.

"She's a doll," said Tony.

"She says the same about you."

"Mrs. Daniels took me to New York over the weekend," said Tony. "We had a great time."

"Holy Cow! What did you guys...!"

"Now she knows, too. I hope SHE doesn't tell Mr. Daniels." Tony could feel himself drowning in a huge black pool. "How do you think I should handle this? Once I let them know in Philly, I was out of a job in three months."

"Jarvis and Sherry call the shots here. They're more than fair," said Charles.

If it wasn't for Alex...nah!

On Thursday, the fifth of November, Sherry Weinstein left the emergency meeting of the "A" lawyers in a pent-up rage. The lawyers had been briefed by Jacq and Jarvis regarding the importance of the Colby trial: how imperative it was for the jury to find Nathan Colby innocent of the murder charges brought against him. The two killings, though distracting, were considered isolated incidents by the media, thanks in part to the efforts of Jacq and his influence within the local TV networks.

Sherry stormed into her office and gave the door a resounding kick. She sat down in her hand-carved highback chair and lit a cigarette, puffed, and coughed repeatedly.

Amy, sitting at her desk, was proof-reading copy when the phone buzzed. She picked up the receiver and removed her large pearl and gold earring. "This is..."

"Amy—it's Sherry. I need to see you right away!"

"Sure. I've got to stop at the print shop for a minute. Be right there."

Feeling a little huffy today, are we?

Sherry rubbed the remains of her cigarette in a silver ashtray, then immediately lit another. Amy rapped lightly on the door and entered the room.

"Sorry about the smoke," said Sherry, "but I need your help with the Colby trial." She crushed her third cigarette. "A favor, quite frankly."

"What can I do?" asked Amy innocently.

Sherry stood and fanned at the malodorous haze. "I feel so sorry for Mai and Brandy. Really, I do. But my main concern, at this moment, is the negative publicity these killings would have on my firm...THE firm...if J.D.'s name becomes linked with them in any way."

"Why are you telling ME this? The Chicago police, with Richard's help, are handling the case. I can't do anything." Amy looked perplexed, her brow furrowed.

"You can," said Sherry, "by convincing Richard that we can't afford to involve Jacq personally with the Colby case, or with the murders."

"Jacq can take care of himself," said Amy defensively.

"He's basically a naive buffoon!"

Amy, surprised, said, "We're speaking of our leader?"

Sherry's eyes narrowed. "Quite frankly, Amy, Jacq and Jarvis are ready for pasture. In another five years, more likely less, they'll be ancient history."

"Are we looking at Weinstein and Associates?" said Amy with a slow, appraising stare.

"How does Weinstein and Port sound?"

Amy's Italian temper got the best of her. "You're anxious to take over this firm, I see."

Calmly, Sherry replied, "It's still salvagable. As chief counsel for the Colby trial, I have a major stake in this firm. You MUST talk to Richard."

"I can't promise."

"I hope I don't come across sounding like some ruthless wench," said Sherry with a angelic smile.

"Oh, no," said Amy. "You have some real concerns."

You ruthless wench!

APRIL 23, 1997

"Remember me?" asked the slim figure as the creaky door opened. He was standing on the porch of an old run-down house outside downtown Chicago. The rotted tongue and groove boards were spongy beneath his weight.

"No, can't say I do," said the bent, white-haired man. "At my age, I'm lucky to remember to shut off the coffee pot." The bright porch light made him shield his eyes with his hand.

The slim figure moved under the bulb. "Now do you remember me?"

"Are you selling something? Come on in. I got all night." The old retiree, using his cane, turned into the small living room, followed by the young man. "Have a seat," said the old man, motioning toward a dirty flowered sofa. "I got my favorite, here." It took the old man a full minute to get comfortable in his LA-Z-BOY. "Want some tea? It's made—on the stove."

"No. I'm in a hurry, Mr. Schlitz."

"Eh? You know my name?"

"Yeah. It's taken me a long time to find you."

"Have we met before, young man?"

"Yeah. A long time ago. You helped me break out of Mansfield in '84..." The slim figure looked nervously at Schlitz.

"Nineteen eighty-four," said the aged man. He rubbed his chin. "That's what, fifteen years ago? I don't remember..."

"Out of the 'closet'. Remember?"

"The closet? At Mansfield?" said Schlitz, grinding his teeth. "Locked in the basement! My God, yes! I remember! That was YOU?"

"Yeah, Mr. Schlitz. I spent years in that hellhole. No thanks to Mr. Colby and you."

Schlitz's hands starting shaking. His voice cracked more than before. "I—I couldn't help you sooner. I couldn't afford to lose my pension!" His face whitened as he tried to swallow.

"You helped me get away in '84," said the slim figure, his eyes narrowing as he peered at the quaking man.

"That was the year I retired," he stammered. "I couldn't stand to see you locked up, like a dog, any longer." Schlitz's heart was pounding. "You're not here to harm me, are you? Please..."

The slim figure stood up and said, "Shut up! Relax. I need one more favor."

"What is it? I'll do anything!"

"Quit yer whining. I need to know why I was put into the orphanage. Why I was never adopted. And..."

"...and WHO was the devil that put you in that dreadful home in the first place!" Schlitz shook his aluminum cane above his head.

"Yeah," said the slim figure. "I'm sure you know. Tell me who it was."

"Now I remember! I gave you knives, spoons...any utensil you could dig with!"

"I want the person's name!" He gave Schlitz a dark menacing glare.

Schlitz ignored him. "I knew the hole was almost finished. I covered the opening with a piece of plywood in the boiler room."

"The name! The NAME!"

"Jacq Daniels! J-A-C-Q" said the old man triumphantly.

The slim figure took a notepad from his back pocket and printed the name with the stub of a pencil.

Schlitz's face stopped twitching. "He's a big shot lawyer. In Chicago, I think."

The slim figure continued to write. He looked down at the old man and said, "You were my only friend, Mr. Schlitz." For a moment, he looked incurably sad.

Relieved, Schlitz asked, "How did you find me? I've been retired for fifteen years."

"It took me a long time. I was chasing every Schlitz I could find, mostly from phone books. I saw a cop show on TV last month, where this guy called the social security office, complaining about his lost check, saying he moved and wanted the checks sent to a new address."

"It must have been agonizing."

The young man curled his lip. "It took me fifty or sixty calls to the social security offices before I got some dummy that gave me your home address. I kept asking them if they had the address right, I told them I wasn't getting the checks, and this stupid woman gave it to me, asking if the numbers were right!"

"Very clever, young man."

"I had plenty of time to work it out."

"By the way, son," said Schlitz, "what is your name?"

"I don't know. but you can call me—Harry."

"What are you going to do now, Harry?"

"See if there is an opening in Daniels' company," he said smugly. *I'll give him something more to worry about than his prostate!*

Iris, a half hour early as usual, maneuvered her green Ford Taurus into her assigned space in the firm's parking garage and turned off the ignition. Rosie was waiting for her, sitting in the large van with its blue handicapped tag hanging from the rear-view mirror. The garage smelled of motor oil, exhaust fumes and wet tires.

Rosie climbed out of her van, waved, and shouted at the Taurus. "Iris, got a minute?"

"Yes, what is it?" Iris lowered the passenger window.

"Can we talk?" Rosie had a silly, dazed look on her face.

"Sure—hop in. What's the matter? You look like you haven't slept at all."

Rosie's makeup was a day old, her red lips faded. "I didn't. I need to talk to someone. A woman."

"That's me, all right." Iris felt foolish once the words came out.

"I didn't mean to sound so dumb. You know what I'm trying to say," said Rosie.

Iris reached across the front seat and put her hand on Rosie's. "I'm sorry. How can I help you?"

Rosie looked up at the damp concrete wall, then back at Iris. "I have a little problem. It's about my mother."

"You've come to the right place. I was a mother once." Iris' face reddened.

"Really?" said Rosie. She appreciated Iris' changing the subject.

"I never heard you speak of kids—or a husband."

"I had a baby when I was very young. Never got married," said Iris pensively. "The father took my baby." She blinked, sat up straight and said, "That's been my experience being a mother."

Rosie hesitated, not knowing what to say next. She took a deep breath and said, "My mother's always ragging on me. Constantly complaining. She never lets up. I try to be considerate of her needs, but she drives me nuts."

"I'm sure it's not easy being a mother in today's society, today's environment. She has pressures to deal with, too."

"Is that a reflection on me?" asked Rosie. She looked hurt.

"Oh, no!" said Iris quickly. "I didn't mean it in THAT context. I'm talking in general terms."

Rosie studied all the gauges and buttons on the dashboard without saying a word for the longest time. "Can I confide in you?" she said finally. "I mean really confide?"

"You know you can."

"Well, here goes." She closed her eyes and blurted out, "I told Jackie the biggest, stupidest, most asinine lie in the world!"

"That would keep most anyone up all night," said Iris. "You want to talk about it...right?"

Rosie nodded. "Yeah, I do."

Then I'd like to hear more about YOUR child.

ROSIER

Rosie skipped lunch. She was waiting on the Riverside Plaza bridge. She watched a small group of musicians playing Mozart, the afternoon sun warm on her face.

Jackie jumped out of a cab near the corner and walked quickly to her. She gave him a weak smile as he approached the mid-section of the arched bridge.

"Hello, Rosie."

"Jackie." Her eyes were glassy. She stared at the musicians grouped at the base of the bridge.

"I have the money. Nobody knows about this." Jackie looked sadly into her eyes.

Rosie held his gaze. "I changed my mind," she said. "I don't want it."

"What!?" Jackie's eyes widened. Shocked, he said, "You need it, for the abortion!"

"I don't NEED it, Jackie. I'm not having a baby. I lied to you. I don't WANT the money!"

"I don't know what to say." He turned his back and watched the rappers and their gyrations across the street. He turned to face Rosie. "If you need the money, for whatever reason...it's yours."

"I feel lower than dirt, Jackie. Lately, for quite a while now, you've been so good to me."

"I needed to wise up. I had a great teacher!" said Jackie sarcastically.

"Your father, no doubt."

"Yeah. Jacq has lost every decent relationship he's ever had."

"Iris told me about one of his affairs this morning." She felt the weight of the world on her shoulders. "I was in shock."

"Jacq's got his own problems. But what about you? Why the lying for the money?" Jackie had a wounded look in his eyes.

"You mean extortion, don't you?" Rosie gazed into the brown water, wiping away her tears. "Jackie, I was a fool. I wanted the money so I could afford to put my mother in an assisted living home. They needed a hundred thousand dollar deposit. It was the only way I could do it."

"Rosie..."

"I had my eye on a great apartment in the city, near the office, for me."

"And you changed your mind? Just like that?!" He grabbed Rosie's arms. Her body tensed.

"Not just like that!" said Rosie. "It was something Amy and Iris said to me." Her blue eyes were focused on Jackie. "I have teachers, too. After talking with Iris this morning, even my mom won't bother me as much."

"Oh? What brought this..."

"Besides," said Rosie, "you sorta grew on me." She looked deep into Jackie's eyes.

"When we started fooling around, Rosie, that's all it was. But now..."

"Now what?"

"Frankly, my dear," said Jackie, smiling, "I'm in love."

"With..."

"With YOU, you gorgeous creature! I love those eyes! I'd do anything for you."

Rosie's mascara was streaming down her cheeks like a spring brook.

ROSIEST

The van purred west on I-90. Rosie was fighting the sun, low on the horizon, one hand on the wheel, the other turning the knob, searching for a more up-beat sound to match her mood.

A half-hour later, she pulled into the driveway of a neatly kept bungalow, fitted the van into the one-car garage, and entered the house from the back door.

Her mother was in the kitchen, sitting in the dark. "Is that you, Rosie? Where the hell you been? It's way past my supper time!"

Rosie went up the two steps into the kitchen and turned on the overhead lights. "Yeah, it's me, Mom. Sorry I'm late."

"Get your butt in here! I'm starved! You look like something the cat dragged in!"

"Okay, Mom. I love you, too," she said under her breath.

"What? I didn't hear that!"

"Nothing."

I've grown accustomed to your face...

BIRDMAN

"You have to go to the police with this information," said Richard. He sat in a secretary's chair, facing Molson, studying the glossy photographs. Ricky was sitting on the edge of a desk. Malty, the parakeet, was perched on his shoulder, pecking on a shirt seam.

"I can't," said Molson, his voice straining. "If word gets out I'm making trades in the market on these computers, I'll be thrown out of my apartment. I can't afford to get caught."

"You're working out of your condo?"

"Yeah. I'm my own boss. I make a lot more this way."

"It's riskier," said Richard. "You'll be shut down and out of here by next week."

"Not if you don't say anything."

Richard held one of the pictures up to the light. "That's the camera, in the kitchen window, that took these photos?"

"Yeah," said Ricky. "It's a fantastic camera. It's got telephoto lens, the best you can buy—programmed to go off every fifteen minutes during the morning hours, what I consider the best feeding times. I built those bird feeders at the edge of the woods last summer."

"A few yards from where the car was abandoned." Richard stared at the second photo. "That looks like Sherry's Miata. The car was reported stolen shortly before the murder. You can see a woman behind the car, carrying something heavy, by the way she's got her head thrown back. Half the face is hidden by the car's pillar."

"It looks like a woman," said Ricky, "or somebody with long hair."

"This other shot is definitely Mai's car." Richard studied the print. "By the shadows, you can tell it was closer to mid-day. Lieutenant Miller said one of the security guards reported the car being there about six hours."

"My camera stops taking shots around twelve-thirty."

"You've got only two pictures?"

"It was a roll with thirty-six exposures. The rest were of some birds and things. You wouldn't be interested."

"Let me be the judge," said Richard. Molson handed him a large white envelope. "You're a part-time photographer, too?"

"An amateur, really. I spend a lot of time in my apartment. Most of it at the computers." The four monitors were flashing and beeping.

Richard smiled as Malty burped a beep. "You're like a...computer nerd?" He thumbed through the slick photos.

"No. I'm what's known as a trader. I buy stocks when the market opens, and usually sell the same stocks before the end of the day."

"Sounds tricky."

"It is," said Ricky, "but you can make hundreds a day, if you're lucky."

"Do you feel lucky today?"

Malty was pecking at the computer screen. Molson leaned over and turned the Packard Bell off. "Look, I had my reasons not to get involved. But when I saw in the papers another girl was killed, working for the same company, I had to do something."

"It's not enough," said Richard bluntly. "You have to go to the police, with this photo especially. With the film-enhancing technology available in their labs, they can blow up this image behind the car. Perhaps identify the person, at least the gender."

"This whole setup is down the tubes." Molson waved his arms toward his computers.

"Help solve the crime. Maybe there's a reward," said Richard.

"Hey, yeah! I can open up my own business..."

"Let's do it this way. You get rid of all your computers and printers. Everything that might tie you to the trading you're doing."

"Wait a minute!..."

"Then, we'll call Lieutenant Miller and show him the photos."

"I can't do that! I'll be..."

"You'll be off the hook," said Richard, "otherwise, Miller and the press will blow the whistle on your fancy scheme. Take your choice."

Ricky looked at Malty. They both rolled their eyes. "Give me a couple of hours."

X

At five that afternoon, Lieutenant Miller was in Molson's apartment, looking at the two slick photos in his left hand, the phone in the other. Malty was pecking on the top rim of a lamp shade. Mike Miller was on hold with the video expert at Central Precinct.

"I have the photos AND the negatives. Yeah." Mike turned to Molson and asked, "You do have the negatives?"

"Yeah, I do."

"Look," said Miller, "I heard about the possibility of freezing frames and pictures for identification of suspects using a film enhancer." Miller popped a Tums. "We've got that capability at the lab there, right?"

"You gotta be kidding!" said the video expert. "Sammy's on vacation, the new guy don't know his ass from a hole in the ground, and I don't know the first thing about the machine."

"This is top priority!" said Richard. Miller repeated the words into the phone. Molson was on the other side of the room, fine-tuning his telephoto lens.

"I can send it to Cincinnati," said the video man. "They'll do a work-up for you."

Miller repeated, "This is a top priority! Read my lips!"

"I hear ya! I can send it to Cincinnati."

Miller sighed and closed his eyes, then glanced at Richard. "How long will that take?"

"I dunno. Couple—three weeks."

"Three weeks, Richie."

"I'm glad I'm off the force," said Richard shaking his head.

"Get Sam back from his vacation!" demanded Miller.

"No can do," said the video guy. "He got married Sunday. He's somewhere in the South Seas, with the new missus."

"You and your damn union!"

"That's why we got it, Mike."

"Donny's bringing the negatives in A.S.A.P."

"No hurry," said the video expert. "I'm done for the day. Leave it on my desk. I'll do the paperwork Monday sometime."

"Hell!" Miller slammed down the receiver. The phone rang immediately.

Richard reached out and pushed the speaker button. "This is Richard."

"Is the Lieutenant still there? This is Dos."

"Yeah, I'm here. What?"

Donny said, "I have good and bad news."

"Go!"

"Two officers answered a 911 on the South Side. They found our buddy, Schlitz."

"Good," said Miller.

"The bad news is—he's dead."

Marcus leaned back in his chair and breathed a sigh of relief. He and Kristie, teamed to work on the Colby case, had finally put the finishing touches on their part of the project.

Kristie straightened the stacks of files and announced, "Thursday, November 19th. Write it down! We're done at last!"

"Let's celebrate," said Marcus. "How about some coffee, hot and dark."

"I'd love to, Mr. Lambrusco, but my Neon is in the shop. I really should be going."

"How are you getting home?"

"I'm staying down the street tonight at the Carlyle. I can grab a cab."

"Please, at least let me see if Guinness is free to drive you."

"No, thanks," said Kristie with a demure smile. "I hate to impose."

"I usually get a taxi downstairs anyway. Let me drop you off."

"In that case, a cappuccino sounds divine. What time is it?"

Marcus looked at his stainless watch. "It's eight-thirty."

Kristie's face was radiant. "The night is young!" she said cheerfully.

"Why do I feel like an old antique?" Marcus rubbed his back, stretched, and struggled into his cashmere coat.

"But you're a FINE antique, Mr. Lambrusco." Kristie playfully helped Marcus with his coat. She accidently touched his hand. She pulled back when she felt a spark.

"Oh—wow!"

"What's the matter?"

"Nothing," said Kristie.

X

The cab circled several blocks and came to a stop in front of Billy's Coffee House on Franklin Street. Marcus and Kristie selected a booth at the rear of the converted storefront.

"You've been great to work with, Mr. Lambrusco." She was admiring the heaping foam and chocolate sprinkles on her drink.

"As a mentor should be."

"I mean, as a friend, too." Kristie wiped her upper lip with a paper napkin.

Marcus' voice was relaxed, mesmerizing. "Thank you," he said. "We've learned a lot...together."

"This last month has been the best of my two years with Daniels and Rumm." Kristie toyed with the sprinkles, then licked her index finger.

Marcus smiled. He took a sip of coffee. "You are every bit as refreshing as this cappuccino. Please, call me Marc."

"Now that we're on a first-name basis," said Kristie beaming, "I've been meaning to ask. Are you married?"

Marcus, surprised, said, "I was married. Divorced."

"Oh, I'm so sorry."

"That's okay."

"Children?"

"Luckily, no." He looked up from his cup and gazed into Kristie's pale blue eyes. "My wife left me."

"Oh, no! How could she do that to someone as sweet as you?" She reached for his hand.

"You don't know the real Marcus." His brow became furrowed, his eyes darkening. "Susie left me during a drinking binge."

"A what?"

"I'm a recovering alcoholic, Kristie. Ten years now. I recover every day of my life."

"I'm so sorry. I didn't know."

"The principals in the firm know. Most of the time I hide it pretty well." Marcus' coffee cup was empty. He exhaled deeply. "I haven't had a drink in a year and six days." He looked at his watch. "And seven hours."

"You're handling it wonderfully, Marcus."

He rubbed his leathery face. "Jarvis informed me two weeks ago that I'll be the second chair, next to Sherry, in the Colby trial. He says she'll do the bulk of the work, the cross-examining and all the rest. My job will be to see that she stays on the right track."

"And to fascinate the women jurors," she said smiling. "No, really, you'll do great. I know you will, Marc."

"I love that enthusiasm." Marcus smiled at her.

"That's my middle name!" said Kristie, fidgeting in her seat. "Try not to worry. I have a good feeling about the trial. We're prepared."

"The jury is going to find Colby innocent?" Marcus' face brightened.

"I don't know about that," said Kristie, "but you'll handle whatever comes."

"The firm's reputation is in jeopardy."

"Let's take it one day at a time. Please call me Kris."

"Sound advice...Kris...from someone so young. What's your stake in this?"

"Just a learning experience." She felt she was aging right before his eyes.

"No stake at all?"

"Except you," said Kristie. "Do you still love your ex-wife?"

X

Marcus' taxi dropped Kristie off at the Carlyle shortly after 10:00 P.M., then continued on to his loft at Wabash and eighth.

He was sitting on a leather sofa, in the dark, the moonlight casting shadows across the pale wall and his framed Cooley Law School diploma. Marcus sat staring at a bottle of scotch. A glass, with ice, glistened in the semi-darkness next to the bottle.

His hands were shaking now. He was thinking of Kristie—and Susie.

It's probably the cappuccino.

CHAPTER LIII

Kristie pushed the button for the twenty-first floor. The only other passenger in the elevator was an elderly man who kept looking at her. She turned her head away, then glanced back at him.

"He's still staring at me," said Kristie under her breath. *"I hope the old guy doesn't hit on me!"*

The elevator doors opened without a sound. The elderly man looked at Kristie again before he got off on the nineteenth floor and said, "Miss—I really should tell you. You have chocolate all around your mouth."

A contented, childlike smile was on Kristie's face as she searched her carryall bag for the keys. She pushed the door in with her shoulder and was surprised to see her sister Lisa sitting on the couch, watching television with the sound off.

Lisa popped several cashews into her mouth and said, "Well, it's about time! We had a date for dinner...remember?"

Lisa wore a long print skirt with a tight-fitting T-shirt. Her navy blazer was thrown over the back of the sofa. She was two years younger than Kristie. She thought she was at least ten years more mature.

"Oh, my gosh! You're right! Geez...I'm sorry."

"I waited for you in the dining room for two hours." Lisa pushed her blonde hair behind her ears with her hands.

"I know. But I had a chance to have coffee with one of my bosses. He is a doll!" Kristie tossed her bag on a small desk, sat down, and pulled off her shoes. "Uhh. That's so much better."

"I gave up studying for my finals to meet you here!"

"Yeah, but you don't know Marcus. He is the cutest lawyer we have, and we have some great-looking guys!"

"Forget that," said Lisa. "Did you have dinner with him?"

"No, just coffee. We talked."

"Aren't you hungry? Why don't we go downstairs and grab something?"

"I think the dining room is closed." Kristie was massaging her toes.

"Then let's get a hamburger in the deli next door."

"I'm game." Kristie headed toward the bathroom. "Give me a minute to freshen up. The coffee's running through me."

"Yeah...and get the chocolate off your mouth."

X

"What'll it be?" The lanky young man with a crisp white apron dealt menus to the girls. He smiled as Lisa handed the menus back to him.

"Two chicken salads and two de-caf diet Cokes."

"You ordering for me, too, or are you that hungry?" Kristie looked up at the smiling waiter. He showed the space between his front teeth.

"I know you eat like a bird," said Lisa. "I'll eat what you leave. I'm starved!"

The lanky man brought the Cokes and set them on the marblized tabletop. Kristie took off her black leather jacket and started picking at her nail polish.

"This Marcus must be hot to make you forget about me. I was starving to death in the dining room."

"Oh, he is! And he's available if I want him. There's a definite spark," said Kristie excitedly. "I felt it!"

"Did he?"

"I don't know." Kristie sipped on her straw, making little gurgling noises. Then she said, "He left his wife."

Spare her the details right now. Spare her the truth?

Lisa drank from her glass without a sound. "Is he that good looking that you'll give up your dream of being a lawyer some day?"

"Maybe."

"Kristie, you don't NEED a relationship at this point in your life. Not this kind!"

Kristie leaned back in her cushioned seat. "Marcus is a huge catch...if I can catch him."

Lisa reached across the table and grabbed Kristie's hand. "What about your career? All I ever heard you talk about since you were a little girl was how you wanted to be a respected lawyer."

"I haven't forgotten."

Lisa squeezed Kristie's hand. "Remember how it was when Dad left Mom?"

"Yeah. But do I want to be lonely like her?" They held each others' gaze until Kristie finally looked down at her long black fingernails.

The waiter balanced the salads on a tray and set them in front of each of the girls. He smiled, pushed his black curly hair aside, and said, "I get off in half an hour. My brother works in the kitchen. We could all go..."

Kristie and Lisa looked at each other and rolled their eyes.

Kristie tilted her head back, her mousey brown hair flying. "My lawyer boyfriend is waiting for me, upstairs at the Carlyle."

"He's waiting for me, too," said Lisa.

The girls smiled at each other as the waiter, shaking his head, carried the empty tray toward the kitchen.

Little white lies come in handy on occasion.

REUNION

Sherry and Jacq were lounging lazily in the glass-enclosed lanai behind her condo. Both sported white terry robes with flowing ties. The pool boy, on the other side of the windows, closing up the pool for the winter, kept peeking into the patio between his vacuuming and furious scrubbing.

"Nice of you to drop by so early." She turned her head and waved at the pool boy.

Jacq was watching the boy watching Sherry. "I told DeDe I was going to the club."

"Thank you. I need a bit of a diversion on a beautiful Saturday morning." Sherry smiled coyly at Jacq. "Won't DeDe ask questions?"

"Nah," said Jacq. "Guinness always backs me up." Jacq kept looking at the blonde ruggedly-built young man glancing repeatedly in through the windows.

"Just ignore him, darling."

"He's a nosey punk."

"He's harmless," said Sherry, smiling.

Jacq went to the windows and dropped the blinds. Sherry dropped the long tie on her robe.

"I'll mix us a drink," said Jacq. He saw the tie fall to the floor. "Another scotch?"

"You've had two already," chided Sherry.

"Who's counting?"

X

"I thought we were an item, sweetheart," said Sherry, half-joking.

"Baby, we are. But I've GOT to get going." Jacq was nursing his umpteenth drink. "It's after five."

"You've got a strange way of showing it!" Sherry displayed her best pout.

"I can come back tonight."

"What time?"

"Tenish."

"What about DeDe?"

"I'll blame it on Colby," he said with a devilish grin.

"I'll be waiting. At least no harm will come to you while you're here."

"Like hell."

She pulled the drapery aside and peered out the front window. "You'd better call Guinness."

X

Shortly after ten, Jacq parked his Jaguar near the side door of Sherry's condo. She opened the door, carrying a cue stick in her hand, wearing a pale pink, daringly low-cut slip gown.

"You look super," said Jacq. He kissed her playfully.

"You're in a good mood," said Sherry. She led him into the game room. The pool table's felt matched the color of her skimpy gown.

"It's late. Let's forget the game, and get right to it."

"You know the rules," said Sherry. "Sink all the balls first!" She bent over the cue ball, her gown falling loosely over the table, showing her cleavage. "I like the feel of the felt under my nude body as much as you do."

The cue ball glanced off the triangular formation and scattered the striped and solid balls at one end of the table. One of the striped balls flopped into a corner pocket. Jacq tipped two striped balls into a side pocket with his hand as Sherry walked around the table lining up her next shot.

"That's me! Behind the eight ball."

"What do you mean?" said Jacq. "You're not behind the eight ball."

"Playing second fiddle to DeDe, I mean."

"You're my first violin, Sher," said Jacq, playfully. He put his arm around Sherry's waist from behind and kissed her.

Sherry turned her head, her hair softly brushing against his face. "You've been promising me for so long," she said suddenly.

"Look," said Jacq, trying to appease her, "as soon as the Colby trial is over, Rumm tells me he'll be retiring."

"Really?"

"The firm will belong to me—AND you."

"What about DeDe?"

"She'll be history, I keep telling you! I've got no reason to be tied down by her. All she cares about is the money, anyway. She's got plenty."

"Sweetie," cooed Sherry, "I'm extremely concerned about you. I love you sooo much—you big baby." Sherry put her arms around Jacq's waist, the straps of her slip gown falling off her shoulders.

"You're my best girl," said Jacq, still flirting.

"Girl, hell!" exclaimed Sherry as she pushed him away. "I want to be a partner in the firm...AND your wife!"

Jacq laughed, not knowing how else to react. "Hey—that's my goal, too."

"When?"

"Well...some day. Pretty soon."

"You've got until the end of the Colby trial! Otherwise, I go to DeDe!"

"You wouldn't dare!"

"Try me!" said Sherry.

I can help you self-destruct!

HAPPY TURKEY DAY, DEDE

Dewars had been wrapped and taped in a camouflage blanket, thrown into the trunk of Labatt's Plymouth, then driven to the Skokie Lagoons. Labatt exited I-94 at Willow Road and turned north onto the county blacktop. He stopped at a secluded spot around the bend of one of the small dams. Labatt could hear the drone of the traffic as the sound cut through the early morning haze high above the Edens Expressway. When no headlights were in sight from either direction, he pulled Dewars' body from the trunk. The blanket hit the ground with a thud.

"So long, it's been good to know you," hummed Labatt. He rolled the body over to the brim of the ravine.

Labatt gave the corpse a swift kick. "See 'ya in the Spring, sucker!" The body rolled down the embankment into the shallow, muddy water.

X

Shortly after 2:00 A.M., Labatt parked his old Plymouth in front of a small, four-room bungalow Dewars had rented while he was in the Chicago area. He crawled into the plush leather seats of Dewars' '85 Riviera and maneuvered it up the ribboned driveway, into the one-car garage. The front bumpers of the Buick touched up against the bare wall studs. Labatt lowered the garage door and entered the house from the rear. He gave the refrigerator a glance, opened a can of Bud, then ripped into a bag of pretzels. He sat on a stool in the kitchen, holding a black notebook, scanning the numbers marked with an asterisk.

"I got unfinished business to do, J.D.," said Labatt to himself. "Unfortunately, I don't think you'll be home to get my call." Labatt pulled the phone down and dialed one of the marked numbers.

"Hello, Mrs. Daniels?"

"No, madam is napping in the study," said a snooty female voice. "At this late hour, I'm sorry I can't..."

"She'll take this call. It's important."

"Well," said the snooty voice, "whom shall I say is calling?"

"Tell her it's Mr. Moneybags. She'll come to the phone for me." Labatt snickered, wiping the beer off the side of his mouth.

"Hello, who is this?"

"Mrs. Daniels," said Labatt, "you don't know me, but I have some good news for you."

"Who is this? What do you want?" DeDe ran her fingers through her fiery red hair, shaking her head, trying to get oriented.

"I have information that you'd KILL to get your hands on."

"What do you mean?" demanded DeDe. "I'm not interested in..."

"Hold it, baby!" said Labatt. "You'll be interested to know your precious J.D. had a kid by another woman." DeDe was silent. He could hear her breathing. "Now you interested?"

"What you're saying is absurd!"

"Ah, I got your attention. It's true," said Labatt smugly. "I have documentation."

"Why tell me all this?"

"Money, DeDe."

"Hah!" said DeDe contemptuously, "I'm not paying for Jacq's

indiscretions."

"You will, if it means money in YOUR pocket."

"What are you driving at?" DeDe was wide awake now.

"Divorce, baby," gushed Labatt. "This information will do won-
ders in a divorce settlement." Labatt knew he had her—hook, line,
and giant sinker.

DeDe tried to regain her composure. "I'm not going to
lower myself to your level, whoever you are, and be a party to
such..."

"Do you see your life crumbling around you, too, DeDe?"
Labatt took a swig of his beer. "Colby is guilty and your cheating
husband is going to go down with his ship. I know that for a fact
DeDe Bacardi."

"How do you know my maiden name?"

"That's my job, baby. I also know you don't give a damn about
Jacq. Only his dough."

"I'm not concerned about his health, if that's what you mean!"
said DeDe, fighting back.

"Only if it's tied to his life insurance," countered Labatt.

"You are a crude man, Mr..." DeDe began to feel as if she were
talking to a 900 caller.

"Call me your secret admirer."

"What do you want from me, secret admirer?"

"Five hundred thousand dollars. For the original files."

"You MUST be joking!"

"Not by a long shot. They're worth at least two million to a good
lawyer. Know where you can find one?" Labatt chuckled.

"I don't seem to have much of a choice," said DeDe, subdued
and nauseous.

"Not if you play it smart. And I think you will." Labatt crammed
the last of the pretzels into his mouth.

"When can we meet?"

"I'll call you next week," said Labatt. "Happy Thanksgiving, DeDe, my pet!"

Where can a working stiff go to make easy money like this?

OCTOBER, 16, 1998

"This is it!" whispered the slim figure.

"Today's the DEADline!"

"He's always in on the weekends!"

"The S.O.B. won't live to see Monday!"

Shortly after 6:00 P.M., Harry locked the door to the print shop from the inside. He positioned a four-foot ladder under the room's cold air return vent, wiping away the accumulation of dust and spider webs from the twenty-four-inch cover. Harry climbed higher on the rungs and opened the hinged vent by turning the screw out several turns with a small screwdriver. He lifted up on the cover, propping it open with a pine furring strip.

The inside of the vent was large, a two-foot by four-foot rectangle. A metal ladder was attached to one wall in the vent. Using a flashlight, Harry could see the two upper stories, to the twenty-first floor, where Jacq's office was located. Looking down, he could see the vent disappearing into a black bottomless pit.

Harry climbed up two stories to the twenty-first floor. Each floor was conveniently designated with a white number painted on the opposite ladder wall. He clipped the vent's screw from the inside with a small bolt cutter and swung the cover into Jacq's spacious office. The vent was located above Jacq's buffet/bar, to the left of a beautiful antique desk. Harry stepped down onto the top of the bar, pulled his carryall bag from the vent and carefully closed the cover. He appreciated the putty gray paint on the vent cover that complimented DeDe's wallpaper selection.

I don't sleep anymore! I don't care how long this takes!

To the right of the bar was Jacq's bathroom.

A perfect place to wait!

Harry removed a hunting knife from his carryall bag and sat on the toilet, and waited. And waited.

X

The junk food was gone by late Sunday afternoon. Harry was nervous and distraught, his face a dark mask. Ready to kill the first person he saw. He didn't see a soul.

X

The curved blade of the knife flashed forward and deep into the desk top. Repeatedly, as the rage increased, the thrusts grew in intensity, gouging into the mahogany's smoothness. Criss-cross slashes.

How does it feel, huh? Feel good? Well, too bad! This one is for YOU KNOW WHO!

The whispering stopped. Then silence, except for the shallow breathing. A hand-held flashlight cast an eerie shadow on the paneled wall. The knife remained imbedded in the desk top. The handle was carefully wiped clean with a fine-stitched linen handkerchief. The door to the office was quietly closed. It was 11:45 P.M.

Just another Sunday in Chicago.

Harry was drained. He slumped into Jacq's chair, his arm brushing a copy of the New Yorker. The Jack Daniels ad on the back of the magazine caught his eye. Harry ripped off the last glossy page and rammed the knife into it. As he wiped off the hilt, he spied the sticky notepad. Harry, in crude block letters, wrote: YOU ARE NEXT.

Not a very good night's work!

Harry retraced his steps down through the vent to his print shop and fell asleep on the collating table.

SHARE AND SHARE ALIKE

The exclusive Professional Club Room was sparsely occupied the day after Thanksgiving. Dinner hour was over and the remaining patrons were making small talk as they shuffled toward the outer hall to the elevators. Jarvis and Jacq were looking out of the heavily draped second-story window. Guinness' limo was parked at the curb in a handicapped zone.

Jacq sat down, leaned back into an overstuffed chair and offered his partner a Don Diegos cigar. He held his usual scotch and water in his manicured hand.

"We haven't done this in years," said Jacq.

"I don't think we've EVER done it."

"I can't believe that, Rumm."

"Take my word." Jarvis settled into a rust-colored high-back chair, which was adorned with hundreds of brass hobnails. He took another puff from the cigar. "Why did you ask me here?"

"For old time's sake," said Jacq wistfully. "We don't talk much anymore. Remember, Jarvis, when we were kids..."

"About twelve or thirteen..."

"Yeah. We swore we'd be friends forever. And partners, just like our fathers."

Jarvis watched the smoke curl above their heads. "They had it tough during the Depression."

"Ha," said Jacq, staring at a painted nude behind Jarvis. "They told stories of running booze from Canada to Michigan, across the Detroit River."

"Yes, and they were so young. Barely out of high school."

"But they broke the law," said Jacq smugly. "That's our heritage, whether we like it or not."

"Well," said Jarvis, savoring the cigar, "that's water under the bridge. Luckily for us, both of them made it through law school. That bond is what made this firm."

"What it is today?" Jacq's face saddened.

"Our best days are ahead of us."

"I hope you're right." He closed his eyes for a moment, reminiscing, deep in thought. "Ah, the rich flavor!" Jacq inhaled deeply. "Enjoy the perks, Jarvis."

"While we have them."

"Don't worry so much. The Colby trial is well prepared." Jacq waved to the waitress for a refill. "Sherry and the rest have done a damn good job."

"They've been working like troopers."

"We're ready," said Jacq firmly. "I'm staking my reputation on it."

Jarvis took a long drag on his hand-rolled cigar. "Speaking of reputation, what's this I'm reading in the papers about our shares of stock?"

"Aw, you know how the press exaggerates." The waitress bent down toward Jacq as he lifted his glass of scotch from her silver tray. He couldn't help but notice her ample bustline. He made her day with his patented wink. "Besides, it's a matter of record."

"I always thought we owned equal shares in the firm," said Jarvis softly. "Your father and mine were equal partners. That's what they agreed to years ago."

"I had nothing to do with it, Rumm." He took a large gulp and wiped his chin with his palm.

"The newspapers played up the discrepancies in the share amounts of the two principal stockholders...you and me."

"I remember now," said Jacq. "My father bought over half of your father's shares, just before your old man died. I wasn't a party to it."

"My father had lapses of memory as he got older." Jarvis crunched his cigar in a marble urn. "He probably didn't know what he was signing."

"I wasn't aware he bought the shares...honest." Jacq gave him a pious gaze. "You can't blame me for that."

"You've done some low, despicable things in your life, Jacq."

"I'm still alive and kicking."

"You've devastated Iris. You've lied to DeDe. Now Sherry is..."

"Mind your own damn business, Rumm!"

"This IS my business! If Colby's found guilty, your so-called empire will come crashing down around you. If the killer doesn't get to you first!"

"I'm a big boy! I can take care of myself." Jacq shoved his fat cigar into his drink and glared at Jarvis.

Jarvis glared back. "What did you really get me down here for?"

"I want to buy you out," said Jacq cooly. "Jackie wants to be partner, and your shares would make a nice wedding present."

"Jackie's getting married?" Jarvis was genuinely surprised. "To whom?"

"Rosie, our receptionist. Can you believe it?"

"I've noticed they've been spending a lot of time together. I wish them the best."

"Well, what do you say...about the shares?"

"I'm retiring in a year or two. Maybe sooner," said Jarvis in a melancholy tone. "I want to salvage what's left for the people like Richard, Amy...and Gina."

"Yeah, you and your Gina," said Jacq. He turned to catch the eye of the roving, bosomed waitress.

"It's strictly business, Jacq."

"Yeah, and I'm a Boy Scout."

"These kids deserve to be partners," said Jarvis, "especially if they can salvage the Colby case."

"You're getting way ahead of yourself, Rumm."

"I've sold my shares to Gina."

Jacq recoiled. "You're a bigger fool than I gave you credit for!"

"It's done," said Jarvis calmly. "Can I borrow your cell phone?"

Jacq removed his flip-phone from his suit jacket and tossed it at Jarvis.

Jarvis punched in the numbers with the tip of his Cross pencil and waited. "Come on up." He stood and stretched his weary bones.

"What gives?"

"I have a surprise for you...for old time's sake."

Guinness exited the elevator on the other side of the room. He approached the two men, wearing an expensive Italian suit.

"What the...?" said Jacq in disbelief.

"Hello, gentlemen," said Guinness in his best British accent. "Thank you SO much for inviting me to join you for a drink."

"There's a first time for everything," said Jarvis. His pale blue eyes crinkled with delight.

"We may never have this opportunity again," said Guinness. He smiled down at Jacq.

Jacq finished his scotch, ashes and all.

The major players in the conference room on the twentieth floor were a-buzz with anticipation. Jarvis tapped his gavel on the Italian marble and cleared his throat.

Something definitely is brewing! thought Amy.

Iris sat to the right of Jarvis, ready to take the minutes of the Friday afternoon meeting. She scribbled in shorthand, then circled a large 'Nov.27/ 4:00 P.M.' on the top corner of her steno pad.

"All accounted for, Iris?"

"Yes. Everyone who should be here is present."

"As you can see, folks, Jacq and Jackie couldn't make this meeting," said Jarvis. "They're with Colby, from what I understand, doing the final prepping, going over his testimony one last time."

"If I hear the name 'Colby' one more time, I'll scream!" joked Amy.

"I concure," said Sherry. "The trial starts Monday. Agghh!" All the women giggled. Sherry made a choking motion around her neck with her hand.

"You're in good voice today," said Richard. "Better save some of that enthusiasm for the trial." He glanced at Amy and smiled.

"People," said Jarvis as he tapped the gavel again, "I want to thank each and every one of you for your exemplary efforts preparing for the trial." He smiled at Sherry who was staring at

Amy. "Especially Sherry, Richard, and Marcus, and their assistants, who have worked tirelessly for the past few weeks, involv-
ing many late-night sessions. And don't forget—Jacq has worked
just as hard."

Amy's eyes met Sherry's. "He's been under tremendous pressure," said Sherry.

"Not to mention the threat on his life," interjected Richard.

"I'm pleased with our preparation," said Marcus. "Lieutenant
Miller is still looking for another nurse to corroborate Colby's—you
know who I mean—innocence. We'll be ready for—you know
who!" Everyone looked pleased and proud.

Tony sat next to Charles, tapping nervously on the glass tabletop with his fingers. Beads of perspiration dripped from his forehead.

Jarvis raised his hand. An anticipatory hush fell over the
small group. He cleared his throat and said, "I'd like to make
an announcement." The participants held their collective
breaths.

Iris stopped her scribbling, her pen poised in mid-air. "What is
it, Jarvis?" Her voice wavered slightly.

"I've decided to tender my resignation, effective after the conclusion of the trial, win or lose." Jarvis swallowed hard. He glanced
quickly at Gina, settling his eyes on Sherry.

Richard was the first to speak. "Why not wait until the first of
the year?"

"I'll be in Sarasota by then!" said Jarvis grinning.

"You've given this matter all the attention it so obviously
deserves?" asked Sherry. Her pale green eyes had darkened a few
shades.

"For your information, I've sold all my shares in the firm to
Gina Collins." Jarvis smiled pleasantly at Gina.

The hugs and congratulatory handshakes took several minutes. Jarvis looked as proud as the proverbial peacock.

Tony went to the other side of the table and embraced Gina and all the other women. He had an anxious look on his face.

Sherry sat in stunned silence.

Jarvis rapped his gavel.

Tony stood up. "I know I'm the new kid on the block...but I'd like to make an announcement of my own. If Mr. Rumm has the courage to resign at this time, the least I can do is muster enough courage to let everyone here know...what some of you already know. I'm gay." He exhaled and surveyed the faces around the table.

Richard looked at Marcus, who shrugged his shoulders. Charles sat erect, ready to defend his applicant. The women seemed disinterested...with the exception of Rita.

"When I worked for the firm in Philadelphia, I informed them shortly after I started," said Tony. "I was gone within three months. I like it here..."

"You're not in Philly, Mr. Martini," said Jarvis.

"Again...welcome to the firm, Tony," said Richard heartily.

"You want to stop for a bite, Gina?" said Amy.

"Who's got the latest issue of Sports Illustrated?" asked Charles.

"I've got to call Mike Miller," said Richard. "See you, folks."

"Thank you, people," said Jarvis. "Meeting is adjourned." He walked around the marble table and put his hand on Tony's shoulder. "Welcome to the firm, young man."

X

Jarvis sat back in his chair and sighed heavily. He closed his eyes for a second, reflecting on the events of the meeting. Iris broke the trance.

"I didn't know you were leaving so soon."

"It's time. I'm tired." He looked at Iris fondly, as if for the first time. "You've been a peach through all this...all these years."

"A peach?"

"Sorry," said Jarvis. "I don't know what else to call you," he said, smiling at her as she headed for the door.

"I can't call you 'Jar.'" said Iris as she winked at him. "How about 'J.R.'?"

"Thanks again...peach!"

TRUTH OR DARE

DeDe stormed past the empty outer office, her cashmere cape flying, and pushed Jackie's door open with a dramatic gesture.

"Is it true? she demanded. "Answer me!"

"Is what true?" Jackie was startled. "You mean about me and Rosie?"

"NO! I mean about Jacq, and his illegitimate offspring!"

"Oh, yeah, it's true. It seems I'm not the only heir to the throne." At that moment, Jackie felt, and looked, older than his mother.

"Where is this other person?"

"I don't know Mom."

"Jacq's not in his office. Jarvis is out! Where is everyone?"

"The Colby trial starts today. They won't be back 'til late."

"How could this have happened?" lamented DeDe. She gritted her pearly white, beautifully-capped teeth. "Who is this so-called heir's mother? Do you know?"

"Please. Calm down," said Jackie. "The mother of Jacq's son, is Iris."

"OUR IRIS?"

"Yes," said Jackie calmly. "Our Iris."

DeDe threw her cape over the back of the sofa and collapsed in the cushions. She fluttered her eyes and put her hand to her forehead and wailed, "What have I ever done to deserve being humiliated like this?"

"You want it all in writing?"

DeDe's stare would have penetrated a lead partition. She regained her composure and said, "I want divorce proceedings to be started immediately."

"You'll need proof," said Jackie. "We'll need to locate Dad's son, too."

"Like hell we do! I have all the proof I need!" said DeDe defiantly. "I don't need Jacq...or his son!"

"You sure?" asked Jackie.

"Absolutely! By the way. What is this about you and that Rosie person?"

CHAPTER LX

Judge Forest Glen, a burly man with eyebrows hanging over the top rim of his glasses, threw open the door from his chambers and marched to his bench as the Deputy Clerk bellowed the familiar words: "All rise!"

"...in the matter of the State of Illinois versus Nathan Colby, case number 27-9120..."

Judge Glen, an African-American with more than thirty years on the bench, took a moment to wipe his wire spectacles with a tissue while the photographers captured his entrance. He surveyed the jurors, four men and eight women, as he adjusted his glasses over his ears. Most of the jurors looked bright-eyed and bushy-tailed on the first day of the murder trial. They had read in the newspapers it was going to be a short, cut-and-dried case. Two weeks tops.

Colby sat, properly attired in a navy suit with a red, white, and blue tie, next to Sherry Weinstein, his defense attorney. She was flanked by Marcus Lambrusco, her first chair. Richard Port was at the far end of the long oak table.

The prosecuting attorney, Terry Taittinger, sat facing the judge, her hands folded, smiling confidently. She was in her late forties, with beautiful features and naturally curly hair. She wore a tight-fitting red suit. The Colby trial was her first major case.

Judge Glen began a short, concise dissertation to the jury,

reminding them they could not discuss the trial with anyone or among themselves.

"Are you ready to proceed?" asked Judge Glen.

One of the women jurors raised her hand, waving frantically at the judge.

"Just a moment, Ms. Taittinger," said the judge as he turned toward the frazzled woman. "This is highly irregular!"

"I know, your holiness! But I got to go...BAD!"

Judge Glen called a fifteen-minute recess.

X

"Are we finally ready to proceed?"

"Yes, your Honor." Terry Taittinger rose from her wooden chair and walked toward the front of the courtroom.

"Please call your first witness."

"The people call Ms. Jennifer O'Doul," said the auburn-haired attorney.

Jenny O'Doul made her way to the witness stand and was sworn in by the bailiff. Her black hair was pulled back in a ponytail. She was in her late thirties, with a muscular build. Jenny wore a dark brown pantsuit with a beige blouse.

"State your full name."

"Jennifer Leah O'Doul."

Taittinger put her hands on the rail of the stand and said, "You work on the afternoon shift in the Glenview Nursing Home in Glenview, Illinois, is that right?"

"Yes," said Jenny, "I rotate shifts every month, though."

"On the night of August 28, 1998, you were working the afternoon shift?" Taittinger placed one foot on the step leading to the witness stand, revealing her shapely leg. The men jurors stirred, as did one of the women.

"Yes, I was."

"Tell the jury what happened in room 238, while you were making your final rounds before leaving for the day."

"I work the patients from rooms 215 to 240," said Jenny. She moved slightly closer to the microphone. "Usually around eleven or so, all the patients are in their beds. Once in a while, I have to help them to the bathroom, or change a diaper..."

"What happened in the room, please," said Taittinger.

"Well, mostly I can go through the bed checks pretty fast. I was ready to check on La Grande in room 238 when..."

"This is Mrs. Sarah La Grande, the murdered woman?"

"I object!" voiced Sherry loudly. "No one has been murdered, your Honor."

"Sustained. Don't get cute, Ms. Taittinger," said the Judge. "The jury will disregard the comment."

Terry strolled toward the jury box, then turned and faced the witness. "Continue. You were going into Mrs. La Grande's room, and...?"

"I stopped to pick up a large paper clip on the floor, right by the door. I pushed the door open as I balanced myself, to keep from falling. The door opened about a foot."

"And you saw Mr. Colby pushing a pillow into Mrs. La Grande's face?"

"Objection!" Sherry stood immediately. "Leading the witness, your Honor!"

The Judge gave Taittinger a royal scowl. "Just ask the questions."

Terry walked to the stand. "What did you see when you pushed the door open?"

Jenny pointed a finger at Colby. "That man there, the director of the home..."

"Mr. Nathan Colby?"

"Yes. He was pushing a pillow over the face of Mrs. La Grande, as hard as he could!"

The courtroom spectators erupted in "oohs" and "ahhs," as did the press and the jury.

Judge Glen banged his gavel repeatedly. "Order! Order in the court!" A hush fell over the crowded room. "Please continue."

"Was Mrs. La Grande struggling with him? Fighting or trying to push him away?"

"No," said Jenny, "I think she was too far gone by the time I saw her."

"Objection!" said Sherry. "Witness is not an expert..."

"Ms. O'Doul," said Glen, "just answer 'yes' or 'no'."

"No. She wasn't struggling. I think she was dead."

"OBJECTION!" Sherry stood, with her hands on her hips.

"Jury disregard!" said the judge. "The answer to Ms. Taittinger's question is 'NO'!"

"Your witness," said the plaintiff's attorney.

Sherry fluffed the lapels of her pale green Armani suit as she approached the witness stand. Her platinum blonde hair was an exact match to the conservative men's button-down shirt that was open at her neck. She smiled politely at the jury, then at the expectant witness.

"Ms. O'Doul. Jenny," said Sherry in a motherly tone. "How long have you worked in the Glenview Nursing Home?"

"A little over four years."

"According to your records, you previously worked at the Northbrook Seniors Facility, also owned by Mr. Colby?"

"Yes. I worked there two years."

"Who hired you then, Ms. O'Doul?"

"Mr. Colby."

"So you've known Mr. Colby for at least six years?"

"Yes." Jenny O'Doul felt her blood pressure rising.

Sherry's jade-colored eyes sparkled as she asked innocently, "Did you know Mr. Colby, other than professionally?"

"I don't know what you mean." She glanced quickly at Colby, then the judge, and back at the mike.

"I'll simplify. Did you and Mr. Colby ever sleep together?"

"Objection, your Honor!" Taittinger glared at Sherry. Sherry looked as innocent as a newborn babe.

Judge Glen bellowed, "Objection sustained. The question has no bearing on the case, Ms. Weinstein."

"I think it does, your Honor, as you will soon see."

"Rephrase the question," said the judge.

"Ms. O'Doul, have you and Mr. Colby ever gone out, after hours, and had a cup of coffee?"

"Once or twice."

"So, you met socially?"

"Yes, once or twice." Jenny put a hand to her wrist and felt her pulse racing.

"Dinner?"

"Yes, a couple of times. But that was it."

"You two didn't get along...socially?"

"We felt it better not to get involved." Jenny noticed a slight crack in her voice.

"Good decision," said Sherry. She walked to the oak table, nodded, and picked up another file handed to her by Marcus. "I have the latest employee evaluations here, dated July, 1998. Are you familiar with this?"

"We have one every six months. Company policy."

"I see Mr. Colby rated you below average in every category."

"I can't be perfect all the time."

Sherry waved the report at the jury and said, "Six years of above-average performance. Then, all of a sudden, your work is BELOW average?"

"Objection!" said the curly-haired attorney. "Witness is not on trial here, your Honor."

"Objection sustained. Make your point, Counselor."

The woman who had asked for the bathroom break was as white as a sheet.

"Did you get a salary increase after this latest appraisal?" asked Sherry.

"No."

"Why not?" Sherry raised her eyebrows as her eyes bore into the witness.

"A rating below average gets you nothing."

"So," said Sherry, "you were angry at Mr. Colby for not rating you higher?"

"Sure. I didn't think I deserved it."

"You were angry enough at him to get him into trouble?"

"Objection!" said Taittinger.

"Sustained," said Glen. "Let's have a direct question, Ms. Weinstein."

A hush fell over the courtroom. Judge Glen took off his glasses and wiped his eyes with a pink tissue.

Loud stomach noises emanated from the white-faced woman in the jury box. She hunched over and rubbed her mid-section.

Sherry didn't appreciate the distraction. "Were you angry enough at Mr. Colby to lie on the stand? He was trying to save that woman's life, wasn't he?" Sherry rattled off the questions quickly. Jenny looked at her lawyer, begging for help with her eyes.

"Objection!" Taittinger said louder than before.

"He was performing CPR on Mrs. La Grande when you saw her! Isn't that the truth?"

"OBJECTION!" yelled Taittinger.

"No further questions." Sherry felt like a fat boa constrictor.

OCTOBER 28, 1998

Harry Heineken leaned next to his wire cart on the twenty-first floor, pretending to sort through the stacks of mail. He started to push the cart past the conference room toward Jacq's office. Harry saw the elder Daniels and a detective-type stranger coming out of the corner office. They both passed him in the hallway, heading to the elevators. Harry looked at his Timex. It was 4:10.

The S.O.B. is never alone!

Harry had a handful of envelopes and assorted mail for Jacq and a few pieces marked for Iris' attention. He parked his cart in the hall near her office and pushed the door open. Iris was not in the outer office, but Harry could hear her sliding a drawer open in the adjoining room—Jacq's spacious sanctuary.

Harry tip-toed to the door leading into Jacq's office. Hiding behind the slightly opened door, he could see Iris holding a manila folder, her hands shaking, a shocked expression on her face. Harry retraced his steps without leaving the mail.

This I gotta see!

Harry shuttled the wire cart up and down the corridor, stalling for time until he saw Iris, with her coat and handbag, hurrying to the elevator. Harry shoved his cart into the empty office. He carried a stack of white envelopes and placed them, one by one, on the edge of the desk. In the process, he pulled Jacq's drawer open and scanned the folders from Dewars. Harry felt his blood racing. He took off his wire glasses, closed his eyes, and felt the side of his face twitching.

Ms. Whiskey is my mother?

Harry threw the mail on Iris' desk and took the elevator down to nineteen. He shoved the cart into the print shop, next to the mail sorter, and threw off his beige shopcoat. Harry removed Mai's nickel-plated pistol from his belt and opened the back of the copy machine. He placed the gun inside the machine and fastened the metal cover.

MY TIME WILL COME!

TIGHTENING

"It's too risky. They'll disbar you." Richard kept his voice down, playing with a checkered napkin.

"If I don't," said Jackie, "we'll lose the case. I'm sure of it."

Richard sat in a green leather booth, facing Jackie, sipping a decaf coffee. The deli was jammed with noisy Saturday morning customers, a perfect spot for a clandestine meeting.

Richard balled up his napkin. "It's unethical to pay for information, which might lead to another witness, which may, or may not, help Colby." Richard took a bite of his apple cinnamon donut. "Anyway, people like that have a way of coming back to haunt you later."

"I have to take that chance. My father's firm is going down the toilet if he loses this case." Jackie motioned to the waitress for a refill. "Jarvis doesn't seem to care. Somebody's got to step up."

"I still think he does." Richard set his jaw and looked directly into Jackie's piercing dark eyes. "Is this about your father? Or you?"

"It's about the future of Daniels and Rumm," Jackie shot back.

"You mean Daniels and Daniels, don't you?"

Jackie felt for a moment as if HE was on the witness stand. "No! Honestly, right now, all I care about is saving the firm. And hopefully...Colby."

"And your dad's life." Richard slumped back into the cracked leather.

"That goes without saying." Jackie tossed a five-dollar bill on the Formica table.

"What do you have to do?"

"I'm paying the janitor at Glenview, a guy by the name of Harvey, a sizable sum of money. We agreed on the amount. He wouldn't take anything less. Plus a plane ticket to California."

"And what do you get in return?"

Jackie rubbed his goatee, finished his coffee, and wiped his mustache with a napkin. "He claims he can lead us to a witness that heard the entire conversation in La Grande's room, at the time of the alleged murder."

"Let's do it legally, Jackie. We can get this Harvey guy to..."

"NO! Harvey says he will NOT take the stand. He's had a prior conviction. It's too chancy. Taittinger will tear him apart."

"Listen," said Richard, "I'm sorry. I can't help you do this."

"Then I'll do it myself." Jackie slid out from behind the booth, reached in his coat pocket, and tossed another dollar bill on the table. "I'll have the witness in court Monday morning, come hell or high water!"

<h1 style="text-align:center">X</h1>

Gina's townhouse, courtesy of Jarvis Rumm, was located within jogging distance of the Chicago Historical Society's lavish grounds. The single-story houses were connected in several U-shaped configurations, each separated by attached garages. Natural colors of tan, beige, and terra cotta were used throughout the complex. Floral gardens and gushing fountains created a rich country setting, deep in the heart of Chicago.

The late afternoon sun warmed the doorwall glass of the living room and Jarvis' back as he made himself comfortable in a white overstuffed sofa. Gina carried diet drinks from the kitchen and set her drink on the slate hexagon table.

"Thanks. If I were a few years younger, I'd be gulping down a couple of martinis."

"The trial's going well, don't you think?"

"Under the circumstances, yes. It's going very well." Jarvis didn't sound convincing. "It could go either way."

"Is he guilty?"

"Perhaps. For our sake, I hope not."

"The trial is in good hands, with Sherry and Marcus." Gina formed the Allstate logo with her hands and smiled.

"The projection is to wind it up this coming Monday."

"Less than two weeks."

"Right. They've gone through most of the people working in Colby's homes. He has some enemies...very few friends."

"Reminds me of Jacq." Gina pushed the sleeves up on her jersey. "It'll be up to the jury to decide his fate."

"I don't know what call I'd make," said Jarvis. "Anyway, it'll be over by Wednesday, at the very latest."

"Great! Then we can get back to normal." Gina sat down next to Jarvis, curled up her legs, and sipped her drink. She wore a bright Redwings jersey and black skintight pants. "I can't begin to tell you how much I appreciate all the help you've given me. Especially, making that announcement last week at the meeting."

"It's been my pleasure," said Jarvis. He looked affectionately into her green Irish eyes.

"You've made it so much easier than I ever dreamed. I owe you a debt I'll never be able to repay." She fought back the tears.

"It's time I stepped down." He reached out and held Gina's ringed fingers. "You'll be a great addition to the firm."

"Jacq has his hands full. I truly believe he'll turn the reins over to Jackie."

"Not Sherry?"

"Sherry's my friend. She has a lot of years invested in the firm."

"She is a survivor," said Jarvis firmly. "She would still be welcome if she wants to stay, don't you think?"

"She's very proud." Gina looked away at a cascading fountain through the domed window. "If Sherry can't be the top banana, she might just go off on her own."

"That sounds more like Sherry," said Jarvis, his pale blue eyes crinkling.

"What about Jackie?"

"It looks like he's settling down. He's learned from his father." Jarvis glanced at his watch and the setting sun hiding behind the bricked garden wall.

"Yes, I know. Whatever Jacq did, Jackie tried to emulate...for years."

"Now, he seems to look at life differently."

"Amy says Rosie's in love." Her Irish eyes twinkled.

"With Jackie, right?"

"I think so. There are wedding bells in the near future."

"Wonderful!" said Jarvis. "Out of the ashes and smoke, we'll forge a new beginning."

"Pretty melodramatic." Gina stretched one of her shapely legs.

"Be that as it may," said Jarvis, "I look forward to a new beginning, the end of the Colby trial, and a new millennium."

"Speaking of millennium, I'm meeting Amy for a morning jog around Belmont Harbor."

"I've got to get going myself. If I wait 'til it gets too dark, the oncoming lights bother my eyes."

Gina leaned over and gave Jarvis a warm, compassionate hug. "Thanks again for the stock shares and all you've done."

"You've worked hard. You deserve it. And I promised your mother."

Gina gave her white-haired benefactor a tender kiss.

"Good night, honey," said Jarvis.

"Thanks again—and good night...Uncle Jarvis."

THE NOOSE TIGHTENS

Early Monday morning, Iris hurried to her office on the top floor of the Bank Building. She switched on the light and saw her chair with its back to the wall. Immediately, a feeling of uneasiness came over her.

Someone's been here!

Iris checked her closet. She slowly opened the door to Jacq's office. It was empty. Most of the staff were at the courthouse, watching the conclusion of the Colby trial. Iris pushed the bathroom door open and peeked inside. Empty. Her hands were shaking. She didn't notice the note on her desk until she tossed her handbag on top of the plastic file rack.

What's this?

X

Richard was listening to yet another boring testimony when the bailiff nudged him and whispered, "There's an urgent call for you in the office, Mr. Port. Follow me, please." The barrel-chested bailiff led Richard across the hall to the courthouse offices where a blue-haired woman handed him a blinking telephone.

"This is Richard Port."

"Richard," said Iris haltingly. "He's here! Somewhere in the building!"

"Whoa! WHO'S there? What are you talking about?"

"My SON! The one we've been looking for!" Iris was hysterical, gasping for breath as she spoke. "He left a note on my desk that says, 'I'M DOING IT FOR YOU, MOTHER'."

"My God!" exclaimed Richard. "Listen! Get out of the office immediately. I'll meet you on nineteen, by Rosie's reception counter. Whatever you do, DON'T take the stairs."

"I'm on my way!"

"Wait!" he cautioned. "If you have your cell phone with you, take it. And DON'T get on the elevator alone. I'll be there as soon as possible!"

X

In the courtroom, Taittinger, the prosecuting attorney, began stacking her briefcase with the Colby files. To her, the case was over. And in her mind, the State had won. She was shocked when she heard Sherry's voice.

"The defense would like to recall Mindy Michelob to the stand, your Honor."

Terry looked at her assistant with a worried glance. "What's this all about?" He didn't bother to answer.

Mindy, sitting in the first row, made her way to the stand in a navy pantsuit, dramatically accented by a large floppy green bow at the neckline.

"You understand you are still under oath," warned Judge Glen.

"Yes, Judge." Mindy felt her stomach fluttering.

Sherry approached the witness stand and smiled briefly at the jury. "Ms. Michelob, you testified last week, stop me if I am incorrect, that you were on duty on the night Mrs. La Grande met her untimely death?"

"Yes, I was."

"To refresh the jury's memory, you are a night nurse on staff at Glenview, and work the 10:30 to 6:00 A.M. shift?"

"Yes. There are six of us on duty at any one time."

"And we know from your previous testimony, that Mrs. La Grande was one of your patients." Sherry folded her arms in front of her and smiled demurely. "Explain to us once more, in your own words, what happened that fateful night."

Mindy, sitting with her hands folded in her lap, touched her wrist with her thumb. Force of habit. She glanced at Colby, then back at Sherry.

"Well—on Friday night," repeated the well-rehearsed woman, "I know the afternoon shift wants to get off a few minutes before the regular quitting time. So I usually make a quick round of my patients so there won't be any surprises once the girls leave."

"Again, just to clarify, and in the interest of time," said Sherry, "according to last week's testimony, you made the rounds, and stopped outside of Mrs. La Grande's door. You said the door was slightly ajar?"

"Yes. I could see in. Jenny..."

"Ms. Jennifer O'Doul, the afternoon nurse?"

"Yes," said Mindy. "She was standing just inside the door. She was watching Mr. Colby push the pillow over Mrs. La Grande's face."

Terry Taittinger leaned over to her assistant and whispered, "What the hell is she doing? She's cutting her own throat!" The assistant gave her a wide-eyed gaze. He made no reply.

Sherry continued. "She made no attempt to stop Mr. Colby ?"

"No. She must have been in shock. I know I was."

"Then what happened?"

"Like I said before, I went into the room as soon as I composed myself. They both looked at me. I could see the woman was dead. She was all white. Her lips were bluish."

"You've seen people in that state before."

"Yeah. Lots of times."

"What happened then?"

"Then Mr. Colby made a call to the resident doctor. About an hour later, they took the body away."

Sherry tapped the edge of the witness box. "Let me get this straight. A few minutes ago, you said, and I quote, 'She was standing just inside the door. She was watching Mr. Colby push the pillow over Mrs. La Grande's face.'"

"I got a bad feeling about all of this," whispered Terry to her silent assistant.

Sherry, her voice raised slightly, said, "My question to you, again, the same as I asked last week, is this what you saw when you looked into the room?"

The courtroom buzzed with anticipation. One of the juror's awoke with a start.

Mindy bit her lower lip. "I saw the same thing Jenny did. Mr. Colby was pushing the pillow on her face!"

The courtroom was silent. Terry's assistant sneezed on her manila folders. He wiped his nose and brushed the files off with his handkerchief.

"You are absolutely positive?"

"Yes! Absolutely positive."

From the back of the courtroom, a heavy-set woman stood and proclaimed in a loud, shrill voice, "SHE'S A LIAR!"

"Order! Order in the court!" bellowed Judge Glen.

"That is NOT what happened!" yelled the woman.

Photographers came out of the woodwork and began taking

various angled shots of the woman. She remained standing for their benefit.

"SHE IS LYING!" she repeated.

"Order!" said the judge. The cameras continued flashing. "Quiet, or I'll have all of you thrown out! Order!"

Several reporters ran from the courtroom. Taittinger's assistant was talking furiously with a third assistant. The jury sounded like a women's afternoon tea party.

Judge Glen banged his gavel with all the strength he could muster. The bailiff ran out of the courtroom and returned with three uniformed bodies. Just in case.

"The court calls a recess until one o'clock this afternoon!" Judge Glen marched to his chambers. He threw his gavel into a leather-lined wastebasket.

Taittinger glared at Sherry, who shrugged her shoulders and looked innocently at the prosecuting attorney. Terry, with her brief-case in hand, approached Sherry.

"What are you up to? I've seen her in the courtroom before. Who was that person?"

"I don't know."

"If the judge would have let me use the $1.3 million willed to Colby, this trial would have been over last week. We both know Colby's guilty!"

"That was a hell of a cause for motive, but he didn't, sweetie," said Sherry. "We both know why."

"With Daniels and Rumm's reputation, I'm not surprised at anything."

"Ta-ta, Terry. We'll have two hours to get to know our new witness." Sherry smiled at Marcus as Taittinger abruptly turned and left the courtroom.

Jackie was right! His strategy worked PERFECTLY!

YOUNG KING COLE

The elevator door opened on the nineteenth floor. Iris was sitting with Rosie, behind the reception desk, her face ashen, eyes large as saucers.

"Wait here!" said Richard, running to the desk. "I'll check upstairs first and work my way down. Rosie! Let me know if any one on our staff leaves the building."

Rosie jumped to attention. "You got it!"

The executive offices on the top floors were locked. Richard made a thorough search of the conference and exercise rooms. The kitchen and lounge were deserted, attesting to the fact that most of the staff was at the courthouse.

On twenty, his office and Sherry's were also secured. Richard made a check of the other offices and a token look into the supply and storage rooms near the rear hallway.

He searched the print shop, the law library, and the remaining offices on the nineteenth floor, working his way down through the front and back stairwells. His last stop was the long hallway opposite the rear freight elevators.

Where the hell are you?

Richard hurried down the corridor to the reception desk. Iris appeared more relaxed. She was smiling at Rosie, thumbing through a bridal catalogue.

"All clear. Not a soul on any of the floors. See anyone go by, Rosie?"

"No, but Mr. Rumm called from the courthouse. They're in recess until one o'clock this afternoon. Something about a new witness."

"I could have guessed," said Richard.

Rosie shrugged. "Oh, Richard, I haven't seen Mr. Daniels come in today. That's not like him." The phone began ringing.

"Try to reach Guinness on the car phone," said Richard. "He most likely knows where Jacq is. I need to talk to him."

X

A bleary-eyed Colada Jones was reviewing the silent video tapes in the living room of the house on 36th and Parnell. Cole wore small black earphones, simultaneously listening to the music of Justin Wilson. The music made the tedious tapes much easier to abide. He was reviewing the last of the seventy-two hours of boring tapes for the third time. His list of people, coming and going, was detailed on several sheets of yellow paper. Cole was sure of the results. Everyone in the firm was accounted for...with one exception.

X

"Richard," said Rosie, "It's for you."

He grabbed the phone behind the reception counter. "Hello, this is Richard."

"Mr. Port. It's me, Cole Jones. I've got news for you."

"What is it, Cole?"

"Plenty! According to the tapes, there was only one person that NEVER left the building on that Friday night."

"Who was it?"

"I don't know who, but he's a young guy...with long blonde hair."

Richard's mouth fell open. He looked at Iris and grabbed her arm. "Get down here as soon as you can! Bring the tapes. I'll be in my office."

Iris dropped the bridal magazine on the floor.

"Who is it?" she asked.

"I can't believe it. It's Harry!"

"Where's Sherry?" asked Marcus.

At ten minutes to one, he was genuinely concerned. He kept looking at the double doors at the rear of the courtroom. Gina was sitting at the long oak table with Colby. She looked flustered, but not as irritated as Colby appeared to be.

"Did our gorgeous blonde jump the sinking ship?" asked Colby.

"I don't know where she is," said Gina. "She called me a while ago and told me, quote, 'to get my you-know-what down here to help you.' What she had to do couldn't wait."

"What the hell could be more important then saving my ass?" Colby loosened his red, white, and blue tie.

Marcus reached for his pen and jotted a note on the corner of a legal pad. Gina saw his hand shaking, then looked away toward the doors. Marcus opened a manila folder and said nervously, "Looks like it's you and me, kid!"

Gina gave him a pat on the hand as the bailiff looked up at the clock and shouted, "All rise!"

Judge Glen walked stiffly to the bench. He faced the bevy of attorneys. "For the record, I'm not going to tolerate any more of those 'Perry Mason' tactics this Court was subjected to earlier this morning. You have both had ample time to deal with the new witness, Brenda Ballentine." He looked sternly at the counselors.

"I want this trial over, and done with, TODAY! Now, who's calling the first witness?"

"Your Honor..."

"I don't see Ms. Weinstein..."

"Your Honor, Ms. Weinstein is unavoidably detained. I will act in her behalf."

"Well, let's get the ball rolling, Mr. Lambrusco."

"If it pleases the Court, I would like to call Brenda Ballentine to the stand," announced Marcus.

"Your Honor," interrupted Terry Taittinger, "the people would like to waive our cross examination, but reserve the right to call the witness at a later time." Terry wore a striking aqua suit with black accents. Her skirt was shorter and tighter than the one she had worn the previous week.

"That's fine, Counselor," said the judge. "Just make sure we wind it up today!"

Brenda Ballentine was sworn in. The courtroom was abuzz. She had been instructed to wear a bright-red dress with navy accessories.

"Please state your full name," asked Marcus. He wore a dark charcoal-gray suit, pale gray accessories, and black leather wing-tipped shoes. The women jurors perked up immediately.

"My name is Brenda Beth Ballentine."

"And where do you work, Ms. Ballentine?"

"I work at the Glenview Nursing Home. I'm the supervisor of nurses on the afternoon shift."

"Why is it, Ms. Ballentine, that after almost two weeks of testimony, you haven't come forward until now?"

"I didn't think I had anything new to offer, until my boyfriend told me, in no uncertain terms, I better tell what I know!"

"Were you threatened by your boyfriend?"

"He didn't hit me, if that's what you mean."

"I'll withdraw the question, your Honor. Tell the Court, Ms. Ballentine, what you saw, or heard, on the day of Mrs. La Grande's death."

Brenda took a deep breath and paused for effect. "I was on duty at my nurses' station. It was close to eleven-thirty. I heard the buzzer go on in Mrs. La Grande's bed. She, I guess it was her, was pushing the buzzer like crazy. Beep! Beep! Beep! I flipped the intercom switch..."

"Tell us what happened then."

"Before I could ask what the problem was, I heard what sounded like a sincere attempt by Mr. Colby to revive Mrs. La Grande."

The courtroom erupted. Marcus steadied his hands.

Judge Glen rapped his gavel on the bench. "Calm down, people! Continue, Mr. Lambrusco."

"What specifically did you hear, Ms Ballentine?"

"I heard a lot of huffing and puffing, I think by Mr. Colby, and I heard him say, 'come on, you old bat...breathe!' Like he was really trying to save her."

"In your opinion, he was trying to save her, not kill her?"

"OBJECTION, your Honor!" shouted Terry.

"Overruled!" shouted the Judge.

"Answer the question, Ms. Ballentine," said Marcus.

"I didn't hear a peep out of Mrs. La Grande. Maybe she was dead already."

"Objection!" voiced Terry.

"Sustained," said Judge Glen. "Ask a direct question."

Marcus felt flashes of light-headedness as he approached the jury box. He held on to the rail, steadying himself before he spoke.

"Have you ever seen Mr. Colby socially?"

"No."

"You never went out with him, for coffee, or anything else?"

"Never!"

"Not involved in any type of an affair?"

"Of course not! Mr. Colby is not that kind of a person," said Brenda. Beads of perspiration ran down the sides of her forehead. She wiped her cheek with a small white handkerchief.

This was not how we rehearsed it!

"Your witness," announced Marcus abruptly. "Your Honor, I'd like to request a short recess."

X

Terry Taittinger stood near the rail of the jury box. The scent of her perfume permeated into the second row. She turned her shapely form away from the rapt stares of the four men and eight women. Brenda Ballentine sat in the witness chair, waiting for her cross examination.

"I'll make this very brief, your Honor. Ms. Ballentine," said Terry, "please answer 'yes' or 'no' to the following question: with all the 'huffing and puffing,' as you called it, that you heard over the intercom, could you honestly tell exactly what was happening in Mrs. La Grande's room? Yes or no?"

"Well...not exactly," said Brenda.

"That means your answer is no?"

"Objection!" said Gina. Marcus gave her a congratulatory nod as soon as she sat down.

"Sustained," said Judge Glen. "Clarify the question, Counselor."

"According to the noise you heard on the intercom, Mr. Colby could have been trying to save Mrs. La Grande, OR he could have been trying to kill her. You couldn't really tell which it was, could you?"

"I guess not."

Terry Taittinger smiled. "No further questions." She returned to her seat, her hips swaying freely. Even Judge Glen was impressed.

Marcus closed his eyes and took in several deep cleansing breaths. He could taste the smooth whiskey cascading over his tongue, in the center of the courtroom, refreshing every pore of his body. With each sip, he could feel the tension diminishing, until he felt relaxed enough to continue. He turned from his seat to search out the comforting hand of Kristie sitting in the first row behind him. They touched without touching.

"Mr. Lambrusco. The State rests!" bellowed Judge Glen. "Mr. Lambrusco! Are you ready for your closing?"

Marcus stood up, tucked his tie into his suit jacket, glanced at the woman who was his inspiration and said to the judge, "Your Honor. As our final witness, I'd like to recall Mindy Michelob to the stand."

Terry Taittinger tugged on her black satin lapels. She sat in her oak chair, leaning into her assistant. "Nothing like beating a dead horse!" The assistant rolled his eyes but remained silent.

"Ms. Michelob," began Marcus, "you testified, under oath, you saw Jenny O'Doul standing just inside Mrs. La Grande's door, watching Mr. Colby push a pillow over her face. Is that right?"

"Yes. I did."

"In light of what you heard here this afternoon, with Ms. Ballentine's testimony, perhaps you may want to recant your earlier testimony," said Marcus calmly.

"Your Honor," said Terry, "this is highly irregular!"

"Sit down, Counselor," said Judge Glen. "Proceed, Mr. Lambrusco. Let's wind this up before the next decade!"

"Ms. Michelob?" said Marcus.

Tears welled up in Mindy's eyes. She blotted her mascara with a tissue from the box on the ledge of the witness stand. Mindy sobbed, trying to regain her composure.

"Thank you, your Honor, for your patience," said Marcus. "Please go on, Mindy." He sounded warm and comforting.

"The papers kept telling everyone what an awful man Nathan is. I began to believe that he COULD have killed Mrs. La Grande. I was so angry at him, I didn't want to believe the truth."

"You were angry at Mr. Colby? May I ask why?" said Marcus in a soothing fatherly tone.

"I loved Nathan."

Marcus was caught off guard. He glanced toward the long wooden table where Gina and Colby were sitting, and found himself wishing for Sherry to come barging into the courtroom at that precise moment. Marcus folded his hands in front of him to keep them from shaking.

"During your last cross examination, Ms. Michelob, we asked if you had had an affair with Mr. Colby, and you said 'no'. Now you are saying you HAD an affair?"

"I didn't consider it an affair. We were in love. We were to be married." Mindy continued sobbing and wiping her eyes. "When he found out about his bone cancer, he broke off our relationship."

"Objection, your Honor!" cried Terry.

"Sustained! Mr. Lambrusco," cried Judge Glen, "ask a direct question or get off the pot!"

"I have one last question, your Honor," said Marcus. He was strongly considering trading his right arm for a shot of Canadian Club. "What happened after Nathan Colby broke off the relationship?"

Mindy, red-eyed, said, "I was sad at first. Then, when I found out he was having a sordid affair with Jenny O'Doul, I got angry. I wished he was dead!"

"Is that why, in your initial testimony, you lied, because you wanted to see Mr. Colby hurt. Because of what he did to you?" Marcus felt a calming sensation coursing through his being, knowing the end was in sight.

"Yes, I lied," said Mindy, "but after what Ms. Ballentine said, like he was trying to save the woman, I knew I couldn't live with myself knowing that I saw him, myself, really trying his best to save Mrs. La Grande. And that's the truth!"

"No more questions, your Honor," said Marcus. He glanced at Kristie who mouthed a "masterful job" back at him.

"Do you wish to cross examine this witness, Ms. Taittinger?"

"No, your Honor," said Terry. "The people rest."

"In that case, we'll take a ten minute recess, then hear closing arguments," said the judge.

There is no way Colby could be found Guilty! thought Glen.

The foreperson, a skinny school teacher, passed out small sheets of paper and three-inch-long pencils to the rest of the jury members. The teacher didn't want to spend another night in the run-down Rainbow Hotel.

"Let's take a vote. We can be out of here in ten minutes, tops."

"Yeah," said the pale, pastey-faced man. "The guy's innocent. Gimme a ballot!"

A red-headed woman "X'd" her slip of paper. "Colby was no saint, but this is an open and shut case, people. Here's my decision."

"That slick lawyer tried to make him out to be a monster," said the accountant.

"She WAS slick, wasn't she?" The smiling taxi driver made an obscene gesture with his hand.

The votes were counted by the school teacher. Eleven, not guilty. One, guilty.

The largest juror said, "Look, it's so close to supper time. Let's have one more free meal outta this. We can take another vote after that."

X

Harry was familiar with the caterer's routine: at the same time every day exactly at 4:45 P.M., the truck pulled up behind the building with hot entrees, desserts, and drinks from a nearby cafe. Before unloading the truck, the driver always went into the men's room to relieve himself, wash his hands, and take a few drags on a cigarette. Today was no different. Harry followed him in.

X

The driver wheeled the food trays along the back stairway, escorted by a sleepy-looking security guard.

"Call me when yer done," said the tired guard.

After pushing the food cart into the room, the driver began placing the dinners and a tray of utensils on the conference table. The jury ate as if it were their last meal.

"Hey," said the driver in a loud voice, "I seen some mega news in the papers a while ago, about this guy Colby!"

"We shouldn't be talking about Colby just now," said the school teacher.

"The papers say Colby kept a young boy prisoner in an orphanage, for fifteen years!" continued the driver.

"No lie!" said the largest juror.

"Honest! The papers say Colby tried to burn the orphanage down to cover up the evidence." The driver had their attention. "He couldn't wait to get Mrs. La Grande's millions, either. He's guilty! No doubt about it!"

"We're ready for another vote," said the red-headed woman.

"As soon as we finish our food," said the largest juror.

X

The driver pushed the stainless-steel cart to the truck well and unloaded the wire interior racks. "I forgot the silverware. I'll be right back." The security guard nodded.

The driver wheeled the cart into the men's room and concealed the slumped body in the stainless opening.

"Ya got it all?" asked the bored guard.

"Yep! I got everything I need!"

Harry jumped into the catering truck and drove toward downtown Chicago. Toward the National Bank Building.

"That's great, Mr. Rumm. I'll pass it on," said Rosie. She hung up the extension and buzzed Richard's office.

"Mr. Rumm called from the courthouse. The jury has been in deliberation for quite a while now. He said Marcus did a fantastic job. He's certain the jury will find Mr. Colby innocent."

"Great! Hey, did you say Marcus? Where was Sherry?"

"He didn't say. Oops. Another call coming in. Just a minute."

Richard pushed the speaker-phone button and nodded reassuringly at Iris, sitting across from his desk.

"I can connect you now," said Rosie. "It's Lieutenant Miller on line three."

"Richie, I tried to get you at the courthouse. They said you tore out of there like a bat out of hell."

"I had an emergency here, Mike. I think I know who the killer is."

"That's why I'm calling." Miller sounded more excited than usual. "I was hoping it wasn't too late to catch you."

"It's Harry Heineken, right?"

"Yeah. How'd you guess?"

"It's a long story. You have proof?"

Richard could hear rustling in the background. Miller was opening a large yellow envelope. "The film was blown up, Richie, and I had it enhanced even further. Damn! What luck! You can see his face, barely, behind the Miata, carrying the body. It was the only photo of him that we got. Good enough for a jury!"

Richard felt more frustration than relief from Miller's information. He leaned back in his chair and glanced at Iris. She was straining to catch the details of the conversation.

"The kid's been working here for a little over six months," said Richard. "I found out why he killed the girls, and why he's been wanting to kill Daniels."

"You've been a busy S.O.B. Where is your boy now?"

"That's why I need you. I don't know where he is."

"Sit tight," cautioned Miller. "Send everyone home. Donny and I will be there as soon as we can."

"You got it," said Richard.

"Yeah?" A brief pause as Miller took a verbal message from Donny. "Oh, hell, Rich!"

"Now what?"

"Word just came down. The jury found Colby guilty."

"What else can go wrong!"

And where is Amy?

VENTING FRUSTRATION

On the twentieth floor, in the northwest corner of the building, Richard heard the quick, labored steps echoing down the faintly lit main corridor. The strides slowed as the figure turned right and approached his office. The footsteps halted. He could see an opaque shadow through the fluted glass door.

"Iris! Get down!" said Richard. He crouched, faced the door, and pointed his .38 revolver at the gray blob.

Cole Jones rapped on the glass panel.

"It's me, Mr. Port. Cole!"

Richard holstered his firearm and opened the door before Cole finished speaking.

"I must be losin' it! I forgot you were coming down."

"I got the tapes," said Cole, revealing a plastic bag from a Target store. "I brought all my paperwork from the last three weeks, too." Cole reared back when he saw Iris pop up from behind Richard's desk.

"There's been a change of plans, Cole," said Richard, sounding more like a detective than a lawyer. "I have reason to believe the killer might be somewhere in the building. The police are on the way."

"The blonde guy!?"

"Yeah! I want everyone to get out of here, NOW!"

"I can go with Ms. Whiskey to the parking garage," offered Cole.

"No! Rosie's still here, too. I'll escort the three of you out of the building."

"I'm worried about Jacq," said Iris. "He always lets me know where he is."

"Jarvis is trying to track down Guinness." Richard motioned the two to follow him out. He locked his door. "Don't worry. Jacq can take care of himself."

"What do you want us to do?"

"Grab a cab and wait for me at Mario's."

"We'll be soused to the gills by that time," said Iris, knowing it was more truth than fiction.

"Trust me," said Richard, "I'll be there! As soon as I find Harry."

X

Richard waited until the taxi pulled away, then hurried past the curved glass block wall on nineteen, past the empty offices, into the print shop.

No Harry!

"This is the ideal time to put my vent theory into operation," muttered Richard. According to the HVAC drawings on the blueprints from the building manager, the main cold air return ductwork, adjacent to the print shop, went vertically straight to the roof, branching off into the conference room on the twentieth floor, and also into Jacq's bathroom on the top floor.

Richard carried the small wooden ladder to the north side of the room and opened it below the large metal vent. He could see that the screw holding the cover to the wall was not fastened securely.

The pieces are coming together, Miller!

He pulled the vent away from the wall and held the cover while he shined his flashlight into the vent cavity. Richard could see scuff marks in the layers of dust at the vent's entrance. He could hear the gusting of the wind as it whistled through the cavernous metal structure. Richard thought he heard footsteps, possibly two floors up.

Nah! Just my imagination!

X

Harry stretched his cramped leg and swore under his breath. He pushed the vent cover open leading into Jacq's office and lowered himself onto the gray Corian countertop. He stepped on the seat of a chair and hopped to the carpeted floor, pussy-footing across the office to Jacq's executive bathroom, and unlatched the stall's metal door. Harry sat down on the padded almond seat, feeling his belt for the curved blade.

You're DEAD MEAT, old man! TONIGHT!

Amy was exhausted. She slumped back in her padded chair. At 7:35, she dialed Richard's office again. Still no answer. Amy's makeup was faded and her shoulder length hair resembled the scarecrow's in the Wizard of Oz. Jarvis had informed her that Richard returned to the office to see Iris hours ago. Now they were both gone. "Something was definitely wrong!"

Do I want to make partner this badly?

She dialed Jacq's extension with the same result. Amy had volunteered to begin work on the appeal for Nathan Colby, her initial incentive being another feather in her cap, not to mention she could be near Richard during this turbulent turn of events.

X

The stretch limo squealed to a stop on Clark Street behind the Bank Building. Jacq ran to the driver's side window. Guinness lowered the black glass.

"Are you sure that's what Jarvis told you?"

"I'm positive," said Guinness. "Richard is waiting for you in his office. Although at this late hour, he might be in your office by now."

"I'll try both places," said Jacq. "Wait for me here."

Jacq entered the building at the rear, punching in his special codes. Avoiding the TV crews and journalists at the front entrance was uppermost in his mind. Once inside, on the nineteenth floor, Jacq found Richard's office locked. Instead of backtracking to the freight elevator, he took the north stairwell two flights up to his office. No one in sight. He unlocked the door.

Jacq entered the office.

Harry was sitting in the bathroom stall, waiting, when he heard Jacq's keys hit the desk. Harry turned the knob on the bathroom door, shoved the knife into his belt...then stopped dead in his tracks when he heard the voices.

Sherry appeared in the doorway of Iris' adjoining office.

"Sherry! What the hell are you doing here?"

"I had to see you again. I just heard the verdict." Her face was flushed and contorted. "I can't understand what went wrong! Jackie pulled that witness out of his hat. I heard Marcus did a fantastic job..."

"A damn kick in the teeth. Colby's innocent! We're filing an appeal."

"Don't bother!" said Sherry curtly. "He's dying. You know that."

"The verdict makes us look like fools."

"We ARE fools!"

"What'd ya mean?" Jacq's silver-gray hair looked whiter in the fading light as he brushed it back with one hand. He pulled out his desk drawer with the other.

"Your credibility, Jacq! It sucks!" yelled Sherry. "After our confrontation with DeDe today, I couldn't believe SHE was actually the one divorcing YOU! I had to find out for myself...from Jackie!"

"So she's divorcing me. So what!" Jacq rummaged through his drawer, searching for his lighter.

"She's been using you for personal gain for years!"

"Tell me something I DON'T know."

Jacq lit up a Cuban cigar. His desk drawer remained open. He went over to one of the arched windows and lowered the parchment blind.

"I truly loved you...once," said Sherry, her eyes spitting fire. The same eyes falling on the extended drawer with Jacq's revolver nestled among his Cross pens.

"What a laugh," countered Jacq. "You knew I could never marry you! You were good for a few laughs. That's all."

"I thought you loved me, too," said Sherry sorrowfully. Her eyes blazed. "Until I found out about Iris' child!" Sherry tensed as she reached for the gun.

"I got my own problems, baby," growled Jacq. "You're better off not being involved with the kid. He's trying to kill me." He was staring at the faded Dali print above the ice bucket. "Besides, you know what I am!"

"A sorry son of a...!"

"You know what YOU are. We're alike, baby!"

"Like hell!" Sherry was livid. "You had no intention of marrying me!"

"Welcome to the real world. Now get out of here!" Jacq exhaled a large smoke ring, following it up toward the ceiling with his eyes.

"Your son won't have the satisfaction!" screamed Sherry. She pointed the revolver at Jacq, extended her arms, locked her elbows and pulled the trigger. The bullet tore into Jacq's stomach. He collapsed to the carpet, the cigar smoldering next to his body. The sound of the explosion echoed up through the vent and into the bathroom where Harry was hiding...and waiting.

Sherry calmly dialed 911. "There has been a shooting. Jacq

Daniels." A short pause. "I don't know if he's breathing. I'm not very good at those things." Another pause. "Top floor in the National Bank Building. Thank you."

Sherry hung up the phone, sat back in Jacq's Oval Office chair and leaned into the soft leather.

The check caught her eye. On the desk, next to the lighter, was a check made out to a 'Forest Glen', in the amount of $50,000. Sherry tore up the check and scattered the pieces into the waste-basket.

She closed her pale jade eyes, caressing the gun tenderly, then placed the weapon in the drawer. Sherry kicked off her shoes and waited for the police.

THE PROXY

Harry listened to the conversation behind the bathroom door, surprised at the abrupt turn of events. One hand was on the knob. In his other fist he held the curve-bladed knife. Harry felt an overwhelming desire to plunge the blade into Jacq's chest...NOW!

No—I'll wait until she's gone!

As the conversation escalated, fragments of Harry's life in the orphanage manifested themselves—intense white-hot scenes, flashing in his brain. Years of nightmares. Years of dreaming of retribution.

Harry heard the shot. Instinctively, he felt for his knife in the loop of his belt. For an instant, his mind blanked.

She deprived me of my proxy!

Harry felt the spittle oozing from the corners of his mouth. He turned the knob and pushed the bathroom door open. He cradled the hilt in his hands.

The authority and power to act for another!

Harry froze, the door slightly ajar, his eyes that of a crazed animal.

I wanted to act for my Mother!

Harry shoved the knife into his leather belt.

Sherry acted for ME!

The veins in Harry's neck bulged, reminiscent of his recurring nightmares.

Now I can act for HARRY!

Harry slid down two stories on the rungs of the vent ladder to the print shop. His voice echoed through the hollow sheet metal.

"I'M THE RIGHTFUL HEIR!"

The knife slipped from his belt loop, clanging, banging, and ricocheting into the darkness below.

Harry kicked the vent cover off its hinges, sending it flying against the copier machine. The machine began to churn, spewing blank white pages on the floor. He jumped out of the vent, his face a dark, smoldering mass.

Amy's office door next to the print shop was open. Her computer monitor was buzzing, its keyboard clicking in time with a Michael Crawford tune she was humming.

Harry felt the overwhelming urge again.

"Amy! December 9th! D-Day! DEATH!"

ONE DOWN

Frustrated by the elusiveness of the killer, Richard climbed the two flights of stairs to the top floor, hoping to pinpoint the exact location of the vent in Jacq's offices. Halfway to the upper floor, he heard the shot. Darting up the remaining steps, he jammed his shoulder into the stairwell door. It didn't budge.

"Damn! This door is never locked!"

Richard took the stairs to the floor below, ran down the long corridor to the passenger elevator and pushed the up button. He pulled his gun, just in case.

The elevator doors opened silently. The long hallway was deserted. Richard ran to Jacq's office and pushed the door open, crouching, gun in hand.

The room appeared to be empty. Richard crept into the office and saw Jacq's body on the blood-stained carpet at the side of the desk, next to the smoldering cigar.

Richard knelt and checked Jacq's vital signs. He placed the handgun on the desk.

"Thank God he's still breathing."

He removed his jacket, folded it, and made a cushion for Jacq's head.

"Hang on! You're going to be okay. Hang on!" He loosened Jacq's collar. "Hang on."

Richard got up and reached for the telephone. As he turned, he saw the navy leather pumps on the floor.

Sherry spun around in the chair.

"I called 911," she said blankly.

"What the hell are you doing here?!"

"I shot him. I saved everyone a lot of trouble."

"I think he's going to make it. For your sake...I hope so."

"And for Jacq's sake...?" Sherry turned in her seat, away from Richard.

CONFRONTATION

Amy dialed Jacq's office again. She was surprised, then thrilled, when Richard picked up the phone.

"I've been worried sick! Where are you?"

"Relax," said Amy. "I'm cozy and warm in my office downstairs." She brushed her hair back and began tapping the cursor key. "Burning the midnight oil for Jarvis. I thought you were with Iris."

"Jacq's been shot. He's up here, in his office."

"Oh my God! Is he...?" Goosebumps crawled up her spine, causing Amy to shiver uncontrollably.

"No, he'll make it," said Richard. "Sit tight! I'll be right down!"

Amy wheeled her chair to the computer and continued the rough draft for the appeal. Her back was to the doorway.

Harry pushed the door open without a sound. He tip-toed into the room and stood behind her.

Amy sensed she wasn't alone. She turned. Harry stifled her scream with one hand, the other clutching her throat. He squeezed her neck with all his strength.

Amy grabbed Harry's wrists and pulled at his boney arms until he lost his grip. She kicked her legs out, knocking over the chair, falling backward onto the tiled floor. Harry threw the chair aside and jumped on her.

Amy twisted her body and jabbed an elbow into Harry's ribs. He recoiled from the blow and lunged at her again, his head back, howling like a madman. She yanked her desk lamp from it's socket and swung it at Harry, connecting with a resounding CRACK across the side of his face, bending the earpiece on his glasses.

"ARRGHH! YOU'RE HISTORY!"

Amy ran into the hallway. She slipped on the waxy surface, lost a shoe, and sprawled head first on the tile. She felt the floor come up and catch her between the eyes. Her head began spinning.

The flashes of tiny lights left Harry's eyes. He saw Amy on the floor, pounced on her, and pulled her back into the print shop.

Where am I?

Harry began to choke her with his bare hands, his howls resounding throughout the corridor.

"OOOWWW!"

THE CHASE

CHAPTER LXXIII

Screams! Amy's screams!

Richard threw the door open and ran down the hall toward the screams. Instinctively, he felt for his gun.

"Damn!" he muttered. "It's on Jacq's desk!"

He skidded to a stop at the doorway of the print shop, hanging on to the jambs as he rounded the corner. Harry was near the copier machine, clutching Amy's throat.

"AMY!"

The skinny figure, startled, slammed his fist into Amy's jaw. He scurried to his feet and grabbed a chrome-plated wrench from behind the machine. The access panel fell to the floor, along with Mai's snub-nosed .38. The gun slid across the floor.

Richard charged at him. Harry swung, stunning him with a glancing blow to the cheek. Blood squirted from the gash under his eye. Richard slammed his face into the leg of a metal table.

Harry ran from the room. He raced past the reception desk, veered at the glass block wall, and sprinted to the rear freight elevators. He pulled down hard on the wooden doors and pushed forward on the controls, riding the car down to the employee parking area.

Amy, still groggy, struggled to her knees and crawled to Richard's prone body.

"Richard! It's Harry!"

He shook his head, trying to clear the cobwebs. "I'll get him! Stay put!" He ran down the corridor, past the reception area, then jumped into one of the passenger elevators and pushed the down button to the parking garage.

Amy, her senses clearing, ran after him. She heard the ding of the elevator as the doors closed. The red lights over the doors indicated Richard's elevator was going down. She pushed the express button on the remaining passenger elevator. The car sped to the underground parking level.

Harry's Dodge Minivan squealed out of the lot, burning rubber and filling the exit ramp with clouds of exhaust fumes.

Richard ran from the elevator toward his Chrysler.

Amy darted from the elevator and ran after Richard, shouting, "I'm going with you! Wait!" Amy caught him as he pushed the remote to the Concorde, the door locks snapping open.

"Looks like I have no choice!" yelled Richard, ramming his foot on the accelerator.

Richard revved his golden coupe, crashing through a "Do Not Exit" barricade blocking a ramp used only for delivery trucks.

He followed the trails of exhaust smoke, chasing Harry's van through the one-way streets of Chicago.

Harry turned south on Clark Street and headed toward the railroad yards, the gray clouds leaving their telltale signs.

Harry cut his wheel sharply at 18th Street, the van speeding west. The bridge over the south branch of the foggy Chicago River loomed ahead.

"Hold tight!" yelled Richard. He rammed his car into the rear of the vehicle, causing the van to spin out of control. The van spun backward, careening to the opposite side of the bridge and slamming into a concrete and steel guardrail.

Richard braked, the trunk of his car popping open as the car skidded to a stop behind the smoking van.

The rail had ripped the van's door off its hinges. Harry was thrown from the front seat, across the concrete walk, and over the edge of the suspension bridge.

Richard, followed closely by Amy, ran from his car toward the van. Harry was hanging on to a bent steel bar with both hands. One of his hands slipped off the bar.

"MY SHOULDER! I CAN'T HANG ON!"

"We'll help you!" shouted Richard.

"SAVE ME!" screamed Harry. "I DON'T WANT TO DIE!"

On all fours, Richard reached over the side of the bridge, grabbed Harry's jacket, and pulled with all his might. The slim figure screamed again as Richard yanked on his dangling, numbed arm. Amy ran to help. She knelt next to Richard and leaned over the edge, grasping Harry's other arm. Together, they pulled him to safety.

Harry lay on the sidewalk, his head on a slab of concrete, staring with unseeing eyes. He focused, recognizing his benefactors. Another wave of repressed rage flooded his being.

Richard removed his handcuffs from his belt and snapped them on one of Harry's wrists. The other end he fastened to a warped piece of steel piping.

"You okay, Harry?" said Richard.

"You're damn right!" Suddenly, Harry kicked Richard in the ribs, sending him backward and over the side of the bridge.

Amy screamed as his body disappeared in the darkness. She scurried to her feet and ran to the edge of the twisted guardrail. She peered into the choppy water.

"RICHARD!" Amy's voice was shrill-filled with desperation. "Richard! Where are you?" she yelled. Amy looked back at Harry's motionless form. He was kneeling on the sidewalk, smiling at her.

"My jacket's caught on something," said Richard weakly. "I'm okay...I think. I'm hanging upside down!"

"Don't worry! I'll get you!" she shouted. " Let me call Miller first. I don't want Harry getting out of my sight!"

"Okay...but...WHOA! OOWW!" Richard's jacket ripped further, causing his head to strike a concrete column when his body fell closer to the river. He felt strangely lightheaded. He could see the glistening waves in the moonlight. "Now! HURRY! I can't wait!"

"Hang on!" yelled Amy. She reached down toward him as far as she could stretch her arms. "God! I can't reach you!" She took another glance at Harry. His smile had turned into a wide, devilish smirk.

"My trunk! See what you can find in the trunk!" yelled Richard. "HURRY!"

She dashed to the trunk of his car. "I've got it!" yelled Amy.

Harry was still on his knees.

She ran to the edge with an extra-long length of a jumper cable. She dangled one end over the bridge. Amy gave Harry another cursory glance.

"One foot lower! Good!" said Richard triumphantly. "Now, PULL!"

Harry was on his knees. He was rubbing his cuffed hand raw. Blood dripped down his arm, saturating his jacket sleeve. He pulled the skin off his knuckles as the handcuff flopped loose, dangling on the steel piling.

Amy pulled Richard up through the mangled wire mesh fence. Her knit sweater was shredded and hung loosely over one shoulder. Richard's suit jacket fell into the river below. He glanced quickly at Harry who was still on his knees.

Amy fell into Richard's arms, panting, sobbing, her body trembling.

"I've got you now." He embraced Amy and held her tenderly,

letting go of the jumper cable. She buried her face in his embrace and cried softly.

The jumper cable and Harry hit the water below at the same time.

Richard heard the splash and ran to the edge of the bridge. "He pulled his hand free!?"

"No one could survive that fall," sobbed Amy.

"Thanks for coming down," said Lieutenant Miller. He pushed the chair toward Richard with his feet, scraping the wooden floor in the stark interrogation room. Dos sat hunched over in a corner, a close resemblance to a whipped puppy.

"You guys look like I feel," said Richard.

"Not so good, huh?"

"I'll live...at least I got that going for me."

"Sorry about the outcome of the trial, Richie."

Richard threw his overcoat on the oak table and slumped into the chair next to the lieutenant. The men didn't speak. Richard counted the acoustical tiles on the ceiling while Miller tapped a pencil on his Timex.

Dos was picking his nose, eyeing the two. "We found Ms. Tai's gun in the print shop, in case we need it for a trial."

"Don't worry," said Richard, "there won't be a trial." He stared at Mike Miller for the longest time. "One minute I had him cuffed. The next minute he was gone," said Richard finally. "He must have hit the water with the jumper cables. I didn't hear any other splash."

"Your girlfriend was lucky to grab you," said Miller. "She had no other choice." He closed the Heineken file and slammed the folder with his open palm.

"I know you're right." Richard shook his head. "I had that little rat chained to the fence. No way was he going to get out of my sight."

"I saw the punk at your office once," said Dos. "I knew he looked suspicious. We should have grabbed him by his scruffy hair and hauled his boney ass in for questioning."

Donny fidgeted when his lieutenant glared at him.

"We all know he wasn't a suspect, right Donny?"

"Yeah, I know. I was just blowing off steam."

"I wish I could."

"He's dead," said Miller.

"He's gotta be," said Donny.

"He'd better be," said Richard.

"By the way, Richie," said Miller. "Welcome back."

X

Jarvis closed the last of the portly files on his desk. The corrugated boxes were stacked against the wall, ready to be filled with the hundreds of papers related to the Nathan Colby case.

This is a job that would have been done by Harry, he mused.

Richard rapped on the glass, pushed the door open, and shook what was left of the snow off his shoulders. "I was down to see Miller a while ago. It looks as if he's closing the case on Heineken."

"Good. I have to believe he is dead. Amy could have died that night too, you know."

"She ended up saving my life." Richard pointed at the cartons lining the office. "What's with the boxes?"

"We're putting the Colby case to bed."

"It seems there was jury-tampering evidence," said Richard. "You're not pursuing a new trial?"

"No. Nathan won't last long enough to go through an ordeal of that magnitude, according to his doctors."

"That's probably for the best," said Richard. His eyes fell on a photo of Jarvis and Jacq, shaking hands in their younger days. "What's the status on Jacq?"

"Looks as if he'll make it. For some reason, he's not filing any charges against Sherry."

"I'm not surprised."

"Neither am I. Behind that gruff facade is a very complex individual, but he's salvageable. I've known him for most of my life."

"Pretty tough guy, huh?"

"Yes. But now that his firm has dropped out from under him, he is back to being a baby at heart. Reminds me of when we were kids. We were inseparable."

"You've got a crazy nostalgic look on your face."

"Is it that obvious?"

"Yeah! You and Jacq are up to something."

"Maybe."

Richard fanned through the thickest file on Jarvis' desk. "Then it's true? Colby was really innocent?"

"Yes. He knew he was dying from bone cancer. When he had the once-in-a-lifetime opportunity to help someone, like Mrs. La Grande, he tried his best to save her."

"You could file an appeal and get..."

Jarvis held up his hand. "It's enough for Colby to know in his heart that he did what was right...perhaps the only time in his miserable existence."

"I owe Colby a debt of gratitude in a round-about way." Richard sat facing Jarvis and the stacks of cardboard cartons. "I'd like you to be the first to know. I'm leaving the firm...effective immediately."

"This is a surprise!" Jarvis fell back in his chair, dropping a cluster of files. "What made you change your mind after all these years?"

"Frankly, the Colby case. Chasing Harry, the investigation regarding Jacq's damaged desk. The gum-shoeing...got my blood worked up." Richard pulled himself up from the chair and stared at a pigeon on the window sill. "It took me a while to realize how much I missed police work."

"Seems like it was your first love."

"Yeah, it is...next to Amy."

"We're going to miss you."

"Same here."

Jarvis went to the window and hugged Richard warmly.

"Thanks."

"It is the best decision...isn't it?"

JANUARY, 1999

Rosie came out of Jackie's newly decorated office flashing an enormous diamond. The sun caught the ring's facets, throwing a rainbow of vivid colors against the pale gray walls.

"Just think," said Rosie, admiring her finger. "The new Mrs. Daniels!" Her blue eyes sparkled, competing with the tiers of brilliant stones.

Rosie approached her old counter and waved at the new receptionist, Jean Hennessy. She waved with her ringed hand.

"It's lovely! I'm so happy for you!" Henny flashed a beautiful smile of her own.

"Thanks! And what about you? You've helped Richard and Jackie so much. I don't know how we can repay you."

"For starters, getting me this temp job...and look at these!" Henny pointed to the corner of the desk adorned by a huge bouquet of red roses. The card was from Richard. It read: "Many thanks for a job well done."

"You deserve them."

"But that's not all," said Henny excitedly. "Richard spoke to Lieutenant Miller. He's going to break in a new partner... soon."

"Not you!"

"Yes! Isn't that sweet?" giggled Henny. "If I didn't know better, I'd swear Richard is in love with me!"

Rosie giggled too, held her ring up to the light, and pushed the down button.

"Oh, Mrs. Daniels," said Henny, "did you know that after being trained by Lieutenant Miller, I'll hopefully be teamed with Richard Port? He's going back to work again for the Chicago police as a Detective."

"Humm. Amy will be thrilled to death to hear that bit of news."

X

Labatt was sunning himself, lounging lazily, in one of the beach chairs on the beautiful secluded Island of Rangiroa. From Tahiti, aboard the cruise ship Paul Gauguin, Labatt had toured the smaller islands and beaches, spending money as if it belonged to someone else.

Labatt fondled his glass, sipping on his third tequila of the day.

"It doesn't get any better than this!" he said to himself, gazing into the azure sky.

DeDe unzipped the flap of her cabana and glided across the sand to the empty canvas chair. She wore sandals and an orange cotton wrap, low around her smooth waist. Nothing more.

X

Amy walked out of Jacq's vacated office. The smell of wallpaper paste and paint filled her nostrils, forcing her out of the large suite.

"What an awful smell!" moaned Amy. "Those fumes are horrendous. I"ll be happy when they finish the painting."

Iris smiled as she jokingly staggered into her adjoining office. "Tony's putting the finishing touches on Jarvis' old office," said Iris. "Rosie gave him the okay for Jackie's color scheme this morning."

"Tony's in the wrong business," said Amy.

"He'll be an equally good lawyer one day."

"Who am I to argue with astute female logic?"

Iris picked up the phone on the second ring. "Mr. Daniels' off...ooops, excuse me!" She glanced at Amy. "Amy Amontillado's office. May I help you?"

"This is the Wyandotte Refinishing Company, in Michigan," said the caller. "We got your desk ready. Okay to deliver next Tuesday?"

"Yes," said Iris. "Send the invoice to the same address, but the name of the Firm has been changed to 'The Associates, Attorneys at Law'. And mark on the receipt, the desk is to be delivered to JACKIE Daniels' office."

"I'm not into antiques, but its nice to be able to keep that bit of history within the firm," said Amy.

"I thanked Jackie when he and Rosie made the decision," said Iris.

Richard came around the corner and stuck his head into the room. He winked at Iris and blew Amy a kiss. "I have some great news! Marcus is going back to his wife."

"That's wonderful!" said Iris. "When did that happen?"

"Over the weekend. Marcus tried to reach you, got Jackie instead. That love-sick goon gave Marcus a leave of absence."

Richard looked longingly at Amy. "You look SO beautiful today."

"Oh, really?" Her smile lit up the office. "Only today?"

"Know what else. Jacq and Jarvis are heading for Florida, to start some kind of fishing business."

"Some sort of fishy business?" said Amy grinning.

"They want to rekindle their boyhood dreams," said Iris with a lump in her throat.

"Will you marry me?" said Richard.

"I heard Sherry is leaving to teach," said Amy, completely ignoring him. "I wish I could have had her for my instructor."

Iris backed out of the office into the hall. "She'll be a great teacher, I'm sure," she said, then discreetly closed the door.

"Oh—and yes...I will!" squealed Amy. She jumped into Richard's waiting arms.

The Ferry *Chivas Regal* scraped the edges of the pier, wallowing helplessly in the choppy waters of Lake Michigan. Low-lying fog shrouded the small wooden ticket booth at the south end of Calumet Harbor. A half-dozen people formed a broken line in front of the black and white striped liftgate operated by an old man in a pea jacket and dirty denims.

"Hell of a day for a ride," he said to the group. "Can't see nothin', hardly."

An elderly woman in a wheelchair spoke to no one in particular, "I don't have much fun anymore. The sounds of the boat and the foghorns make me happy. That's why I'm here. It's relaxing."

"I know what you mean, lady," said the man.

"That's one of the reasons." Horns sounded from across the bay and she smiled.

"All aboard!" The gray-haired man tore the tickets in half and shoved the stub into each passenger's palm. A slim figure with a bandaged hand was the last to board.

The mooring lines were tossed to a bundled form on the dock and the *Chivas Regal* labored into the gray mist.

Harry leaned against the low rail, watching what was left of the dock before it faded out of sight.

The wheelchair creaked, coming to a stop next to Harry's skinny frame.

"You look like you've just lost your best friend," said the elderly woman. She maneuvered her chair facing the railing and Harry's bandaged hand.

"Only my father and mother, old lady."

"OH, I'm terribly sorry. You looked so despondent...I had no idea..."

"I don't need no lecture."

"My son works on the ferry. It's the only chance I have to see him." She turned the frayed collar up on her coat. "Family is so important."

Harry wiped away a tear, his first in a long time.

A chilling wind blew across the icy waters, causing Harry and the two other passengers on the starboard side to turn their faces. The old woman saw the hurt in Harry's eyes.

"Do you have any other family, Mr...?"

"My name is Harold J. Daniels."

I'm not a bad person.

"You look so sad. I wish I could do something to..."

"I don't need help."

The old woman reached out from under her blanket and touched Harry's arm. "Harold," she said solemnly, "my grandfather once told me, I think it's from the Bible, 'It is better by far to die for something, then to live for nothing.' I hope that verse helps you."

"I said I don't need your help!...especially with no stinkin' parable!"

Harry pulled his hand away. He turned abruptly and made his way to the deserted stern of the ferry. He climbed over the rail and slipped his fragile body into the murky waters.

The ferry chugged eastward, then disappeared in the dense fog.